A PRE-EXISTING CONDITION

Books by Gene Rontal

The Police Surgeon

Sterile Justice

A Lethal Dose

The Cruelest Cut

A PRE-EXISTING CONDITION

A Detective Ben Dailey, M.D. Mystery

GENE RONTAL

CAVEL
PRESS

Kenmore, WA

A Camel Press book published by Epicenter Press

Epicenter Press
6524 NE 181st St.
Suite 2
Kenmore, WA 98028

For more information go to:
www.Camelpress.com
www.Coffeetownpress.com
www.Epicenterpress.com
www.generontalbooks.com

This is a work of fiction. Names, characters, places, brands, media, and incidents are either the product of the author's imagination or are used fictitiously.

Design by Scott Book and Melissa Vail Coffman

A Pre-existing Condition
Copyright © 2021 by Gene Rontal

ISBN: 978-1-60381-735-6 (Trade Paper)
ISBN: 978-1-60381-736-3 (eBook)

Printed in the United States of America

"The end of life cancels all bands."

Shakespeare: Henry IV, Act III, Scene II

Chapter 1

Six words on a highway sign: That's all an average driver reads at fifty miles an hour. After reading that fact in a college text, I immediately felt the challenge. Being average was not my goal. Thus began a lifetime driving game, me against the billboard. At first glance, tonight's freeway contest was a perfect six: Be An Angel, Stop Devil's Night. But there was more. Not only did I read the message, I also caught the signature at the bottom. Franklin Robinson, Mayor, City of Detroit.

A tinge of anger tightened my jaw as I thought about the message. It was good advice, I guess, but for the more sensitive of us in the car capital of the world, it was just another sucker punch to the belly of a beleaguered city.

Some people scratch their heads, trying to remember what Devil's Night is. Those who associate it with childhood mischief were right, except, for the citizens of Motown, who saw nothing childish about it. It was, in fact, their yearly meeting with fear and disgrace, the night before Halloween.

The event started out innocently in the '30s as an excuse for rascally kids to let off a little steam. For the timid, it was soaping windshields or toilet papering a few trees. For the real troublemakers it was throwing eggs at windows.

After the '67 riots, Devil's Night turned vicious. Whole neighborhoods were set on fire by lawless thugs followed by lurid stories and pictures on the national news. Even books were written about it. The notoriety caused so much publicity that Mayor Dennis Archer called upon the citizenry to form neighborhood watchdog groups to protect their homes. He referred to them as angels. Deputized vigilantes were a better word. This PR campaign did little to change the city's image, and it made me angry. You see, I still love Detroit.

In the middle of this internal discussion my cellphone suddenly rang. It was

George Sennett: Lieutenant to those who worked with him at Detroit Homicide and just plain George to his friends, like me.

"Ben, where are you?" he asked anxiously.

"On my way home. I was at the hospital taking care of an emergency."

"I need your help," he replied. I heard that statement before. Gauging from past history, it usually meant trouble.

Cars were whizzing by, so I slowed into the right lane of traffic, switched off the speaker and put the receiver to my ear. "You sound excited. What's up?"

It took him about a minute to tell me that a woman he knew from the mayor's office was in trouble at City Hospital. The fire department found her in a deserted building set afire on one of those vacant blocks that dotted the Detroit landscape. I didn't ask him how she got there. He seemed too agitated.

No burns, but Sennett said she had severe smoke inhalation. "Will you see her in the emergency room?"

I never said no to George. We had too much history. Or should I say our mutual near-death experiences made me feel I was a volunteer member of the homicide department. But this request might have gone overboard. Without privileges at City Hospital, I hesitated for a moment.

He sensed my reluctance. "Ben, I think you should come down. She had your office card in her purse. You know, the one that says Dr. Benjamin Dailey, Head and Neck Surgeon." I didn't know it at the time, but I was about to enter my own personal weeks long Devil's Night that would test what kind of a doctor—and police adjunct—I really was.

When he told me her name was Sandra Wells, I remembered something about her. But after a few moments, I quickly decided it didn't make a difference.

Whether I liked it or not, the Detroit Police Department and I were joined at the hip. That's why my hand went to the pocket of my jacket and pulled out two items.

The first was my badge. I clipped it onto the visor and glanced at it for a second. It read "Police Surgeon." And in case anyone is going to assume this was a token gesture to build up my ego, forget it. I earned that piece of metal. The second was my package of Juicy Fruits. I unwrapped two sticks and popped them into my mouth. Some habits are hard to break.

My 20-year-old Grand Wagoneer exited at Eight Mile, made the turnaround, and pointed its bulldog front end south, back into the city. Devil's Night was no longer just a billboard.

I exited onto the Davidson Expressway and headed east. The short two-mile length of highway was the first freeway in America, at the time a futuristic means of showcasing the products of the city. In one of urban planning's biggest blunders, the auto barons convinced the powers in charge to build the country's best freeway system. In the process they squandered any chance for mass transit. It was a decision that would haunt Detroit for decades.

A right turn onto the Chrysler Freeway and a quick exit shortly thereafter brought me to Mack Avenue and City Hospital, Detroit's home to the knife and gun club. The hospital provided sanctuary and care for many of the underprivileged and destitute people of the city. It was also a Level One trauma center, capable of taking care of the worst emergencies. As I drove down the expressway, two large cranes next to the hospital appeared in my windshield. They were each outlined in the surrounding streetlights like gargantuan reptiles pointed in different directions, guarding the gates of hell.

Pulling up to the hospital emergency department, I saw three XXL officers loitering at the front entrance. The only comforting things about their presence were the Sig Sauer 9mms holstered at their sides. They suddenly came to life as I parked my car in the "Police Only" spot. I got out, flashed my badge, and walked through the glass doors of the emergency department, leaving them to wonder what they had just seen.

Upon entering, I saw a large, solidly built black man with I-beam shoulders, standing by the triage nurse's desk. He had a square jaw, a heavy, furrowed brow, and a "don't-mess-with-me" glare.

The frown became more imposing as he attempted, without luck, to snap on a temporary ID badge. When he saw me, the glower disappeared, changing him from menacing warrior to jolly giant. George Sennett came up and engulfed me in an almost painful hug.

"Sorry to drag you down here," he said, still fumbling with the badge attached to his coat.

I took the ID from his hand and quickly fixed the plastic snap onto his lapel. "No offense, George, but I'm glad you're not a neurosurgeon."

He was about to reply when I heard a loud shout from down the hallway. The words "crash cart" echoed against the enameled brick walls leading into the emergency department. Several people in scrubs ran toward the sound.

Sennett turned around and led me toward a door that was labeled "Acute Trauma." I followed obediently. We entered a brightly lit large room with metal cabinets filled with instruments, a state of the art anesthesia setup, and the antiseptic smell of iodine stinging my nose. A man and two women in scrubs and masks hovered over a woman on a gurney. I quickly glanced at their badges—two female residents and the staff anesthesiologist. I couldn't see the patient's face, but the rapid beating of the heart monitor echoing in my ears and the sight of blood sprayed over her gown told me she was in real trouble.

"I . . . I can't stop the bleeding," the male of the three doctors stammered. Over a bloodied mask fear sprang from his eyes. "I put a tube in her airway to ventilate, and then she started coughing up blood," he explained. Sennett looked pleadingly at me.

I listened as the doctors spoke. It appeared that none of them had seen any-thing like this before. I looked at the patient. The tube was in her airway, but blood was still coming out the end in large clots. She was barely responsive. Just then one of the physicians called out to get the throat doctor in the room, stat.

"She'll be dead if you wait that long," I said above the din of the cardiac monitor and the anesthesia ventilator.

They looked at me like I was from another planet. That's when Sennett stood in front of them, a striking figure under any circumstances, but now a bellowing bull of a man that demanded attention.

"This is Ben Dailey from St. Vincent's. I think you better listen to him. This is his patient."

The older doc looked at me for a second. "The detective or the doctor Ben Dailey?"

"I like to think of myself as the doctor," I replied. "This woman is my pa-tient, but I don't have her chart. That's about all I know."

He looked at his counterparts. "It's okay. He glanced sideways at me having trouble, and he is her doctor. We can't wait for someone to come down." Then he looked back at me. "What do you need?"

I knew what to do. "Get me a rigid bronchoscope," I said firmly. I was now in command of the situation, no need to yell. I had my coat off and was put-ting on a gown, gloves, and a shielded facemask as I spoke. Within seconds the nurse brought in the rigid metal scope. It was about a foot long and had an angled tip so it could be placed into the windpipe. "I'll need a good suction. We have to see where the bleeding is coming from." I checked the patient again; she had two IV lines in her, pumping blood and fluids.

They attached the fiberoptic cord to the scope and handed it to me.

"Give me a suction and when I tell you, deflate the cuff," I said, clenching hard on the gum in my mouth. I took the Yankauer suction and cleared her throat. As I did, I asked them to empty the air-filled balloon around the tube and slid the bronchoscope into her windpipe.

I saw where the blood was coming from, a laceration in the lining of the throat above the voice box. I removed the bronchoscope and instructed the anesthesiologist to re-inflate the cuff around the endotracheal tube to prevent blood from going into her airway.

"There's a tear in in the lining of her throat, probably from the intubation. That's where the blood is coming from. If we don't control her airway, we won't be able to clean the smoke debris from the fire out of her lungs. Give me some tonsil sponges on a pull-out string."

The nurse quickly handed me the ball-shaped gauze and, with a forceps, I inserted it with pressure against the bleeding area. The bleeding stopped.

"If this continues, she might need a tracheotomy."

I was about to tell them get the setup ready when a group of doctors came up to the bedside. It was the staff physician whom they had called. I looked at him for a moment. He was tall and thin with graying blonde hair, high cheekbones, and an aquiline nose. His face was sallow with penetrating blue eyes, covered by gold-rimmed glasses. The total effect was haughty and imperious. I wasn't wrong.

They stood at the head of the bed, looking at the tube and bronchoscope in place and listening to the anesthesiologist tell him what had happened. While they were talking, they occasionally looked over at me. I felt oddly naked in my street clothes, like I didn't belong.

The staff physician's name was on his coat. It said Charles Fitzhugh. Below the name was an army general's mortarboard of medical, academic, and administrative titles decorating his chest. I listened as the anesthesiologist explained to him that the bronchoscope was in her airway and that I saw a tear in the lining of the pharynx. He said that I was the patient's doctor.

Fitzhugh studied me for a moment; I was dressed in a gown that partially covered my slacks and open collar shirt. "You're a doctor, this patient's doctor, right?" he asked without an introduction.

"Yes," I replied, raising my voice.

"Do you practice here?"

"No."

"And you helped perform a bronchoscopy to stop the bleeding."

Behind my mask I felt my nostrils flare and my face redden as I nodded.

Fitzhugh turned to his entourage. "Do you think for one moment that in Boston we allowed something like this to happen? You see, this is just the kind of crap they hired me to eliminate. We need discipline in this hospital, not a bunch of itinerants performing rogue surgery. And by God that's what I am going to do!"

I studied him for a moment. He was, as one of my professors once said, a jug full of water with the cork rammed home. He didn't know me, but I don't take that kind of shit from anyone. "Tell me something, uh, Doctor Fitzhugh, is it? Were you born witless, or did you have to learn to be stupid? This woman is my patient. If we don't do something quickly, she's going to die!"

His face reddened and his lips quivered. It was the face of an academic bully who wasn't used to having his chops busted by a peon like me.

After a moment of silence, Sennett chimed in. "Look, doctor, I don't care where you came from or where you are going, but one thing is for damn sure, this doctor you are yelling at just saved this patient's life. Now I would advise you to shut up and help this poor woman, or I am going to testify at trial on your behavior."

He looked shocked. In his academic cocoon I had a feeling that no one ever told him how things were in the real world. Fitzhugh recovered long enough to see Sennett's badge, along with the handle of his gun sticking out of his belt. That must have been all the convincing he needed, because he stopped giving orders.

In the midst of this confrontation I heard the anesthesiologist yell: "She's in V-fib!" As he spoke, he started pushing drugs into the IV line. Then he yelled again, this time for the paddles. I could do nothing except watch the monitor as he shocked the patient.

I saw no heartbeats, only an irregular line on the screen. The anesthesiologist reached for a syringe on his table. I knew it was filled with adrenalin. He attached a long needle at the end, palpated the patient's chest for the space between the second and third ribs on the left, and pushed the needle into her cardiac musculature. After emptying the syringe, he looked back at the monitor. Suddenly, the patient's heart snapped back. I looked at the graph. Even I knew what a normal sinus rhythm looked like.

The anesthesiologist peered over his mask, relief in his eyes, and, ignoring Fitzhugh, asked me what we should do.

"I think she needs a tracheotomy to control her airway and then we can stop the bleeding from her throat. But it's up to your doctors now."

I ignored FitzHugh and got up to leave. It felt weird walking away from my patient, so I stood by the door for a few moments, waiting to see what happened. All I could hear was the regular beeping of the monitor and the quiet murmuring of the staff in the trauma room. Somehow Fitzhugh decided that a dumbass like me might be right, because he ordered the nurse to set up for a tracheotomy, yelling for instruments and chastising the staff for not responding quickly enough.

My experience with surgeons like Fitzhugh was that they were cowboys, ready to operate at the drop of a hat with the swagger of a gunslinger and the arrogance of gambler who never lost. Don't get me wrong; sometimes it's necessary. In this business the only proof of right or wrong is whether the patient survives. However, the guys that yelled the most were usually the docs with the least confidence in their abilities.

I had to admit one thing: In spite of his arrogance, Fitzhugh had a good point. I was on shaky ground according to hospital protocol. I motioned to Sennett that we should leave. After all, Sandra Wells was alive and this tight-ass academician obviously needed to show how his superior training would save the day. As we left, I gave a thumbs-up to the anesthesiologist, and he returned the salute. Walking down the hall I angrily tossed my Juicy Fruit in the trash. I knew this was wrong. Administrative rules were forcing me to abandon my patient, and it felt like hell.

CHAPTER 2

WE STUCK AROUND FOR A FEW MINUTES at the nurses' station, then started walking out of the emergency department. Sandra Wells was alive, but not out of the woods. When we reached the end of the corridor, Sennett touched my shoulder and pointed me in the direction of the cafeteria.

I followed him through the entrance and was suddenly awakened by the brightly lit room, filled with empty white Formica tables devoid of anyone, except three residents sitting on plastic chairs. Two of them were staring absently at their half-eaten Danish. The other had his head down next to his food, fast asleep.

George picked out a table beside a window. While he went for coffee, I sat down and stared out at the urban landscape. In the distance I could see the bright lights of the GM building dominating the skyline. I thought about the young woman in the emergency room and wondered how a person's life could come to this.

I didn't have time to answer the question. Sennett returned with two cups of the house blend and put one in front of me.

"Drink this. It'll do you good."

I watched as he took two packs of sugar and poured the contents into the black sludge. He must have seen me staring at him, because he said, "I'm a health nut." He didn't say it as a joke. It was almost as if he was talking to himself.

Whatever the reason, that quip pulled me out of my funk long enough to take a swig from the cup. As I did, I looked over at the residents. They still hadn't stirred from their spots. For a moment I thought they were mannequins put there by the hospital just to reassure people the place wasn't deserted. I turned back to Sennett.

"How did you know Sandra Wells?" I asked. "Was she a friend of yours?"

He told me that he had known her for a couple of years. She worked for the mayor as a staff assistant in the development office. I think he saw the look in my eye, because he ended by saying she was just a friend. George had a rep with the ladies, but no one ever knew whom he was with. That fact didn't take away the look of deep sadness in his eyes.

"What do you think happened?" he asked.

"I don't know exactly what those ER guys got into. At first I thought they might have hit the innominate artery, a huge vessel that crosses in front of the trachea. Now I think it was only a tear in the lining of throat when they put in the endotracheal tube. It must have been a tough intubation."

George swallowed half his cup of coffee, then asked me if I remembered her as a patient. I told him I didn't recognize her on the table, but who could recognize anyone with blood on her face and a tube down her throat? When I got to the office I said, I'd check it out.

Sennett was about to say something when a loud chiming sound echoed through the cafeteria. It was enough noise to vibrate our table. Obviously, that was what the hospital intended, because the resident who was fast asleep on the table jumped from his chair like he was hit by a Tazer. When he realized where the noise was coming from, he pulled a black pager from his white coat and gazed at the message with resigned disbelief.

I looked at him and saw myself twenty-five years ago; on-call, beat, and wishing I'd never see a pager again.

"You see those kids over there?" Sennett nodded. "I was like them, tired, poor, overworked and feeling like I was forever under the thumb of the man. They don't understand how good they have it."

Sennett looked puzzled. "What do you mean?"

"No matter what, they can still pass the buck to their chief. When I was their age, I couldn't wait until I was free of being accountable to the department above me. I wanted to be my own boss. That comes with a price. You can't hide from the responsibility of failure."

He nodded. "Kind of like being at the academy."

"Exactly."

"You're not sorry you're a doc, are you?"

I just smiled and shook my head. Taking risks was part of my profession. But I have to admit, I never operated in a hospital where I didn't have privileges. Yet, even though I might have been wrong in the eyes of a lawyer, I knew that, given that situation again, I would have done the same thing. After all I had been through in my life, I knew right from wrong.

Sennett was about to say something when we saw a light-skinned African American in his late thirties walking toward our table. He was well over six three. His body, which at one time could have been considered athletic, had a paunch that stretched the buttons of his expensive suit. The man's face had a fleshy corpulence that made his freckled skin look swollen. His lips were full and his eyes peered out from droopy lids. At the cuffs of his jacket were manicured nails and a gold pinky ring with a large diamond in the middle. In sum, he had the look of a man who was used to being satisfied.

Next to him was a smaller white guy about five ten and compactly built. He had neatly combed sandy-brown hair and black eyeglasses that rode just below his knitted brows. It was the bookish appearance of someone who spent a lot of time reading reports. The overall effect said accountant, but the confident way he walked suggested he was more than a bookkeeper.

Three look-alikes in dark suits and coiled earphones followed them. Each of the triplets looked like they could play middle linebacker for the Detroit Lions.

As the man in the blue suit walked near us, I could see a Spirit of Detroit pin on his lapel. Sennett got out of his chair and stood at attention as the man approached. He looked over at Sennett and said: "Good evening, Lieutenant."

Sennett stood up and responded with a deference I had seldom seen in him. "Good evening, Mr. Mayor," he said as he extended his hand.

"You remember my chief of staff, Tommy Holiday, don't you?" Robinson said, pointing to the accountant.

"I sure do," George said, smiling. "Tommy and I go a long way back."

Tommy shook Sennett's hand and smiled back. The smile instantly lit his face. His blue eyes suddenly became animated and his ruddy cheeks spoke of a yarn-spilling storyteller, the hit of the Irish pubs.

"Georgie-boy," he said. "We got a bad one tonight, huh?" he said seriously. "Who's your friend?"

"Ben Dailey. He was unfortunately there when Sandra Wells came into the hospital."

"You're a doc, aren't you?" Holiday asked. I could tell he wanted to know everything that affected the mayor. "Weren't you in the papers or something?"

I acknowledged him contritely. "Yeah, that was a while ago." At times like this I wished I were somewhere else.

"What happened to Sandra Wells?" Holiday asked. "We only heard that she was in a house fire."

"She had some problems," I replied tersely. As a doctor, I'm particular about randomly giving out patient information.

"Most people die in fires like that from smoke inhalation, don't they, doc?" he asked.

The tone of his voice was insinuative and demanding. Personally, the way I felt now about leaving Sandra Wells, I didn't give a damn who he was. So I bluntly told him I didn't feel like answering his questions.

He squinted in anger for a moment, as if he was momentarily stunned at being rebuffed; then he recovered. "Yeah, you guys have to keep up with the HIPPA laws, don't you?" He paused for a moment and smiled: "I'll find out anyway."

After an awkward moment of silence, Franklin Robinson turned back to Sennett. His eyes were sincere; his voice was soothing. "When I heard about Sandra, I came down. It's a terrible thing. We have to do something to stop this madness."

"We will," Sennett affirmed. "We will."

Robinson shook the lieutenant's hand and walked on. Holiday didn't bother to say goodbye.

"I didn't know you were tight with the Mayor," I said, surprised.

"I've known him for a while. I really admire him."

"Strange that in a city famous for an imprisoned mayor and a bankruptcy that almost shut it down, he could gain such admiration."

"Doc, this city has been through hell. We need the help of anyone willing to move the pile forward. That man is the future of this city," Sennett said. "Look what he is doing. He already got the City Council to agree to build a new hospital in the face of all this economic chaos."

"What about Holiday?" I asked. "We barely said two words and he was confrontational."

"That's Tommy. When you tell him you can't divulge something, it's like putting a burr under a horse's saddle. The man doesn't like to be told no by anyone."

I left Sennett at the door and walked to my car. By the time I drove out of the hospital entrance, my cell rang. It was Sennett.

"She's dead," was all he said.

The phone clicked off as I stared ahead through the darkness. The few cars that were out whizzed by me in indifference to my pain. The loss of a patient was a doctor's ultimate failure, and I couldn't help but blame myself.

CHAPTER 3

W AS I RESPONSIBLE FOR THIS POOR WOMAN'S DEMISE? Most of the time you can see disaster coming, like an incurable cancer. But there are always those times when instant decisions have to be made. When that happens, you second guess yourself and wonder if you could have done something different. So, on the drive back I did what I always did when a patient of mine died. I went step-by-step over my actions during my care of Sandra Wells.

I learned to do this as an intern at the county hospital. When I made a mistake on a patient's order, one of the attending physicians confronted me about it. I guess he saw I was angry at the rebuke. That's when he told me that the difference between success and failure in medicine is the ability to accept criticism. I took that as my mantra. If I or someone else concluded that I made a mistake, I vowed to learn from it and try to never make it again. Dealing with someone's life is the ultimate responsibility. We all have to get better at what we do.

It was after midnight when I pulled into my garage in the suburban neighborhood of Birmingham. I parked the car, turned off the engine, and sat there with my chin on my chest, staring vacantly at the yard tools in front of me.

Finally I walked out of the car, still thinking about Sandra Wells. I knew that I would have done nothing differently except declining Sennett's invitation to help the poor woman. That and maybe punching the lights out on that bag of wind, FitzHugh.

By the time I walked up the steps and opened the back door, Sandra Wells' death was partitioned into that portion of the brain that holds my experience. Bucky, our seventy pound yellow lab, was waiting for me. A couple of scratches behind the ear and a doggie treat were all he needed. Sometimes I wished humans were that easy to placate.

I took off my coat and went straight to the refrigerator. Inside I found a loaf of rye bread, some turkey and salami, and a package of Swiss cheese. I toasted the bread, then piled on a few slices of meat and cheese, and topped it with yellow mustard. I didn't bother to sit down, I was that hungry. So I ate standing at the kitchen sink. If my wife had seen me eating like this, she would have had a fit. Unfortunately, bad habits from living alone are hard to break.

When I finished, Bucky and I went upstairs where I checked on Joey, my 7-year-old son. He was fast asleep. I left Bucky at the foot of his bed, quietly went into my bedroom, and closed the door. The harvest moon was shining through the large bay window. I followed the rays of light until they illuminated Jordan soundly sleeping.

Looking at her asleep reminded me that I was married to the most beautiful woman I ever met—dark auburn hair, hazel green eyes, and a lithe enticing body. After my failed first marriage, it was a miracle Jordan and I found each other.

I went into the bathroom, got undressed, and peeked at the mirror. I was in my late forties, my hair was slightly gray at the temples, and I was a couple of cans short of a six-pack. But that didn't mean I was falling apart. Muscle-wise I was still pretty strong. I ran regularly and still did a lot of the calisthenics I'd learned playing football in college.

When I finished brushing my teeth, I walked into the bedroom. In case anyone is interested, I sleep commando. It was a habit I developed during my exile from medicine. I was a live-aboard sailor, and I found I liked to travel light. After a while I got used to the routine.

As I pulled the covers over me, my body touched Jordan's smooth warm skin. I could smell the faint scent of her perfume. It was intoxicating. She stirred slightly, then groggily opened her eyes.

"Rough night?" she said sleepily.

I turned toward her and took a deep satisfied breath. I had reached my sanctuary. "Kinda, but not now." My arm lingered on her shoulder as I reached out to stroke back the hair of the most beautiful woman I had ever known.

"Nice," she said, as she rubbed her hand along the side of my leg. Pretty soon she was commando too. Not one to ever turn down the invitation, we became one as City Hospital faded into a distant memory.

When our lovemaking was over, I held her in my arms and told her I loved her. As I did, I looked at her face again. This time I saw through her closed eyes a single tear making its slow journey down her cheek. I knew why and felt powerless to stop it.

I WOKE UP THE NEXT MORNING WITH THE HANGOVER of last night's events still lingering and a clattering noise upstairs that wouldn't stop. I didn't have much of a chance to think about it; I could hear Joey in his room. He was playing with one of those mechanical toys designed to make a racket and wake up his parents.

Joey was our miracle child. Jordan got pregnant before we were married. It was a problem pregnancy. Thankfully, everything worked out, but that was it. In spite of trying, she hadn't been able to get pregnant again. It wasn't that she couldn't carry a baby anymore. After some tests the doctor told us that as a result of her pregnancy she and I developed antibodies to each other. We tried five years of a variety of fertility treatments and then gave up hope. The decision to quit was hard on both of us, especially Jordan. She came from a large family and loved the tumult. Though she put on a tough exterior, I don't think her mind had yet gripped the fact that Joey would be an only child.

I got out of bed, shaved, dressed and then walked into the Joey's room. He looked up. "Look, Dad, I made a rocket ship," he said, smiling. I never understood how he could be that active at six in the morning. The boy definitely had a motor.

I studied the plastic model. It looked much too complicated for me, so I suggested that we go downstairs and get something to eat. He waited a moment while he attached one more piece to his contraption. Then he picked it up, jumped off the bed, and made for the stairs. Joey loved to eat.

When we got to the kitchen, I poured Cheerios into a bowl, cut up a banana, and put it in front of him. I watched him shovel the food into his mouth.

"Slow down, pal. It isn't going anywhere." He looked at me quizzically.

"Yes it is, Dad. It's going into my stomach."

"Who taught you that?" I asked.

"I saw it in a book," he said between bites.

Another doc in the making, I thought. I wondered if his career would be like mine. After what I had been through, I hoped it wouldn't.

When he finished, he picked up his plane and started adjusting the pieces. While he did, I opened the Mochamaster, put in water, added coffee, and turned on the machine. I heard the water bubbling as I turned on the television to listen to the news. It wasn't until I retrieved my coffee that I paid any attention to the speaker. I could hear the newscaster giving a live report from city hospital. That's when I began to listen closely.

She described the death of a city employee, Sandra Wells, who had been the victim of a senseless arson the night before. They flashed a picture of Sandra on the screen. She was a beautiful young woman, bright eyes that spoke of eagerness and a smile that seemed infectious. It was the look of a person with the whole world in front of her, twenty-eight years old, a graduate of the University of Michigan Law School, and gleaming with the promise of a successful career. It seemed odd that while I see a lot of patients over the years, her piercing blue eyes and black hair were hard to forget.

Then the mayor's interview from the night before appeared on the TV. His words were sharp and concise like he was reading from a prompter; his tears weren't.

"We must find a way to stop the plague of senseless deaths that has engulfed this city. We must find an answer. We simply must." The footage stopped and the newsman came back on the screen. By this time I heard steps behind me and turned around to see Jordan.

"Sleep well last night?" I asked.

She nodded and put her arms over my shoulders, hugging me from behind. "Yeah, I might ask for that again," she whispered in my ear. The closeness of her body and the reference to my welcome home last night stirred me for a moment.

I turned around to look at her. In spite of her levity, I sensed a hint of sadness in her face, as she stared down at her empty hands. I had seen it the night before, and I saw it every time we were intimate. It was ironic, the pleasure and tenderness with the man she loved, and the mourning for the love of a child she would never have. She still had not come to grips with the realization of this loss.

Initially, I had trouble understanding her feelings. When we had Joey, I felt my life was complete. But that was me; not Jordan. Her deep maternal instinct took me a while to understand.

I knew that she wanted to talk to me about it, but I looked at my watch. Now was not the right time. I had to see Allan Davis before my office started. When I told her we would talk about "the situation" later, I could see disappointment in her eyes, and it made me angry that I had to leave. The anger was made worse when I realized that what happened at City Hospital last night wasn't going away.

Chapter 4

ALLAN DAVIS HAD A SINGULAR WAY WITH PEOPLE; they all seemed to dislike him. Some said his demeanor went with the job, Wayne County Coroner. Others thought it was a lifetime affliction. I didn't think so. I thought it was not so much what he said, it's what he didn't say. His had a disregard for ordinary chatter and a highbrow intellectualism that looked down upon the common man. Even his physical appearance seemed annoying—asthenic, with a receding hairline, a beaked nose with dangling wire glasses perched on the bridge and a long, stiff neck that rose above his bow-tied shirt. The overall impression was the animated cartoon character, Gosamer Goose.

I arrived at his Wayne Count Coroner's Building at eight o'clock. After parking in the covered garage off Mack Avenue, I made my way through the empty halls of the morgue to his office. The stark white tiled walls and the pungent smell of formaldehyde left no doubt as to where I was.

As I walked to his office, I steeled myself for the meeting. I knew that as soon as he found out that I needed something from him, he would envelope himself in his most august imperiousness, making sure that I paid homage to His Excellency. What I needed were the final autopsy results on Sandra Wells. Unlike other people he would brush aside, I knew he would give them to me.

I was probably one of the few people in Detroit who tolerated him, most likely because I was the only person in Detroit who had ever ruined his façade. I once had an intense dislike for him. Now I just saw him for what he was, an insecure person hiding inside an academic stuffed shirt.

My opinion was not without justification. You see, it was his testimony that cost me my medical career. He was smug and self-assured in front of the jury when he testified I had left a sponge in the patient's wound.

Five years later, I proved him wrong. It was an egregious mistake on his part. The sponge he claimed I mistakenly left in the patient had been planted. None of us are perfect, but Allan was a forensic pathologist. That's his job. A guy like him doesn't make those kinds of errors.

I had known him since medical school. He was the smartest guy in our class. I think he reveled in this intellectual adulation, because no one would have mistaken him for a great athlete or a ladies' man or even a doc with great bedside manner. His arrogance was a "screw you" to every bully that had made his life miserable when he was a kid. In contrast, I was one of those college kids who found his career path by trial and error. I liked sports, music, and hanging out. I'm sure he looked at me as an academic misfit.

I remembered on surgical rounds once, when the professor asked me what Sampter's Triad was, I couldn't come up with the answer. Davis quickly pushed his way to the front of the group and gave the correct response. I remember the self-satisfied look he gave me after he spoke.

Now I had him. His mistake in my case cast an indelible tarnish on his reputation. I vowed to punish him one day for what he did. Then I remembered what my dad always told me: "You don't get big by making other people small." All doctors have the proverbial skeletons in their closets. I also knew that I might need him someday. This was going to be one of those days.

As I walked in, I heard the high-pitched whine of a centrifuge. Davis was sitting behind his grey metal desk. When he saw me, he immediately put down his recent issue of Golf Digest and shut the machine off. Aside from dissecting stiffs, Davis was consumed by the game of golf.

Leaning back in his chair, I saw his head drop a little, the eyebrows sag, and his body shrink into his chair. "What brings you down here this morning, Ben?" By this time he was nervously polishing his wire-rimmed glasses. Without the specs he looked almost human.

"Al, I'd like to see the autopsy results on the woman who died at City Hospital last night." I called him Al, which I think he liked.

"You mean the one that died in that abandoned house?" The glasses were now back on and the old Davis reappeared.

I nodded. "Did you find anything in particular?"

The first thing he asked me about were the HIPPA laws that cover dissemination of this type of information. I told him this wasn't about the legal ramifications. I was merely a treating physician asking for information.

He seemed surprised that I treated this patient. When I nodded, his demeanor changed. He first suggested that he could give me the information after he filed the complete autopsy report. I told him I couldn't wait that long.

Reluctantly, he said there were no abnormalities on gross examination, except for the laceration I had noted in her throat and diffuse smoke inhalation throughout her lungs.

"Anything else?" I asked."

"What's that?"

"Whoever performed her tracheotomy didn't do a very good job." I think he believed I had done it, because he had a wrinkle of a smirk on his face.

"Why?"

"They put the trach in too high. If this patient had survived, she probably would need an extensive reconstruction procedure. That said, I believe that she died of a PEA."

When I told him to speak in English, he looked over his wire rims and said," pulseless electrical activity—too many drugs, too much debris in her lungs causing her heart to stop with irreversible brain damage. They got her back, but by that time it was too late. Whatever happened in that emergency room incident didn't matter. From the look of her lungs she was a goner."

I asked him about drugs in her body. He seemed distracted and just shrugged his shoulders, saying they were working on it. His face became pensive; he seemed lost in thought for a moment. Then he did something I wasn't expecting. "Let me show you something unusual. Follow me back to the storage room."

With that he raised his lanky, uncoordinated frame from his chair and walked back into his laboratory. I followed. Inside stacked cabinets and metal racks were glass containers holding preserved tissue of dead people. I'm a doctor, but looking at preserved body parts still gives me a chill down my back. I remember seeing the same bottles and the planted gauze covering the tissue that incriminated me. As if guided by an unseen map, he ignored the specimens and went up to one of the cabinets packed with files.

He thumbed through the names on dozens of folders until he came to the one he wanted. I could see the name Sandra Wells on the tab. Once he found her file, he pulled out a photograph of her left hand.

"It's no big deal, Ben, but look at her little finger."

I studied it for a moment. "It looks a little shorter than I would have expected."

He rubbed the back of his neck. "That's right," he said, with a touch of disappointment that I had actually noticed. "It's strange, but the tip of the finger appears to be gone. I don't know how it happened. It's possible that something with the fire may have caused it. I just thought you might be interested. No big deal. I barely mentioned it in my report."

I had no idea what it meant and neither did Davis. I think he just wanted to prove to me how thorough he was. With an air of disappointment he put the folder back and closed and locked the cabinet.

"Have you ever seen something like that before?"

"Not that I can remember," he replied, obviously puzzled by the finding.

He had nothing else to add, so I thanked him for his help and walked toward the exit. I looked back at him as I walked to his office. It was depressing. Standing there forlorn among the rows of specimen bottles and filing cabinets, I almost felt sorry for him.

When I left the morgue, I had mixed feelings: a sadness for Sandra's passing and personal relief that I had done nothing to lead to her death. On the way back to the office my cellphone rang. It was my nurse, Karen. She said the president of City Hospital wanted to see me in his office tomorrow. It was something about operating in a hospital without privileges. A feeling of unease gripped me. I could see hospital administrators and lawyers crowding around me, all trying to ruin me once more. This time I shook the idea out of my head. Not in this lifetime.

CHAPTER 5

THE CHIEF MEDICAL OFFICER and some other officials might want to meet with me in the morning, but I wouldn't speak with anyone without checking with my attorney first. That discussion didn't turn out as well as I had hoped. He succinctly pointed out that the courts disapprove of doctors performing surgery without hospital privileges. I understood that, but the facts were what they were. I decided that I was going to go on my own. After what I had been through in my life with the medical profession, there weren't enough hospicrats in this city big enough to scare me.

That afternoon, as I pulled up to the entrance, I noticed the radiance of City Hospital during the day. The bright, imposing glass tower of the new medical campus replaced the oppressive dread of the inner city at night. Next to it were the two cranes, no longer mechanical monsters. These were the implements of hope. This was the city's focus on revival, a billion dollar development that would bring Detroit a world-class hospital complex.

At least that was the pitch the city government gave its constituents. Being a cynic, in a city on the verge of bankruptcy, I assumed some political pork barrel in Washington was going to bail the government out.

Instead of rushing up to the emergency room as I had two nights ago, I parked in the visitors' lot and walked in the entrance. A couple of minutes of instructions from the lady behind the information desk, and I was on my way to see the powers-that-be.

The walk to the boardroom at old City Hospital had an eerie reminiscence to it—long, fluorescent-lit corridors leading to polished, dark wooden doors. I made a similar trek to another boardroom seven years ago. Except that visit signaled the end of my career as a physician, president of the medical staff, and highly respected member of the community. It also spelled the end of my first marriage and a downward spiral that left me destitute and homeless, living and acting like a bum. All because of a setup by the Chairman of the Board at my hospital, St. Vincent's. All in the name of money and greed.

I uncovered the plot, but not before my patient died. That death bothered me more than all the monetary and personal grief I suffered. I captured the son of a bitch who did this to me, but it almost cost me my life. His name was Charles Thornton, a tycoon, who thought he could manipulate the world. Now he spent his days behind bars with nothing to think about except his ruined life.

When I walked into that boardroom seven years ago, I was in a maelstrom of accusations I couldn't fend off. Today was different. I tried to save someone's life. Now punishment was going to be my reward. I was certain that I did nothing wrong and confident that after what I had been through, they would not shake my resolve.

There was no slouch in my gait as I reached the ornate paneled doors and pushed them open. The room I stepped into was on the third floor, low enough to be partially shielded by the tall blue spruces of the inner courtyard and high enough to catch the afternoon sun shining off the glass windows of the new hospital though the floor to ceiling windows. In the middle of the room was a long, polished mahogany conference table crowned by two stainless steel carafes and white coffee cups emblazoned with the hospital's logo. Surrounding the table were enough high backed leather chairs to accommodate thirty people. Today there were only seven.

Six of the chairs contained officious looking men dressed in expensive suits with pocket squares, polished cap toe shoes, and regimental ties. It was the new dress code of corporate medicine. Of the five occupants, three were doctors: Arthur VanEngle, M.D., Chairman of the Board of City Hospital, Horace Stanford, M.D., Chief Medical Officer of City Hospital, and Charles Fitzhugh. Of the other three, one of them was the hospital's attorney, Jamieson Cartwright and one was Turner Davidson, Mayor Robinson's opponent in the upcoming election. The sixth person was Tommy Holiday.

When Holiday saw me, he jutted his chin and flashed a confident smile, almost a smirk. "How are you doing, doc? I told you I'd find out what happened." I just ignored him.

After the introduction it was all business. I was expecting a tongue-lashing and a series of legal threats regarding my medical attempts to save the young woman. In fact, that's what I got.

Stanford matter-of-factly laid out the illegality of working at a hospital without privileges and how it placed the hospital in a precarious legal position. Sandra's death could cost them millions of dollars they didn't have. I cynically thought to myself once again how naïve I was. Medicine was now run by bean counters; the human element was MIA. I was impassive through Stanford's diatribe. Never let them see you sweat.

After a half-hour lecture on the legalities of medicine, Stanford suddenly changed the subject. "How long had you known Ms. Wells?"

"As a patient?" I asked.

"Was there something else?" he asked.

"What are you implying?"

Stanford backed off. "Just curious if Ms. Wells indicated to you what she did for a living."

"Even if I did, I have no reason to tell you," I said defiantly.

My response didn't satisfy the cabal in the room. That's when VanEngle jumped in.

"Ms. Wells worked for the mayor. She was his assistant, focusing on the new project at City Hospital. We need to know if discussions took place with you regarding her job, and whether her death had anything to do with her employment."

"Is that why you have the mayor's chief of staff at this meeting? Look, I'm a surgeon, not a psychiatrist. If conversations took place about her job, I can't divulge that, or maybe you haven't seen a real patient lately to know the HIPPA laws. If you have something you want to say, let's get on with it."

Seemingly unfazed, he went on to tell me that the new City Hospital is the most important building project the city had ever had and the Mayor's office couldn't allow any bad publicity. Obviously, he meant me, because he followed with a threat to pursue legal action on me for operating at the hospital without privileges.

I gave him a hard stare. "Let me ask you a question," I said, speaking deliberately. "If you drove down a highway and up ahead saw an accident with a person lying face down on the pavement, under your theory, you would keep driving, right?"

Stanford blustered for a moment. "Well, that's a different situation."

"Is it really?" I asked, "or is that the knee jerk response from a physician who sees only the bottom line? Have you forgotten what it means to be a doctor?"

Stanford was about to reply when Cartwright jumped up and told his client to keep his mouth shut. It was probably a smart piece of advice.

"Dr. Dailey, I know your history. You are something of a legend in the medical-legal circles in Detroit. But that does not give you the right to flout the law."

I waited for a moment, jamming my teeth against the gum in my mouth to control my anger. "I'm not afraid of you or your staff or, for that matter, the mayor's office. I did what a real doctor is supposed to do. If you or your pencil-pushing associates don't like it, you have your legal alternatives. I'll take my chance with a jury of real people "

When I finished, the lawyer jumped in, pointing his finger at me while holding up a piece of paper that delineated the credentialing process at City. He then referred to the requirement for malpractice insurance by every physician working at the hospital. Since I was not on the staff, it left them wondering what to do. It also left me responsible for damages.

His speech took another five minutes, during which he continuously took his glasses on and off as he read from the papers on his desk. He had an annoying nasal twang that made him sound like a whining teenager.

As for Holiday, he just sat there and took in the whole process without saying a word. He had a pen and a legal notepad on the table, and every now and then he would write something.

VanEngle took a piece of paper in front of him and handed it to me. "This is a letter from the hospital spelling out City Hospital's position on this matter. It includes a section from the by-laws requiring proper credentialing and acceptance to the hospital staff before a physician can provide services within its confines. I suggest that you read it over carefully; you may want to contact your personal attorney. I can tell you that City is going to disavow any connection with the incident. Should the hospital be sued, you would be personally responsible for any damages."

I looked at the letter. It was signed in a chicken scratch that read "AVE." I took note of it. This matter was obviously beneath his dignity to sign his full name.

If he thought he was going to scare me, he was wrong, dead wrong. I saw this movie before and faced the consequences of failure. I knew I was too tough for him. From the way sweat gathered on his upper lip at me I think he knew it too.

I took the paper, crumpled it up and threw it back on the conference table. I felt like telling him to go fuck himself, it might be the best time he ever had. Instead, I took a piece of paper from my pocket and deliberately made them wait as I slowly wrote down a couple of words. They all looked annoyed at my insolence in making them wait.

When I was finished, I looked down at the words I wrote and told them that instead of pounding bureaucratic papers in front of them, I actually did something positive regarding Sandra Wells. I then explained that I went to the coroner's office and went over the autopsy.

I looked over at FitzHugh. "It turns out that your hotshot, stuffed shirt surgeon from Boston screwed up big time. He couldn't find the right place to put the tracheotomy in and went into the cricoid cartilage. Had this patient lived, she would have had a miserable existence as a respiratory cripple. He said he needed to get rid of the riffraff in City Hospital. Maybe he should start with himself. And by the way, if this becomes a legal dispute, I intend to testify on his ineffectual bungling."

I suppose no one had ever told FitzHugh the facts of life in the real world of medicine, because he ranted for five minutes on his training, abilities, and academic record. Then he accused me of being incompetent and a few other things. By the time he was finished, spittle was gathering at the corner of his mouth. It was in some ways amusing. I was definitely under his skin.

When he finished, I got up and put the paper back in my pocket. At the door, I stopped. "Gentlemen, as far as I'm concerned this meeting is over. There is one thing I think you should know. Whatever happens in your legal attempt to intimidate me, I have the conscience and the knowledge to know that I acted as a physician, something that you administrative sychophants lost a long time ago."

With that, I walked out of the boardroom. In spite of my outburst, I didn't slam the door behind me as I had done the last time I had faced the powers-that-be at St. Vincent's. Somehow, in the back of my mind, I realized these guys might have a case.

CHAPTER 6

I WALKED OUT OF THE HOSPITAL AND found my Jeep Wagoneer in the lot. I got in and sat behind the wheel for a moment. I had a thing with my car. It was old and finicky, but it was part of my life. That's why I had spent untold thousands of dollars keeping this 20-year-old beast alive.

When I turned on the ignition, I heard a slight coughing sound as it came to life. It almost growled in appreciation.

It was late afternoon by the time I reached my office on the campus of St. Vincent's Hospital, a thousand-bed facility just north of the city limits of Detroit. The mere fact that it wasn't in the city gave it a cache of safety and, accordingly, superior care. Sometimes this was more perception than reality.

However, the perceived reverse racism of the then mayor, Coleman Young, gave impetus to the white flight of the seventies and doomed the city of Detroit to a downward economic spiral. Every service in the city suffered—schools, police protection and even medical care. By the time the state government took over the management of the local government, hospitals had sprung up all over the suburbs and the suburban population flocked to them. Ironically, the residents of the inner city, recognizing the superior care, went with them.

St. Vincent's was the biggest and most powerful of these institutions with a well-trained medical staff, a level one emergency room, and a medical school affiliation. It seemed incongruous that my office was at a hospital that had nearly ruined me, but you can't hate forever. When Charles Thornton's plot was uncovered, and I was vindicated, the hospital begged me to return. It didn't hurt that they made a large financial settlement and gave me an office for free.

After a couple of years the pain disappeared, and I immersed myself in medicine again. I restored my reputation as a voice specialist and head and neck surgeon. However, I never seemed to be able to shuck my involvement with the law. As a reluctant detective, trouble always seemed to find me.

I parked my car, walked into the medical office building, and made my way to my office on the third floor. The late autumn sun was hanging on for its last glories of the day, magnificent in peach, lavender, and glowing orange. The office staff had left, and I was alone. I heard some noise at the front desk, so I walked up the corridor. It was the cleaning crew. They must have been new because I didn't recognize them.

A small waiting room with glass entry doors opened into the office lobby. Behind it were fifteen chairs arranged in groups with small tables for magazines. In the far corner was a hanging television set playing the Home and Garden Network. I went though the waiting area and passed the examining rooms as I moved toward my private office.

My office was in the back corner of the suite. It was a relatively small room with large tinted windows that exposed to the medical behemoth of St. Vincent's on one side and, on the other, the endless sea of traffic moving down the expressway. A photograph of a winter view of the Maroon Bells in Colorado sat behind my desk. On either side were shelves with a number of medical books, and at each end hung my diplomas from undergraduate and medical school at the University of Michigan. Next to them were membership certificates from a dozen medical societies and some awards I received over the years. My nurse, Karen, told me patients like to see their doctor's pedigree, but I never made much about them.

When I walked into to my office, a man in cleaning crew overalls sat behind my desk. I shot a glance at him. My computer was open, and he had a wastebasket on his lap. I had never seen him before. Funny, but his appearance seemed out of place with the usual cleaning crew.

"Where's Caroline?" I asked.

"Oh, sorry. Didn't mean to scare you," he said, getting up from the chair. "I'm working tonight. She's sick and the boss sent me over." As he spoke, he emptied the wastebasket into a larger trash receptacle and then left the room.

Something didn't seem right, so when he was down the corridor, I went over to the trash container and rummaged through the papers. When I looked inside I saw nothing except some newspapers, paper towels, and a few empty cardboard boxes.

I shrugged off the incident and sat down behind my desk. I turned on my computer and frowned as I searched for Sandra Wells' record. I hated the computer. It was a bureaucratic intrusion on my practice. I liked real paper; something to hold and make notes on instead of a temperamental mouse that took a break every five minutes.

But my vote didn't count, so I pulled up the file and immediately saw Sandra

Wells' photo on the screen. I was shocked when I stared at her face for a moment. I remembered her, a very pleasant, nice-looking young woman with an All American smile. I quickly scanned her records and saw nothing special. She had seen me a several times over the past two years—sore throat, sinus trouble, nothing serious.

Looking at her picture again, I was reminded of something else. I strangely recalled conversations with her covering a wide-range of non-medical subjects—art, politics, sports, that kind of thing. Whatever it was, I remembered these discussions were insightful. I guess in one sense I could have thought that she had something else in mind with me besides medicine, but it wasn't like that. I sensed that she was genuinely interested in what I thought. It was almost as if she was interviewing me.

I also recalled that she worked for the mayor and that someone there had referred her. She said before she came that she had looked up my bio. Since she was a lawyer, my history intrigued her, especially the way I solved crimes.

I usually didn't like talking about my past. I was a doctor, not a policeman, but somehow she wasn't obtrusive. With every visit she seemed to find another question. Not on a personal basis, but as if she was collecting information.

As I thought about her, one incident did stand out in my mind. We were in my office discussing her condition, when she saw a picture of me taken twenty-five years ago. It was one of those posed pictures that the athletic department at Ann Arbor took of each player on the football team, regardless of how good he was. It was old school. I was dressed in my uniform, without a helmet, down in a three-point stance. I have to admit I looked good, but that was about as far as it went. When it came to ability, I was just a practice squad player.

She said she wasn't much of a football fan, but she knew from working in Michigan about the Ohio State-Michigan rivalry. Then she asked me an odd question: Would I let my child go to Ohio State? I thought a moment and said my child's life wasn't about me. If that's where he wanted to go and he had good reasons, I would support his choice. I just wouldn't root for his football team. She smiled and nodded her head in an almost approving manner. Just like that the interview was over.

A couple of weeks later I received a package in the mail. I opened it up and inside was a small maize and blue football with a Michigan emblem on it. Attached was a note from Sandra Wells. I remembered what it said. "To Joey, Go Blue to a future Wolverine." I thought it was a little strange, but when I showed it to Joey, it became the staple of our afternoon football games.

My phone suddenly interrupted my thoughts. It was Jordan.

"You walked into a real mess, Ben." She sounded excited.

"How did you find out about City Hospital already? Was it that big a news story?"

"I don't know anything about City Hospital. I'm talking about the death of that young woman and her relationship with the mayor."

I asked her what she meant. "It seems as though his honor had a thing for Sandra Wells, and Mrs. Franklin Robinson wasn't too happy about it."

"Did they say this was an attempted murder?" I felt like I was back in familiar territory I didn't want to be in, solving crimes.

"I don't know for sure. They had just gotten the information through the Freedom of Information statute." Apparently, the mayor lied to the press when he said he didn't know anything about Sandra Wells. His cellphone was filled with text messages between them. Setting up meetings at night.

"Okay, the man is cheating on his old lady. How is that a Federal crime?"

She said that he was using a government phone, so this took his relationship with Sandra Wells into the public domain. I was about to ask her what she thought, when she said she had to run and hung up.

I sat at my desk for a moment, staring out the window. All I could see was trouble. This was going to be national news and my wife was going to be in the center of it. My head was beginning to throb. I hated the press.

I rummaged through the remaining mail until suddenly my gaze landed on a green medical journal I had left on my desk. I casually opened it up and glanced at the articles. One of them piqued my interest, "Tracheal Hemorrhage—Diagnosis and Management." I was going to put it down, but I couldn't help but read it. Even though it reaffirmed that I did everything right, it still couldn't take away the sadness of Sandra's death.

CHAPTER 7

MY OFFICE WAS CLOSED ON WEDNESDAYS, so I arranged to meet Jordan for lunch. It was a crisp late October day. In this part of the country it's called Indian Summer—temperature in the low seventies, maple trees blazing with red leaves, and a filtered sun low in the horizon, announcing to all that winter was around the corner. It is that few weeks of the year when everything seems perfect.

I parked my Wagoneer at the curb and filled the pay meter with quarters. I quickly realized I didn't have enough for two hours, but I decided to take my chances, praying that I not stoke the city coffers. I walked down the street and saw a woman coming toward me. The sun was glinting off a silver barrette that pulled her highlighted auburn hair away from her face. In her silky white dress with a pink sweater pulled close to her chest, she looked lithe, athletic, and definitely eye-turning. I'm older, but not too old to check out a nice-looking woman. It wasn't until she got closer that I had one of those stupid flashes of guilt. I was ogling my wife.

I kissed her on the cheek, and we walked together for a block, until we reached Elie's, one of the best Lebanese restaurants in a city. We waited at the entrance to be seated.

"The way you stared at me I almost believed you were checking me out. Did you think I was someone else?" she asked

"It's my eyesight. You know as you get older . . ."

"It's okay, Ben. I liked it." As she spoke, the waitress came outside and ushered us to a table. Next to it were five men in dress shirts and ties, crowded into a table for four. They were eating shrimp, drinking beer, and laughing loudly about some kind of airplane one of them owned—the upscale businessman's lunch. I bet they drove BMWs, wore Gucci slip-ons, and were all scratch golfers.

A couple of them looked at us. I was sure they weren't looking at me.

I glanced around for another table but none were available. Jordan didn't seem to care.

"Did Joey give you any trouble about going to school this morning?" I asked as we sat down.

Jordan picked up her napkin, placed it on her lap, and proceeded to explain her entire discussion with him, including the negotiation that left his teddy bear in his bed.

"He has the devil in him," she said. "I left him for a moment to get something out of the closet. When I came back, he had taken out all the glasses from the cupboard and set them on the counter on a series of plates at different levels. Then he took the water nozzle from the sink and started pouring water from the top one down. When I came in water covered everything."

"What did he say?" I asked, laughing.

"He told me he was making Niagara Falls; it was an experiment." She saw I was smiling. "I know you're laughing, but you didn't clean it up."

I proceeded to tell her my mother said I did the same thing when I was his age, except I used baking soda and vinegar to make a volcano. I could tell she wasn't impressed, so I asked her what she did with Joey.

She said it was very simple; every bad action has a reaction. "In this case, he helped me clean it up. Apparently, he thought it was the funniest thing ever."

I thought it was funny too. "No wonder, you are a Federal prosecutor. Joey didn't stand a chance."

Jordan became serious. "You know, Ben, no matter what Joey does, I'm soaking it in. We only get one chance; I want to make the most of every moment." Her eyes widened, trying to avoid the inevitable tears. She brushed them away with her napkin.

"Maybe we should consider adoption," I replied.

"Maybe we should," she said.

I was about to respond when one of the guys jumped up from the table next to us, spilling his wine glass on the sidewalk and shattering it into a thousand pieces. I looked up annoyed and then realized his face was turning beet red as he held his hands up to his neck.

One of his friends at the table yelled, "Someone help him! He's choking!"

I pushed back my chair and yelled at his friends, "What was he eating?"

"A shrimp," one of them said. "He was talking and drinking at the same time and then he started to choke."

By this time his face was turning blue. He was a big guy, about six three and two-forty. I didn't waste any time telling them I was a doc. Instead I jumped in front of him, spun him around, and put my arms around his upper abdomen.

With my fist jammed into his solar plexus, I squeezed suddenly and forcefully against his rock hard abdomen. Nothing happened. I had a sudden epiphany. It was Sandra Wells all over again, except I wasn't going to let it happen. With all my strength I pushed once more against his stomach. I heard him cough and suddenly half a shrimp shot out of his mouth.

He coughed again and took in a breath. His airway was clear. As he gasped for more air, normal color returned to his face. That's when he sat down. By this time a crowd formed, trying to see what happened. I heard someone calling 911.

"Are you all right?" I asked, checking his pulse. Pale and still breathing heavily he nodded weakly. I looked at him more closely. Wavy black hair with a dimpled chin, and a tanned face with a hint of a 12 o'clock shadow. He smelled of expensive cologne.

I took the napkin from the table, dipped it into his water glass and held it against his forehead. He brought his hand up to hold the cloth in place and wiped his face. The heavy sound of his breathing eased.

The firehouse was right across the street. In short order the EMS guys arrived. I stepped aside as they gave him some oxygen, took his pulse and checked his blood pressure. When they mentioned the hospital, he shook his head, seemingly embarrassed at all the fuss that was being made over him. I probably would have felt the same way.

One of the techs frowned, as if to say he was making the wrong decision. That's when I stood up and told him I was a doc. After I described what happened, he nodded and reluctantly packed up his gear.

I understood their position; giving advice to someone who had almost choked to death and then listening to him tell them he was okay isn't what they wanted to hear. But not every decision is black and white, and this was one of them.

I watched as they walked back to their truck, remembering the number of times someone ignored my advice as a physician. I always told them they were the CEO of their bodies and they had the right to decide what they wanted to do. The patient isn't always wrong.

By the time I turned around, the guy whose life I saved was out of the chair and straightening his tie.

"Jeff Taylor," he said in a slightly hoarse voice and stuck out a hand emblazoned with a gold Rolex Daytona. He had the slow smile of relief

I shook his vice-like grip. After giving him the Heimlich maneuver against an abdomen as solid as his, I wasn't surprised. "I'm Ben Dailey," I said.

"I heard you tell the EMS guy you were a doc. My lucky day."

"Even a blind squirrel can find an acorn."

"Well, I guess I'm glad I was the acorn," he laughed. It was the nonchalant laugh of someone who was used to being lucky. He reached into his front shirt pocket and handed me a card. "If you need anything, give me a call. I owe it to you."

As he walked up to the waitress to pay his bill, I glanced down at his card. It read Empire Investments, Jeff Taylor, CEO. The way the economy was going I was half-tempted to take him up on the offer.

I sat back down at the table and watched as the five amigos sauntered down the sidewalk. The waitress came over and I ordered a Labatt Blue. Jordan had a Pinot grigio. Opposites attract.

"Do you look for trouble or does it just find you?" she asked, sipping at the straw.

"You know, some people make their living on the misery of other people."

"If that's the case, you should have asked for his Blue Cross card."

When I told her she should be my office manager, she shrugged and said she had trouble balancing her own checkbook. Then she looked at me seriously and asked when I decided to be a doctor, if I thought it was saving lives like Jeff Taylor's.

After a long sip from the glass, I admitted that I had no idea what it was going to be like when I went to medical school. All I could see was the excitement of the operating room and helping people. No one told me about how hard the rigors of a medical school was going to be.

She asked what I meant. In reality, unless you have actually lived it, it's hard to tell someone what it's like constantly studying for examinations every five weeks, doing scut work until all hours of the night, having just enough money to get by, owning a life that wasn't your own. How could I explain to someone the feeling of accomplishment after I finished my training? I was about to get serious, when I suddenly began laughing.

"What's so funny?" she asked.

"Multiple choice tests. I never knew when I went to medical school, that my life would be ruled by the multiple choice test."

"Your point?"

"They drove me crazy. Four answers, two of which you knew were wrong and two that could be right. I was going crazy until I figured it out."

"How did you do that?"

"The "C" rule."

"Huh?"

"When in doubt the answer is always 'C.'"

Jordan smiled and said it was no different in law school. "Except our problem wasn't multiple choice; it was the essay test."

I told her it was perfect for a lawyer, because they get paid by the word. She laughed. "Lawyers and doctors are like oil and water."

"They actually have a lot in common," I said. She looked at me quizzically. I responded with my favorite line. "Lawyers are pre-med students that can't stand the sight of blood."

She reached out and touched my hand softly. "Not really. I might know more than you think. Like mouth to mouth resuscitation."

"What do you mean?" I asked, twirling the bottle on the table.

She pursed her lips into a small circle. "Oh, I don't know. Take you, for instance. A little oral resuscitation might do you some good." I felt her hand slide off the table and touch the inside of my leg.

I looked around to see if anyone was looking. The coast was clear, so I smiled. The agonies of my past now seemed like a distant memory. My short arm was pointing in a different direction.

CHAPTER 8

I WALKED IN TO MY OFFICE THE NEXT DAY through the back door and there, sitting on my desk, was a huge fruit basket, filled with apples, pears, kiwis, three kinds of cheese, crackers, and a couple of bottles of what appeared to be expensive wine. I looked on the handle and saw a card. It read: "I will never be able to thank you enough for what you did for me yesterday. If I ever can do anything to help you, please call. Jeff Taylor, Empire Investments." Nice gesture, I thought. I put the card into the drawer of my desk and quickly forgot about it.

It was a nice start to the day and things went smoothly. There were no emergencies, and I finished on time around noon. That didn't mean my work was over. There was another two hours of completing records, going over patients' tests, and returning phone calls.

After walking back to my office, I sat down in front of the mail on my desk. As I did, I glanced out the window at St. Vincent's Hospital behind me. An emergency vehicle pulled up to the circular drive next to the helicopter pad. The driver rushed out of the cab and raced to the back of the van to open the doors. He reached inside and pulled out a stretcher. Next to it was a tech holding a facemask over the patient, pumping oxygen furiously into the patient's lungs. Good people, men and women at work, saving lives, trying their best.

I was just getting ready to go through the mail when Karen came in. George Sennett was on the line. I picked up the phone and listened.

"Ben, how about going with me to look at the house where Sandra Wells was found?" When I asked him why he wanted me to go, he said something about me being able to see things he couldn't.

I was surprised. "Come on George, you're the crime dog, not me."

"It's the truth, but if you don't believe me, then come along for the company."

I shuddered at the idea of getting involved. Did I need this? Then I thought for a moment about Sandra Wells' death, the problems I had with City Hospital, and the card she had in her purse with my name on it. After a few moments I replied, "You know, I wouldn't say no, didn't you?"

"You took longer than I thought. I'll be at your office in twenty minutes."

"WHERE ARE WE HEADED?" I ASKED, as I got into his car.

"West Chicago Boulevard and Livernois Avenue. It's rated the number one most dangerous neighborhood in the country." He shrugged it off when I asked him if I should be worried and advised me that if I stayed next to him I should be fine.

We turned down Woodward Avenue past shops, restaurants, high-rise buildings, and most of all people. The downtown part of the city was starting to revive after decades of deterioration. On the way I asked him if he had any new developments on the death of Sandra Wells.

"Nothing yet, except for a trace of cocaine, and I'm not sure it wasn't planted. I knew Sandra Wells. She was a straight arrow. That's why I'm treating this as a homicide until proven otherwise."

He steered away from the handsome seven and a half mile redevelopment strip that symbolized the beginnings of a new city and toward the "old Detroit." As he turned, I asked, "Would anyone benefit from her death?"

"If you call a couple of hundred thousand dollars in a savings account something to benefit from, I would say so. We don't know where the money came from, but there is nothing to suggest it was illegal."

"Maybe she inherited it," I suggested.

For a moment he didn't answer. His eyes ranged from side to side and his body stiffened as we moved into an urban wasteland of deserted streets and empty buildings. It was literally acres of abandoned land.

He didn't start to relax until we turned down the ramp and onto the expressway. When the car was headed north, he re-started the conversation. "In her safety deposit box was a life insurance policy and the card of an insurance agent named Mark Crandall. Someone had written "important" next to his name and below it was a smiley face."

When I said that the insurance policy should make some relative happy, he said she didn't have anyone else, except a cousin who lived across the river in Windsor. Her parents are both dead, killed in an auto crash ten years ago. He didn't say anything else for another mile. The farther we drove, the more his words became clipped and the body tension returned. He seemed to be looking for something he didn't know was there.

It didn't take me long to realize why he was uneasy. By this time we were exiting the Jeffries Freeway onto Elmhurst, which we followed to Broadstreet, driving past deserted, dilapidated shops covered with graffiti. The only businesses still open were a convenience store and a barbershop at the corner. On the street a couple of cars made their lonely exit from the neighborhood. Every now and then we saw a few people walking, collars turned up, heads bent down, on an endless trek to nowhere. Poverty has a way of doing that.

We turned down Cortland. At the corner three young men, probably in their late teens or early twenties, leaned on a light pole and looked at our car. One was tall and skinny with his pants hanging near his knees. The other two were short with oversized FUBU jackets and Jordan high tops, looking like stuffed mannequins.

Sennett raised his eyebrows, as he turned down the street. "Drug deal going down." I asked him if he was going to call it in.

"It does no good to stop. They'll just run away and find some other place to do business. These gang members have no respect for the police. They laugh at them until they get busted."

"Yeah, and if you do catch one of them and somehow they get injured, people will accuse you of police brutality."

Sennett pulled at his ear. "Doc, I used to walk the beat. Law enforcement is really hard. Just think, if someone wants to steal your wallet, you don't want a policeman reading a law book to the criminal. You want someone to physically protect you, a big man with a gun. On the other hand those kinds of policemen are tough guys. Sometimes too tough. In the heat of the moment they're not looking at the constitution for answers."

I was about to ask him what the answer was but he was silent again, slowing down and looking for an address. Staring at the homes that were still standing, it was hard to imagine that this was once a flourishing middle class neighborhood in the fifth- largest city in the country. Now Cortland Avenue consisted mostly of boarded up houses. Those structures that survived had an occasional car in front of weed and dirt lawns. This was the home of crime and drugs in the city.

Half a block down the street Sennett found what he was after. It was a house, or what remained of it, its singed walls tottering on a brick foundation. In front was a black and white with two officers standing by their unit. Sennett didn't take chances.

He got out of his car, greeted the two men, and chatted for a few moments. When he introduced me and told them I was a doc, they looked at me curiously, like who the hell was I going to save? Sennett picked up the glance.

"Don't worry about the doc. He can take care of himself."

I felt a flush of trepidation redden my face. "Don't forget, George, you're the one with the gun."

"You're right, boss," he said, tapping the holster on his chest. "Let's go in."

My leg muscles tightened, and I shortened my stride. I think Sennett sensed my fear, because we moved slowly up the driveway to the side of the house. What was left of the side door remained open. Even though it was daylight, Sennett took out his flashlight and sprayed its light inside the entrance. Before we walked in he unclipped his shoulder holster.

The first thing that greeted us was a rancid, musty odor—a mixture of charred wood, mildew, and urine. Light filtered in through the front window, exposing what I assumed had been the living room.

"They found her in a corner of the living room," Sennett said, as he pointed the light in the darkest area. Debris and cinders covered the floor. In the corner stood an old mop handle that had somehow avoided the fire.

He picked it up and started moving the debris away. The old carpet had been destroyed and so had some of the flooring, exposing the floor joists.

"Be careful."

I looked down at the floor as his light danced off it. From the angle where I stood, something caught my eye. "Wait, aim your light a little to the right near the corner." I pointed my finger. On the floor was what appeared to be some writing with a blue Sharpie.

I got on my knees and stared for a moment at the writing. "What do you think this means?" I asked.

Sennett looked over my shoulder, then shook his head. "I don't know how the crime guys missed this. Probably with all the smoke and debris they didn't see it." The writing included a number: 13675.

"Any ideas?"

"I don't know, but it's the other writing that's interesting."

"What's that?"

"It says Cal Finney. He's a cop in the special investigation unit."

"What the significance?"

"Nothing, except wherever he is, trouble isn't far behind." He backed up carefully so as not to disturb the message. As he did, we suddenly heard a couple of hard cracking sounds against the outside brick wall. The thump of bullets hitting the house was unmistakable.

Sennett quickly threw the mop on the floor, and we raced to the side door. When I looked out, the first thing I saw were the three guys from the street corner walking down the other side of the street.

I looked back at the police car. The two officers had their guns drawn and were creeping along the rear end of the squad car. Claustrophobia gripped me. We were trapped in this house with a shooter outside.

"Stay behind me, Ben."

I followed Sennett's shadow as he moved around the corner of the house, screened by two large bushes. I looked down the street and saw the tall, skinny kid from the street corner swaggering down the street, his low riders almost touching his knees. His two buddies were right behind him. At his side he held a long, cylindrical object. The closer we got, the more it looked like some kind of weapon.

Another shot struck the front of the house. One of the officers drew his gun and aimed at the three men.

"Stop!" Sennett yelled at the officers. "Get down."

The cops hesitated at Sennett's command and then got behind the squad car away from the house. In the meantime the three young men, apparently scared by the officer's gun, dispersed, running back toward Broadstreet. The tall, skinny kid dropped the object in his hand and grabbed his belt, pulling his pants up, so he could run. Under other circumstances it would be humorous, but not now. The officers were already calling for backup.

The three boys were directly across the street from me now, but two of them were running fast. I assumed they were the ones that started the shooting. The tall, skinny kid had dropped farther behind his friends. I decided that if we caught him, we might get some information.

I bolted across the street heading straight for him. He didn't see me until the last second. That's when I plowed my shoulder into his back. He screamed in pain as he went down on the sidewalk. I saw his two companions look back and then take off. Friends to the end, and this was the end.

Panting heavily, I stood over the kid and looked around for his weapon. All I could see was a black object on the ground about ten feet from where he was. I picked it up and was chagrined to find it was only a small branch from a tree, which from a distance had looked like a gun. Suddenly another loud bang resounded from inside the house. This one was more like an explosion. Immediately, flames engulfed what remained of the living room, and it wasn't long before the rest of the house was on fire.

I dragged the kid off the sidewalk and, using him as a shield, made my way back to the squad car. We kept ourselves between the line of gunfire and the car and finally came up to the two officers. In the distance I heard the increasingly shrill wail of a siren.

By the time we reached the squad car, I could hear Sennett yelling at the other two cops. "You guys are lucky," he said. "If you weren't, your names would be all over the newspaper tomorrow."

"Why?" one of them asked.

"Line of shot. It was coming from the opposite direction." Then he pointed at the object dropped on the sidewalk. "That thing the kid was carrying was a stick. These punks do that all the time in this neighborhood when the police are around to scare them. You would have killed three innocent teenagers."

My heart sank. He was right. The two policemen looked at each other with a new lease on life, while Sennett and I waited for the fire department to douse the blaze. By this time, the only goal was protecting other houses on the street.

The police officers cuffed the kid. He must have been seventeen or eighteen, with a sullen, insolent demeanor. It was a rule with these kids to never show fear to the police. Sennett frisked him and pulled a couple of plastic bags from his pants. After he read him his rights, he pushed him into the squad car, protecting his head with his hand. I bet he wished he never picked up that stick.

Three more police units surrounded the area looking for the shooter. It was to no avail. Whoever was firing at the house escaped the net.

With nothing left for us to do, Sennett motioned me back to his car. On the way out I asked Sennett what the hell happened.

"Somebody has been watching that house. They didn't want anyone to go inside. Now they've made sure of it."

"What about your friend Cal?"

"Calboy is on my list. By the way, that was some kind of lick you put on that kid. Your coach would have been proud."

"Yeah, until he found out I risked my life for a stick."

"My point. It does no good to be a hero. Besides, if something happened to you, I'd have a lot of explaining to do."

CHAPTER 9

SENNETT CALLED CALBERT FINNEY and arranged to meet him at his favorite watering hole to talk about Sandra Wells. Then he asked me if I had time to go with him. When somebody starts shooting at you, you want to know why, so I told him I'd go.

On the way over he gave me a thumbnail sketch of Finney. Sennett knew Cal Finney for twenty years. He called him the toughest sombitch on the force, part of the Big Four. That was the squad they sent in to bust up gangs, do the heavy work. He got the name Calboy from working with them. Sennett said he saw him in action, describing him like he was Wyatt Earp at the O. K. Corral. According to the lieutenant, Finney did his best work undercover, but was always loyal to his badge.

It was three in the afternoon when we entered the Long Ride, a titty bar in the Cass Corridor. I'm not sure what the "Long" referred to but looking at the four ladies stripped to their G-strings, gyrating around floor to ceiling poles, it didn't take much imagination to guess who wanted to be riding whom.

The sensory assault was penetrating—high decibel thumping rock, the conglomerated smell of booze, sweat and cheap perfume, and a smoky haze hanging over the dance floor. In the middle of the stage the naked women bumped and ground their pelvises while shoving their silicone breasts in the faces of men at crowded tables. In return, the "audience" spent their time pushing money down their ladies' strings. Every now and then the bouncer would come by and gently remind the patrons not to touch the merchandise, at least not here. At the corners of the stage were a few single men just watching the show and drinking beer.

Sennett found Finney at the bar behind the dance floor, talking to the bartender. Two or three empty shot glasses were turned over in front of him next to a half empty pack of Lucky Strikes. When he saw us, he got up from the barstool.

I could see why they used him for the "heavy work." He was at least two inches taller than me, and I'm six two. He had a big chest on a frame that could have belonged to a nose guard. His face was creased under the graying stubble of a beard, and a deep scar ran across his chin. When Sennett introduced me, he shook my hand with a nicotine-stained meat hook that felt like it could crush someone's windpipe in seconds.

We moved to a spot at the end of the bar away from the music. Finney ordered another Jack on ice and told the bartender to give Sennett the bill. Sennett and I both ordered Cokes.

"What's up, George? This must be important. You don't usually make the rounds of my bars." His voice was deep and raspy. I figured it was too many Luckys.

Sennett told him he had found his name on the floor of the Cortland house where Sandra Wells died. He wanted to know what Finney had on Sandra Wells.

"Sandy and I were friends. I met her when Tommy Holiday asked me to check out a couple of things for him."

"What kind of things?"

"Can't say. I promised Tommy I'd keep my mouth shut, but it sounded to me like he was on the opposite side. Like how he could get a piece of the action." Sennett raised his eyebrows in surprise and asked what he knew about Wells.

Finney took another cigarette from the pack, lit it, and washed the taste away with his drink. He said she was working on the new City Hospital project. His take was that in the city government bribes and contracts were always a bad mix. Her job was to make sure whatever transpired was clean. "Sandra was a nice gal, and I feel real bad that she died like that."

Out of curiosity I asked whether Sandra ever said she felt in danger of anything. Finney looked at me, his eyebrows raised. "Funny you should ask that. The day before she died we met for lunch at a place on Griswold. She acted nervous. You know what I mean? Looking around like she was being followed. I asked her if she was in trouble. She said she felt someone was watching her."

He nodded when I asked if she had any idea who it was. He said she thought it was someone in City Hall, but she didn't tell her bosses. I asked him why, but he had no answer.

Finney extracted another cigarette from the package in front of him, pulled out a wooden matchstick from his shirt pocket, and lit it by flicking the end with his thumbnail. "I told her to talk to them, but she was headstrong. You know what I mean? She was the kind of person who needed all the facts before she made an accusation."

When Sennett asked him what kind of person she was, he said, "Sandy was easy to get along with, friendly, and very methodical. Several people who knew her used the word 'organized' to describe her." While he was talking, he crushed his half-finished smoke in the ashtray and rubbed his hands down his pant legs.

Without waiting, he immediately lit a third cigarette, finished the Jack Daniels, and then glanced nervously around the room. After a few moments he seemed reassured and resumed talking about Wells. Apparently, other than a cousin she spoke of once in a while, no one knew about her family. "As far as her social life, sometimes she would go out for drinks after work. Her friends said she was fun to be with, interested in sports, music, that kind of stuff. Hell, if I was younger, I would have chased after her." Finney paused and then reached inside his coat.

"There is one other thing. I saw Sandy a couple of days before she died. It was kind of weird. She said she couldn't trust anyone but me. Then she handed me this paper." He pulled a couple of folded sheets from his corduroy jacket and laid them on the bar in front of Sennett. One of them was a spreadsheet. The other was blank. "She said it was the key to the kingdom," he continued, "and for me to hold onto it. Those were her words. I brought it with me, thinking you guys might know what it means."

As he rearranged the papers, a tall, slender young woman in a tight, short skirt came up from behind him. She had no bra, only an open shirt, leaving nothing to anyone's imagination. The girl had too much makeup for a face that would have been pretty on its own. Finney seemed startled as she bent over his shoulder and said something in his ear.

"Not now, Carrie, I got business to take care of. Maybe later." He turned back to Sennett.

The girl shrugged with a disappointed look and walked away, her tight ass wiggling in front of Finney. I wondered whether they would eventually be doing their own business together later that evening.

Sennett appeared not to notice and continued questioning Calboy. "Did Sandra Wells tell you what she meant by a key to the kingdom?"

"Nope. She said she didn't trust anyone. Now that she is dead, I don't suppose it matters." He stopped for a moment and stared into the empty shot glass in front of him. "Funny you should come here with the doc."

"Why?" Sennett asked.

Finney explained that Wells told him if he couldn't figure out the spreadsheet he should contact me. "She said that Dailey would figure it out, because it had something to do with medicine."

"Do you have a copy?"

Calboy shook his head. "Didn't think to bring one. If you can get one, you can have it. I need to keep the original with me. You know what I mean?"

Sennett nodded. "I'd do the same. Let me see if I can get one made."

Sennett picked up the spreadsheet from the bar. He folded it, put it in his pocket, and then went up to the bouncer at the front door. I saw him flash his badge and then walk into a room off the entrance.

Finney looked up from his drink for a moment and stared at me. "It's strange, even before Sandy mentioned your name, I wanted to meet you. I admired what you did at that hospital. A one man wrecking crew." As he spoke, his eyes again shifted around the bar, looking for something. I asked him if anything was wrong. His eyes seemed to be fixed on a table at the end of the stage. I looked but all I saw was empty tables. He shook his head.

"I'm a computer idiot," I said. "That spreadsheet looked like hieroglyphics to me."

"Give it a shot. You never know," he said hoarsely. I noticed he was getting short of breath as he talked.

"I'd leave that to an expert. Get me a copy, and I'll give it to my wife. She's a Federal prosecutor, deals with that stuff all day."

"I'll do that. I didn't tell the lieutenant, but I always have a back up plan." He took one of the blank pieces of paper and wrote his number down on one of them. He had me write mine own on another and put it in his pocket. "Call me later if you find out anything. I'm interested. " As he handed me the paper with his phone contact, he started coughing again. I folded the paper and put in my coat.

"This is strictly professional. You ever get your throat looked at?" I asked.

"No, I stay as far away from you guys as much as possible."

I was about to reply when Sennett returned to the table with a sour look on his face. "Damn place. They don't even have a copy machine," Sennett said, handing the spreadsheet back to Finney.

Calboy took it and immediately slipped it back in his pocket, saying he would get Sennett a copy. As soon as he pocketed the paper, he stood up and surveyed the bar again, shifting from one foot to the other. I noticed his hands were shaking.

"I gotta get out of here. Doc, I'll stay in touch."

"Are you all right? Do you need a ride?" Sennett asked.

"No, I'm just down the street. Thanks." He walked out, leaving his unfinished cigarette on the bar smoking in his shot glass.

WE HUNG AROUND FOR A FEW MINUTES and talked. Sennett said he had never seen Cal Finney this nervous, like he was scared. Scared enough that the four doubles he had washed down didn't seem to faze him.

"Maybe he should be nervous," I said, "especially with that raspy voice and smoking. I said something to him about it."

"You may be right, but it's not medical. He always said nicotine and booze is what kept him going. By the way, what did he mean he'll stay in touch?"

I told Sennett about what Sandra Wells said. Without the spreadsheet, nothing made any sense.

Sennett looked worried. "I should never have let him go. We've got to get out of here. I've got to find him; he may be in trouble."

"How do you know?"

"Nothing scares Calboy."

Sennett paid the tab and we walked out of the bar and into the fading light of a November afternoon. When he asked the parking attendant which way Finney went when he left the bar, the man pointed left down Cass Avenue and said Finney always parked at a lot off Willis.

We got into the car, made a U-turn, and headed north. Willis was four blocks from us. The A1 Parking Lot was on the corner; the rest of the side street was empty. All that was left were cracked sidewalks with weeds pushing upward from the dirt and a couple of abandoned industrial buildings that built nothing. I looked up and saw the streetlight was broken, not unusual for Detroit.

Sennett continued down the street slowly, but half way along the block he stopped. In the dim light I saw a large object on the sidewalk. He drove closer and then suddenly slammed on his brakes, put the car in park, and ran across the street. I followed him. When I got there, I saw the object was a body on its side.

Sennett rolled the victim over on his back. The disfigured face of Calbert Finney stared at us through lifeless eyes. Blood pooled on the sidewalk coming from the front of his chest, and he wasn't breathing. I checked for a pulse. His skin was still warm, but his heart had stopped.

As I searched for my phone to call 911, Sennett bent over him and spread his coat apart. On his shirt was a deep red stain over the left side of his chest, but that's not what he was looking for. He reached into inside pocket and his hand came out empty.

"The spreadsheet is gone," he said, and then, he carefully pulled up on the arms of Finney's coat, exposing his hands. When he found the left hand, he raised it up and showed it to me. The left pinky finger was cut off.

"We've got trouble, Ben. The killer was in that bar watching us."

CHAPTER 10

WE SPENT TWO HOURS AT THE CRIME SCENE. This included reviewing the security camera tapes at the Long Ride. Most of the customers looked the same, except for a couple of men at the end of the stage. We tried to match them up with the video at the entrance, but they had their heads bent down. Regulars to a place like the Long Ride knew it had camera surveillance.

By the time we finished, it was around five o'clock. As we got ready to leave, I glanced over at Sennett; he looked pissed. Knowing him I suspected he felt to blame. From my perspective, I was glad to get out of there. It's not every day that I talked to someone who was about to get killed, especially at close range.

I slapped a couple of sticks of gum in my mouth and started chewing. After a few minutes the cadence of my jaw muscles started to ease my tension, and I was able to focus. I barely knew Calbert Finney; now he was dead. As gruesome as the crime was, I ruminated on it. I wanted an answer, not a question.

After Sennett dropped me off I drove to a Starbucks on the way home, went inside, and got a tall dark roast. I took a seat by the window and looked around. It was strange. I just left a murder scene and here I was, watching a few kids being tutored after school, a couple of women conversing, and a group of older men sitting around a table, laughing over a game of checkers. Just another day in the burbs.

I sipped at my coffee and looked out the window at the relentless dance of traffic moving up and down the highway, frustrated drivers honking their horns and changing lanes. I wondered if they were as disturbed as I was. Calbert Finney died over a spreadsheet, a piece of paper Sandra Wells thought I could decipher. She said it was something medical. Now it was gone and Finney's life suddenly extinguished. Slowly, I finished my coffee as the rush hour started to unwind. But unlike the drivers framed by the window, I couldn't change lanes. I had no answer.

After thirty minutes of pondering, I pulled out my cell and called Jordan. She had heard what happened and didn't seem surprised. Apparently, Sennett contacted her. He must have known I would wait before calling. The only thing I sensed in her voice was relief.

I think I knew why. She recognized what all law enforcement people eventually realize: They had chosen a profession that was hazardous. That was their decision. She knew it wasn't necessarily mine, but getting in my face about the danger I might encounter wasn't going to make it go away.

At the end of the conversation she repeated what her boss in Miami once told her: "Until this thing is over, walk like you are being followed. Talk like someone is eavesdropping. Never take any chances." Then she paused. I heard a muted sniffle and a slight crack in her voice. The conversation ended when she suddenly reminded me of the parent-teacher conference at five. It seemed incongruous, but life goes on.

I was older when I had a child. Not because I didn't want one, but because my first wife never had the time for it. She always had an excuse—her career as an interior designer, her age, problems with her parents. I was too busy or too consumed with my own practice to make a fuss. Don't think I didn't chastise myself for being so unconcerned. I couldn't face the reality that I had married the wrong woman, so I convinced myself nothing was wrong. Denial is no excuse.

Now that I was remarried and had Joey, everything had changed. I understood what having a family was. Joey and Jordan were my life, and for a guy who spent five years as an outcast, it was an eye-opener. Something else was really weird; Joey was just like me. Always curious, always active, and always getting into mischief. Not a troublemaker, just exuberant. At least that's how I saw him. Somehow, I didn't always think that his teachers perceived it the same way. That was why I dreaded the parent teacher conference.

Jordan and I showed up to the school a little ahead of schedule and waited outside the door to his first grade class. I watched her anxiously fidgeting with her purse strap, and I understood why. She had never been like me. She was the good kid who never got into trouble.

Fortunately, we live in a kinder, gentler America. The teacher was great. She understood Joey like a book. Exuberant, smart kid, he'll outgrow this phase, she said. This wasn't mischief. He has an active brain, filled with curiosity. She said he was especially interested in how things work, machines, cameras, computers. I sat still and kept my mouth shut. When we walked outside after the conference, Jordan asked me why I was so quiet.

"I was the bête noire of my family. I remembered my parents going to the parent teacher conference at school when I was a kid. I thought I was going to get the glowing report of a wonderful student. Instead, all I saw was the glum face of a disappointed father. When I asked what the teacher said, I remembered Mom saying Mrs. Sawyer told her I would never amount to anything. That was the last parent-teacher meeting my parents ever went to."

"That's terrible."

I nodded. "You know my folks, especially my dad. He was a hard working, first generation American. His kids were his life. Say something bad about his family and you insulted him."

She did understand. She might have been the only child of a wealthy family, but she was tough. A law degree, a few years as an assistant DA in Miami and the loss of her FBI fiancée in drug gang shootout hardened her. When we met, we had a common bond of new life that held us together.

We returned home around five o'clock. The smell of falling leaves and the cool fall air gave us a sense of comfort. As soon as we entered the front door, Joey came running. Barking right behind him was our dog, Bucky. Dorothy, our babysitter, stood behind them.

He jumped up at me, and I lifted him in the air. A little tickle under his arms, and he was squirming with fun. Bucky joined the rumpus.

As soon as I put him down, he ran to the kitchen and came back with Jordan's MacBook Pro. "Look, Daddy, I found the number machine. I can add numbers with it." Jordan and I looked on, mesmerized, as he showed us how the computer worked.

"Where did you figure that out?" I asked. He shrugged his shoulders and mumbled something about television.

It took us a while to get him settled down and then put to bed. By the time we ate and cleaned up the dishes it was nine o'clock.

We stayed up for the news. The TV stations had complete coverage of the murder on the Cass Corridor. Stuff like that sells airtime.

CHAPTER 11

THE NEXT DAY SENNETT CALLED and said he wanted to meet me for lunch. I suggested that we go to Los Galenes. After hesitating for a moment, he agreed. Sennett wasn't big on spicy food.

Los Galenes was in the Mexican Village area of southwest Detroit on a sleepy street near the expressway. The restaurant wasn't much to look at, except for the large, exterior mural on the back wall of the building. No one would mistake it for Diego Rivera, but the colorful flowers, a huge monarch butterfly, and the beautiful Hispanic woman with a blue scarf sitting below the restaurant's name made it a landmark. Inside were large tables with high backed wooden chairs in a room with industrial ceilings and windows overlooking the street.

Sennett knew why I picked this spot. I'm a hot food freak. As soon as we sat at a table near the window, I started studying the ingredients of the four bottles of hot sauce in front of me. In the corner, Los Sultines de Ritmo were unpacking their guitars.

It was still early and the restaurant was half empty. Sennett picked up a menu and cursorily scanned it.

"You really like this food, huh?" Sennett asked

"It's great. Remember, not all Mexican food is spicy. Besides, if you don't like the taste, the music is good. Regardless, I'm buying."

While we waited for the waitress, I picked up one of the bottles and looked at it closer. "This is the one, But Jolokia Hot Sauce. It has around a million Scoville Units."

He looked at me as if I was talking in Sanskrit. "What the hell is a Scoville Unit?"

I went into a dissertation on Wilbur Scoville, a pharmacist in the early

1900's, who developed a hot scale based on the amount of capsaicin in a dried chili pepper. Capsaicin was the ingredient that sets your mouth on fire. Scoville made his units based on the amount of sugar and water needed to make the substance undetectable to a group of tasters. The Bhuta Jolokia chili is one of the hottest.

Sennett stroked his throat and grimaced. "You still haven't told me why you want to use this. It sounds like something the Marquis de Sade would put out in his parlor."

"Taste, George, it's the taste." I knew he hadn't suggested meeting because of his culinary predilections, so I changed the subject and asked if there was anything on Cal Finney.

Sennett shook his head. "No one in the department knew what was going on. No papers, except that spreadsheet. All his files are gone. Cal was a loner and kept everything close to the vest. People told him things, and he stored it away until he needed it. Every now and then he found something big. Like Sandra Wells, for instance."

While he was talking, I motioned to the waitress to take our order. When she came up to the table, she asked in broken English if I had decided. I ordered the chimichanga. Sennett played it safe and got the rice and beans.

As she left, I asked Sennett what Finney was working on. He mentioned a vacant lot scam. It was a routine cover for everything else he did. He said Detroit has so many vacant lots, the city couldn't provide adequate services, including electricity, garbage, and police protection. Even in a city that's broke, there will always be some contractor who tries to screw the public. Apparently, Finney uncovered a company that bilked the city for a few hundred thousand dollars, claiming they cleared out neighborhoods they never touched.

"Live off the miseries of other people and you'll never be poor." I said

He nodded. "Now he's dead, and we may never know what happened. The killer got away and nothing was left behind, except the slug in Cal's chest."

"And a spreadsheet with numbers on it that we have no idea what they mean."

He spent the next ten minutes talking about the Mayor's personal involvement with Sandra Wells. Robinson denied everything, but the press, anxious for a story, was muddying the water. At a news conference that morning, the mayor flat out denied any accusations of misuse of his office, calling Sandra an able and valuable assistant. Apparently, his opponent for the election was having a field day with the story.

When I mentioned to Sennett that he didn't look confident about the situation, he said, "For the first time since I've known Franklin Robinson, I'm worried about the mayor."

"How did Robinson respond to the question from the press?"

"Tommy Holiday picked up the microphone during a press conference and stopped the proceedings."

I knew this hurt Sennett on a personal basis. He revered Robinson as the city's savior, a clean guy who could close the gap between the black and white communities, something that had festered for over fifty years. The last thing anyone needed was another selfish politician using the office for his own personal gain.

Before we discussed anything else, the waitress arrived with the food. Sennett watched as I kneaded the hot sauce into shredded chicken, refried beans, and Monterey Jack cheese. I took a bite and smiled.

"Sure you don't want a taste?"

"Not unless I'm interested in driving the porcelain bus," He smiled.

I stopped insisting. Instead we both ate in silence. He didn't speak again until his plate was clean. With a satisfied look, he set down his fork and looked up at me. I think he was surprised that he found something he liked on he menu.

"When you looked at the spreadsheet, did you recognize anything?" he asked.

"Other than numbers? No. I'd need an expert to find out what it means." He wondered if I knew what Calboy meant about Sandra Wells's comment that the spreadsheet was something medical, and she thought I could find out what it meant.

"I'm not sure. Maybe she figured I was something more than a doctor."

"It's funny. I thought the same thing."

Sennett didn't pursue it further, but to my surprise, he picked up the tab, despite what I'd said. He never did that before. I think he actually liked the food.

I walked with Sennett back to his car and then drove to my office. Halfway there I got a call from Jordan. She sounded irritated. I soon found out why. Some kid in Joey's class had shown him how to use a cell phone to text messages. When I asked her why she was upset, she said this is where the problem of kids and cellphones starts. I didn't think it was a big deal and told her it was part of growing up. What did she expect from a kid who loved gadgets? Somehow I didn't think she was buying what I was selling.

CHAPTER 12

SENNETT CALLED ME THE NEXT DAY. He said he was meeting with a couple of women at their office that afternoon regarding Sandra Well's death, and suggested I go with him. I realized this was turning into something more than the investigation of the death of a government employee. Somehow, I felt I was being drawn into a set of circumstances where ignoring the invitation was not an option. I had seen this movie before and it was making me anxious.

It was late in the afternoon when I met him at Police Headquarters. I walked into his office, only to find him barefooted and lying on his back flat on a foam rubber mat. His legs were extended backward over his head and his toes touched the mat.

"Are you okay?" I asked.

"Sure, just doing a couple of yoga stretches."

"Really? It looks more to me like you're trying to find a way to get hospitalized."

He didn't reply. Instead he continued to hold his legs while he talked. "It's Halasana, the plow pose. Good for stretching your legs and spine."

"Funny, you look more like a twisted pretzel. When did you start yoga?"

"About a month ago. It's a great workout. You should try it."

I admired his flexibility but ignored his suggestion. "Do you go shopping at the mall afterwards?"

Sennett laughed as he brought his legs down. "I was getting too bulky with the weights. A friend of mine told me about yoga, so I talked with this instructor. He explained their philosophy—strength without flexibility is rigidity and flexibility without strength is instability. It made sense. I go twice a week, and

I feel a lot better. I'll tell you one thing, it sure beats all that gum chewing that's ruining your teeth."

"Nothing is worse than someone who has found religion and talks about it. I suppose you bought the outfit too."

"Sure did. Hey, I'm the only guy in a room with twenty women. What are the odds? I gotta look good."

"Let me ask you one question." He looked at me quizzically. "Do you close your eyes during downward dog?"

"Doc, I'm still a man," he said with a laugh.

I pretended to wipe my brow. "I was beginning to worry."

He got up from the floor, stored the mat under his desk, and put on his socks and shoes. From his office we headed to the garage and found his car. As I slid into the passenger's seat, I asked him where we were headed. He said the name of a motel on the east side of Detroit. I gave him a puzzled look. "Don't worry; it's just a couple of prostitutes."

We drove out from Police Headquarters and turned on to Jefferson Avenue. No matter what direction we drove, the farther away we got from the reconstructed core city and its big buildings, the more the few pockets of organized hope seemed to dwindle. Direction didn't seem to matter. Outside the shiny new downtown, it was still the same empty blocks of abandoned buildings and indistinguishable bedraggled people, chin to their chests, shuffling down the sidewalk in a daze. It was going to take time and hard work to get rid of the old Detroit look.

At Harper, we turned left and crossed the expressway. About two miles from I-94 were a string of cheap motels, single story, non-descript units with full parking lots. Sennett pulled into one with a neon palm tree in front. A sign read Cabana Motel.

He said that these motels held much of the prostitution in Detroit. Twenty-five dollars for two hours, forty for the night. We parked near the motel office. Sennett brushed past the manager and walked to the first unit on the right. Without knocking, he pushed open the unlocked door. The pulsating sound of rap music filled the room. Inside were two women, naked and kneeling over a tall man, probably in his thirties, equally naked and lying on the bed. The older of the two was an African American woman with enormous breasts that swayed from side to side as she gyrated her crotch over the man's face. The other girl was white, maybe in her early twenties, and had the man's cock in her mouth. I heard a lot of moaning and groaning and wondered how much of it was pretend. Suddenly, the man convulsed as he ejaculated into the woman's mouth. This all happened in the thirty seconds we walked into the room.

I don't think either of the women noticed us, as they nonchalantly climbed off the john, like two employees leaving the factory. Suddenly, they saw Sennett and scrambled for their clothes. The man, for his part, had an instasoft and darted for the bathroom.

I looked at the older of the two women. She stood next to the bed, unabashed, with tight dreadlocks, smeared bright red lipstick, and a gathering of crow's feet at the corners of her eyes that said her youth was in the past. A silver ring shone from her navel and another one peeked out from the light Brazilian at her crotch.

The other girl lay on the bed with the sheet half covering her naked body. I saw some blood crusted at the end of her nose, and her face appeared swollen. In spite of the injury, something about her was familiar.

"Lieutenant," the older woman said in a husky, smoker's voice, "you know you got no right busting in on a working woman trying to make a living." As she spoke, she came a little closer to Sennett and started massaging her nipples. Then she slid her hands down between her legs until she found a spot that gave her pleasure. That's when she looked up at Sennett again. "That is, unless you need a little bit of enjoyment from my sweet pussy."

He must have known her, because he called her by her name. "C'mon, Queenie, tell that to the judge when he looks at your record," Sennett replied. "We need to talk about Calboy." As he spoke, Sennett looked toward the bathroom. I assumed he was worried about the guy inside, because he unclipped his holster and put his hand on his Sig Sauer. When he looked back at the woman, her face became clouded.

"What you want with that man?" The derisive way she said "man" made the word sound like she and Finney weren't on the best of terms.

"Last time I heard, you and Calboy were tight."

"The only time we were tight was when he was fucking me. Not too many guys who could handle the Queen. We were a perfect fit." She eyed Sennett for a moment, especially his crotch. "You know what, Lieutenant, you ain't so bad yourself. Maybe you could be my new main man." As she spoke, she began putting her clothes back on.

"Not a chance, Queenie. I want to stay alive on this earth. Being around you would probably kill me. Like your friend, what happened to her?" He pointed to the blood on the other girl's face.

"The man got rough with her. It's the only way he can get hard." She looked serious for moment and then glanced at me. "Who's this honkey with you? Did you bring him here to get a piece of the Queen?"

"Forget it. He's my silent partner." Just as he spoke, the door to the bathroom burst open and out rushed the john in a business suit, with his head hidden behind his overcoat. I noticed a ring on his left fourth finger.

Sennett reached for his Sig. "Stop!" he growled in a voice loud enough to stop a bear.

The man, probably in his late thirties, was tall with a muscular neck pushing against his spread collar. He turned and impatiently faced the lieutenant, like he had better things to do than deal with the police.

"Let me see your ID," Sennett growled, his voice now steely serious.

With an insolent frown the man retrieved a license from his wallet. As he handed it to Sennett, I noticed some blood on the knuckles of his left hand, partially smeared on the gold band of his ring finger.

Sennett handed back his license and told him if ever saw him again down there he was going to jail. It didn't make much of an impression, because the cheater turned his back on him. When he saw me, he purposely ran his shoulder into mine, almost knocking me over.

I felt my face flush and my pulse quicken. Ordinarily I would have let this go, but some things in life I can't tolerate. Physically abusing a woman was one of them, so I flipped my switch. Grabbing his arm, I spun him around. We were face to face. I sized him up quickly—cocky smile, pretty boy, a muscular body bought in a gym, standing tall in some kind of Kung Fu stance. My coach taught me two things about physical contact: you have to act fast, and it's the opponent who stands straightest that's most vulnerable. I don't think he knew what to make of me, so I didn't wait for a discussion. Instead, I feinted a head slap feint with my left hand, lowered my body, and moved upward with a right forearm shiver under the chin. He screamed out in pain as blood dripped from his split lip.

I grabbed him by his suit collar as his body sagged onto the floor. Blood and saliva continued to drool from his mouth, and he shuddered with fear. "We're you born to be stupid?" I yelled. He didn't say anything, so I slammed my fist just below his rib cage, doubling him over.

"We're you born stupid?" I yelled again. "Cheating on your old lady and beating up women, huh?" This time he nodded his head in resignation.

Sennett got between the john and me and pulled the guy up from the floor. "The next time I see you here it won't be so easy," he said, as he grabbed him by the top of his suit jacket and pushed him out of the door. He was gone before either of us could say anything. Just a businessman's lunch, I guessed.

"See that, Lieutenant, you and your friend just cheated me out of my client," Queenie said.

"Unless you're interested in getting beat up, a man like him isn't worth the money," Sennett replied.

Queenie rolled her eyes. "When you do what I do, you take chances. You know what I mean?" Sennett nodded. "Besides, I've taken his sugar before. He got some big-time money, some weird habits, and one of the biggest dicks I ever seen on a white man."

Sennett ignored her. "I'm sure you heard about Calboy." She shook her head, so Sennett was forced to tell her that her former lover was now dead.

For a brief moment the woman appeared stunned. She recovered quickly and merely shrugged her shoulders.

"It was bound to happen, knowing the guys he was running around with."

"What do you mean?"

"You have to ask Carina over there. She and Cal were friends."

While Sennett was talking with Queenie, I examined the other girl's face. She sat passively on the side of the bed, holding the sheet to cover her chest. The bleeding had stopped, but she had some swelling over the dorsum of her nose. I touched the nasal bones. They didn't appear to be broken, but some soft tissue swelling was beginning.

I took a closer look at her. Her face was sallow, colored by some rouge on her cheeks, a ridge of dark mascara over her eyelashes, and a bruised, purple coloration on her upper eyelid. She had dirty blond hair and a vulnerable, waif-like appearance even with the heavy makeup. When I finished examining her, I told her to put some ice on her nose and see a doctor if she continued to have problems with bleeding or breathing. She nodded her head slowly and got up from the bed.

As she did, the sheet fell down, exposing her naked body. She contrasted sharply with her partner, narrow hips and a flat stomach. No tattoos ornamented her chest, only two rings on the nipples that jutted from her perky breasts. Her expressionless face and blank stare spoke volumes about her emotions and perky wasn't one of them.

Sennett walked over to the bed. As he did, she retreated toward the bathroom, pulling the sheet from the bed to cover herself again. Standing naked on the floor, she looked imperiled and defenseless. He reassured her in a soft, comforting voice that he wasn't going to hurt her and suggested that she get dressed. She seemed to relax.

The girl began shuffling through the bed for her clothes, seemingly embarrassed. We turned away for moment. While she continued searching, Sennett picked up her purse and spilled the contents on the table next to the bed. Her keys bounced loudly against the Formica surface along with her wallet, lipstick, and a package of condoms. Inside the wallet was a hundred dollars in cash.

When we turned around, she was already in pink tights that highlighted the cleft between her legs. Carina was tall, probably around five-ten. Now that she was dressed, she seemed to be more in control of herself.

Sennett continued. "Queenie says you and Calboy Finney were friends."

"Is he really dead?" Carina asked in a slow, girlish voice. Sennett nodded. Soon after tears appeared at the corner of her eyes.

Sennett waited a few moments and then asked her a couple of questions about her relationship with Finney. She remained silent as she wiped her nose on the back of her hand. This went on for a while, but it was clear that she wasn't about to say anything. Finally, Sennett said: "You know, Carina, I can take you downtown, book you, and send you to jail for prostitution. If you don't have a previous record, the judge will probably only give you two to four months. But who knows what's going to happen in jail, if you know what I mean. Now tell me, how old are you?"

"Nineteen." She stared down at the floor as she spoke. By this time she had her V-neck cotton knit sweater back on, leaning over just enough so we could see her breasts and the pink nipples that jutted forward.

I studied her face again, particularly her eyes. The look she gave me seemed smarter than my preconceived idea of a prostitute. I asked her how long she had been working the streets. She said for the last year or so.

"You don't want to end up like Queenie. I know her well," Sennett interjected. "I used to work this beat. She was young then and good-looking and all the johns wanted a piece of her. But she had something else. She was college smart. Then she got a habit. Now look at her."

For a moment it looked like Carina might agree with Sennett. Instead, she shrugged in resignation. "Bullshit," she said, with her head down, looking at the floor. "I'm a hooker. The guys like the one that just left, they come down here and pay us big money to fuck them. They like weird shit, tying you up, three-ways, plastic bag fucking. That says enough, doesn't it?"

She pulled up her thin sweater and gave us another look at her small, firm breasts. "You see that bruise?" She pointed to a dark blue area just below her nipple. "That guy was fucking me so hard, he bit my nipple when he came. Then, I screamed. I think he liked that, cause he got hard right away and fucked me again. It was evil. A hard fuck, like I was some kind of animal he had to dominate. There will never be enough money for me to do that again. You know what I mean?"

As she pulled her sweater down, Sennett nodded and then asked her again about her relationship with Finney. When she hesitated, he suggested that she might be scared about talking with the police about anything, possibly, because her pimp might work her over. He assured her of police protection.

"I'm not worried." A touch of fear crossed her eyes. "I liked Cal. He always tried to protect me."

Sennett asked her what she meant. She said that when he was around, no one messed with her. But that was it, they were just friends. Then he asked if Finney ever mentioned Sandra Wells' name. She shook her head.

I think Sennett knew that he wasn't going to get any farther, so he handed her a card and told her to call him if she wanted to. I think he felt sorry for the young woman, because he reiterated the police could help her get some counseling. She shook her head. I now saw a look of resignation in her eyes. My bet was Sennett had seen that look before.

We were about to leave, when Queenie came over to Sennett. "Do I get one of those cards, too?" she asked.

He shook his head. "You know where to find me without a card, Queenie."

"Well, how about your friend? I could always use some conversation."

"The only conversation you'll get from Dr. Dailey is if you have a medical problem."

Carina suddenly raised her head. "Are you Doctor Ben Dailey?" I nodded and asked her why. She didn't say anything, just shook her head and went back to putting on her clothes. It pissed me off. I've spent the afternoon in a rent-by-the-hour motel with two hookers when suddenly a nineteen-year-old prostitute pipes up like she knows me. Then she shuts up.

I admit to having a short fuse and can be a hardass when it comes to people who feel sorry for themselves. I was about to give her a piece of my mind when I looked at her eyes, which spoke of a misery far deeper than I understood. I decided to keep my mouth shut.

Queenie stared at me for a moment and found my badge sticking out of my front coat pocket. "You're Dailey, huh?"

When I nodded, her face became animated. "I read about you. You're a doctor who investigated a murder. Something about bringing down some rich guy who had framed you over a crime you never did. It was all over the papers and TV. Ain't that some shit. Now I got a celebrity standing right in front of me."

Before I could say anything, Sennett stepped forward. "Listen, Queenie, forget the doc, here. You hear anything, give me a call."

By this time, Queenie was at the door with Carina right behind her. She turned around and looked at Sennett. "Lieutenant, the next time you want to find me, call first. I just gave away my pussy for nothing." With that she walked out with Carina in tow. I doubted we would see either of them again.

I got into the squad car and slumped into the seat, trying to digest what had happened—a sleazy motel, prostitutes, and a low-life, adulterous misogynist. What was this? I felt out of control, as if I was being drawn into something dark and bottomless against my will.

Sennett must have noticed. "It's police work, Ben. One of the guys at the station wrote a sign the other day that sums it up. 'Life's a bitch and then you die.'"

I hoped he was wrong.

CHAPTER 13

Sennett and I left the Cabana Motel and drove back to Police Headquarters. I think he was upset, because he gave me a short lecture about what I did at the Cabana and my personal safety. Then he smiled and said he would have done the same thing, except I beat him to it.

It was four o'clock by the time I got into my car and called Jordan. She couldn't wait to tell me about Joey's swimming lesson. It seemed surreal as I listened, that an hour ago I was talking to a drugged out prostitute in a rent-by-the-hour motel.

By the time I drove up the driveway in front of the garage, I was back in the real world. Joey must have seen me, because as soon as I stepped out of the car, he raced out of the back door and grabbed my arm. "Dad," he yelled. "Can we throw the football?"

I looked over at Jordan on the patio behind the kitchen. She just shook her head in mock dejection. "See, I'll never hear 'Let's go shopping for dresses.'"

I watched as Joey found the Michigan football that Sandra Wells gave him, lying on the ground by the side of the door. It was his most prized possession. For a moment a feeling of sadness crept over me as I thought about Sandra Wells and her gift to Joey. Before I could answer, Joey was in the backyard with me in tow.

"Go straight out and then turn toward the fence. I'll say a number and then you start running when I say 'hut.'"

Joey lined up next to me and I called: "4-84 hut."

He ran toward the fence and turned around about ten feet from me. I lofted a soft throw, and he caught it. As soon as he did, he started jumping around like the players on TV. Then he ran back to me.

As he handed me the ball, he asked, "Dad, why do you always say the same number?"

"It was my number. I played tight end. They used me as a blocker most of the time, but it was on that number that the quarterback would throw the ball to me. It was a secret play. Now it is your and my secret."

The next time I threw the ball it bounced off his hands next to the evergreens that separated us from the Thomases next door. When it rolled back to the patio it stopped next to a small rock. Joey picked the rock up and called me to come over.

"Dad, look at this rock. It has a smooth finish on one side."

I laughed. "That's not a rock, Joey, it's a hide-a-key. Let me show you."

I opened it up and showed him the key to the house. "Mom and I keep it here in case we forget our key. And just so you know, we also have a roll up ladder to get to the balcony outside our bedroom so we can never get locked out." I had a small pole with a hook on it next to the house that I used to pull the ladder down to the ground. It, too, was hidden in the trees.

"You are never to mess with either of them. I just want you to know what they are. Okay?"

Joey laughed. He thought it was the funniest thing ever to have a key hidden in a rock.

For the next hour he ran back and forth trying to catch the ball. Every now and then we connected. I could have stayed out there all night. It was exactly how my dad and I used to play when I was a kid. The only difference was that my dad had no idea what the game was about. He had an awkward throw that never really spiraled, but for me the greatest part of the day was when I played catch with him.

Over the years I tried to explain the game to him, but as a first generation American from Russia, he grew up trying to make a living and keep his family together. I don't think he ever understood football, except that he knew it made me happy. He had no time for idle sports. The only thing he ever wanted was for his kids to live better than he did. He came to all of my games. I was a big deal in high school, an all-conference and all state tight end.

The only problem was that my press clippings weren't as good as my performance. I related that mostly to the fact that the other guys were better. But no one tried harder. For four years in college I was a walk-on that worked on the scout team, getting the other guys ready. In my senior year I finally got into a game and actually caught a ball to the endless joy of my teammates. They mobbed me when I got back to the bench, like I had just won the Super Bowl. It was a no-big-deal catch, a five-yard out cut with no one covering, but to me that catch was the greatest physical feat of my life.

When I graduated, my coach came up to me and gave me a big hug. He said he was as proud of me as any All American he ever coached, and he coached a lot of them. I still had the note from him on my graduation from medical school, telling me what a great doctor I was going to be. He died before my troubles at St. Vincent's. I often wondered what he would have thought of all that happened to me. Knowing him, he would have raised his eyebrows when he heard that I had gotten into trouble, then called to see if he could help. Regardless, I don't think he would have been surprised that I had persevered.

We threw the ball for another five minutes until Jordan called out that dinner was ready. Joey ran in yelling, "Mom, 4-84 hut!" She looked at me for an answer. I held up the football and smiled.

It wasn't until eight o'clock that Joey was in bed. That was a ritual in itself, telling stories, reading books and finally watching him drift off. I knew he would be up at 6 in the morning, ready and raring to go.

When I came downstairs, Jordan was sitting in front of the TV, waiting for me.

"I went to see Tom Bromley today," she said anxiously.

I was surprised that she mentioned it. Tom was her obstetrician. The last time she had seen him, he basically gave up on her having another child. Since then, Jordan rarely talked about the subject.

I sat down next to her. "Sounds important. What is it?"

"He told me a young woman, who is his patient, is pregnant."

I didn't get it. "So?"

"She's not married and doesn't want an abortion."

I felt bad. Why would Bromley discuss another woman's problem? He knew how upset Jordan was that she wasn't able to have another kid.

Jordan must have realized my confusion. "She wants to put the baby up for adoption. Tom thought we might be interested."

I felt stupid. "How do you feel about it?"

"You know how I feel about giving Joey a brother or sister."

"How long do we have to make a decision?"

"She's in her first trimester. Maybe second or third month."

"I'm not against it. I would like to have another child."

Jordan let out a long sigh. I think she thought I was reluctant. "When I talked with Tom, he said he could see us tomorrow. I'll tell him we want to know more about the mother and the father. I think it would be a good place to start." I put my arm around her and hugged her tightly. She put her head on my shoulder.

We sat together for a long moment and then I got up to go to the office. As I did, I saw the newspaper on the table next to where she was sitting. I picked it up. The Free Press can be hard to read at times. It always had a story about a murder or the sad plight of the city. It was depressing.

I was about to put the paper down when something on the front page caught my eye. The headline read, "Mayor's Early Opposition to New Hospital Almost Costs City Its Jewel." As the story unfolded, the article claimed that Mayor Robinson opposed the building of the new facility at its inception on the basis that the city didn't need more debt. It intimated that in his opposition the mayor ignored the health of thousands of poor people in the city. The article finished by throwing support to Robinson's opponent, Turner Davidson. I handed the paper back to Jordan.

"Do you know anything about this? I asked."

She frowned when she saw the headlines. Then she read the article. "Did you see who wrote this piece of crap?"

I shook my head, so she gave the article back to me. I looked at the byline.

"It says Curt Ringle. I know him from my lawsuit. He's a real prick."

"Well, nothing has changed. He writes this column, Uncle Leo's Diary. He is the biggest scab journalist in town. Why are you interested?"

"When I was going to meet the head of city hospital, I noticed the cranes for the new hospital. It seemed like a pretty heavy project for a bankrupt city."

"Curt Ringle is stirring the pot," she said. "He's the king of yellow journalism in Detroit. Now that he's on this story, I'll be answering the phone all day tomorrow. Some of it is going to be about that poor woman who you took care of at City Hospital," she said with a frown.

Then her frown transformed into a look of deep concern. I knew that expression. Every time I involved myself in a crime, something bad happened. She had reason to be worried.

I still felt uneasy over the idea of adoption when I met Jordan at Tom Bromley's office late in the afternoon. We owed a lot to Bromley, saving Jordan's life and delivering Joey seven years ago. After the delivery, he told us that Joey might be the only child she would ever have. Jordan is one of those people to whom you never say no.

When he called us into his office, I had the feeling of being a patient and not a doctor. It was strange. We sat in two chairs in front of a blond wooden desk in his consultation office. On the shelf behind him was a picture of Tom with his family. I studied it for a moment and realized it satisfied an odd theory that I learned in medical school about the body types of doctors. The tall, asthenic body type was usually associated with the "intellectual" internists. The strong, muscular mesomorphs were usually surgeons, such as orthopods. And the pudgy, somewhat flabby endomorphs were usually obstetricians. Tom was definitely an obstetrician.

We talked casually for a few minutes about mutual friends, and then he got down to business.

"Jordan told you that there may be a chance to adopt a baby in the near future. How do you feel about that, Ben?"

"I know this means a lot to Jordan, and I want to be supportive," I said earnestly. "I just want to know more about the parents."

Tom explained that direct adoptions don't come along often. But he indicated that, while he didn't know the father, the pregnant woman was a patient of his for several years. She was a college graduate and came from a good family.

Jordan surprised me when she said that before any adoption took place she wanted detailed information about the parents. Tom mentioned that unmarried pregnant women were often reluctant to talk about the father, but he'd try. I felt in a certain sense that in the adoption business "beggars can't be choosers."

He gave Jordan and me some papers to look over and fill out. Then he stopped for a moment and looked at both of us. "I want to help, but I also want you to understand the realities of adoption. It's sometimes very difficult to know what you are getting into. Everything has a risk."

"How do you make a decision?" Jordan asked.

We listened intently as he described both the objective and subjective sides to adoption. The objective part involved prenatal testing, such as testing for Down's Syndrome and taking a careful history from the parents to detect any hereditary diseases. Those were facts that helped make a decision. In the case of this pregnancy, all the tests were normal.

Jordan clutched her hands tightly. "What about the subjective side?"

"That's the inside decision. How will you accept someone else's child? How will you feel if it doesn't turn out the way you hoped? How will it affect your relationship with your son? Those are questions I can't answer for you, but I will tell you one thing."

"What's that?" I asked.

"If I was the child, I would sign up in a minute. You're great parents."

"Be careful what you ask for," I said. "Our only problem is we don't have a crib big enough for you."

Even though Jordan laughed, her voice carried a hint of nervousness. I could tell that the reality of adopting was more difficult than she realized. I think Tom knew it too, because he suggested that we give it some more thought and call him when we made a decision. We thanked him and walked out of the office. On the way out I looked at Jordan's face and saw indecision, the one emotion she rarely felt.

As we walked silently back to the car, I made up my mind to let her talk first. When we sat down inside, she stared out the window. "I'm so confused, Ben," she said, suddenly breaking the silence. "We have such a wonderful boy, and I would hate to mess things up by my own doing."

"You won't mess anything up. Whatever comes along we'll deal with it. We just have to make a careful decision. I know it's hard to eliminate emotion on something like this, but we've got to be as clear-eyed as possible. I just want you to know that I'm for it." I spoke enthusiastically, trying to avoid the tone of "I'm just doing this for you."

Jordan picked up my hand and held it to her face. She is a strong woman, but time was against her, and she knew it. Having a baby when you are older is tough, especially when you had a kid like Joey. If something went wrong, she would hate to have it impact him. I never said this to her. She already knew.

CHAPTER 14

I WOKE UP THE NEXT MORNING TIRED AND RESTLESS. Too many weird dreams about snakes and pet shelters. I guessed that the combination of the death of Cal Finney and the contemplation of adoption were too much for my psyche.

Fortunately or unfortunately for me, I had no time to dwell on it. When I went to the mailbox, the newspaper was waiting for me. I immediately saw the headline: "Rogue Doctor Performs Illegal Surgery." It was Curt Ringle again. The article went on to describe Sandra Wells' demise, chapter and verse. Even I had to admit it was accurate.

Only so many people had direct access to the information. I thought about the doctors in the emergency room department. I couldn't imagine what they gained by giving out the details. Then I thought about Fitzhugh and his determination to "get rid of the scum" that inhabited his hospital. From my encounter with him he didn't seem like the kind of person who would use the press to do his work for him. The only other people who would have access were those in the boardroom of City Hospital. That's when Tommy Holiday's face flashed in front of me. Of course, it made sense. The question now wasn't "if" but "why."

I stuffed the paper under some magazines on the counter. My watch said 7 AM. If I left now, I would dodge a discussion with Jordan about the article, at least for a while.

When I went back inside, Joey was just coming downstairs with Jordan. I gave both of them a kiss and hustled out of the house. Jordan gave me an odd look as I made for the door.

"Here's your hat, what's your hurry?" she said.

"Sorry," I mumbled. "Early office." Then Joey came up and started asking me questions. The kid was a walking encyclopedia of sports. He wanted to know when the last time the Detroit Lions had won the Super Bowl. I had to explain to him that they didn't have the Super Bowl in 1957. The significance of that statement didn't seem to faze him, as it has every Lion fan for the last six decades. He had his answer.

I was just about to leave when Jordan picked up the paper. Busted. "Was this the reason you had to be at the office?" she asked deliberately, holding up the newspaper.

"Just not in the mood to talk about it right now," I replied sheepishly.

"I can understand that." Then she came over and hugged me with her head on my shoulder. "Call me later," she whispered. She kissed me again, this time hanging on for a few extra moments.

It took me a little longer to get to work on the Lodge Freeway, mainly because of some mechanical genius doing a major engine repair on the shoulder. In contempt of what society thought, his partially covered butt mooned everyone who passed. In Detroit they call this a Lodge car in honor of the Lodge Freeway. Irritating as the backup was, I actually didn't mind. It gave me more time to think about the newspaper article. By the time I reached the office, I decided that I would store Curt Ringle and his character assassination in the junk file of my brain.

I parked the Jeep, snuck in through the back door, and began seeing patients. By three o'clock Jordan texted me, reminding me of Joey's soccer game that afternoon. It was irritating to be on a time schedule. Not that I would ever miss a game with my son, but I had a hard time juggling my personal life, my job, and now an investigation.

I got to the field after the game started. After watching the kids play, I realized this was going to be a little more than a kid's soccer game. Joey's coach, Aaron, turned out to be jerk. He got into an ugly confrontation with a 16-year-old referee over a penalty kick.

I played sports all my life, coached by a lot of different people. I never liked that kind of coaching. The ones I responded to the most were the ones that made it fun. Even in college, where the stakes seemed so much higher and the demand for excellence so much more intense, I always knew that my coach cared for me and enjoyed watching his players grow up.

It didn't take long before Aaron was in the referee's face, yelling at him and pushing his forefinger into his striped shirt. When I saw what was going on, I was about to pull Joey out of the game. Luckily, Jordan was there, first, because she played soccer in college and second, because she was a Federal prosecutor. Fortunately or unfortunately, Jordan pulled me back and ran onto the field before I could. She put her hand on my shoulder and told me to wait.

Instead of confronting the coach, she walked onto the field and went up to the ref. She said something to him and the young man nodded his head. Jordan then turned to the coach and calmly delivered some type of message. She must have said something right, because he walked off the field, picked up his bag, and, with fifty parents from both sides of the field staring at him, walked to his car. Opening the door, he turned around and glared at the field, his team, the ref, and Jordan.

The next thing I knew Jordan was yelling to the kids on the field to come over. I couldn't hear what she was saying, but they all started laughing. Then she gave them some instructions, and they ran back on the field. The game resumed and Jordan continued coaching the team. They clearly were having fun. When the game ended, I asked her what she said to the coach

"It was simple. I told him that if he kicked Aaron off the field, the parents voted me in as the next coach."

"Okay. So what did you say to Aaron?"

"I merely said that I was a federal prosecutor and an officer of the court. I said if he didn't stop, I would call the police and embarrass him. If he walked away, he would probably avoid a situation and come back next week to coach."

By this time Joey ran up and was tugging on Jordan's coat asking what was for dinner. I was about to walk away when a tall man with dark wavy hair and a dark complexion came up to me.

"Remember me? Jeff Taylor. You saved my life at a restaurant."

I did remember him. "How could I forget?"

"Probably because you were standing behind me trying to get that shrimp out of my windpipe. Now I've got to thank your wife for getting rid of that ding dong who was harassing those kids."

I shook his hand. "Glad to see you. Which one of these kids is your son?" He pointed out a handsome boy about Joey's size. "Nice looking kid."

"Takes after his mother." He stopped for a minute. "You know I sent you my card. I meant what I said. If you ever need anything, call me." He stopped for a moment. "Actually, I'm glad I ran into you. I've been thinking of a way to thank you. I just thought maybe your family would like to go to northern Michigan with my wife and the kids. I have a plane out at Oakland Airport. We go there a lot. Maybe you could join us."

I thanked him for the fruit basket and declined, saying I was a white-knuckle flyer.

"I understand, it takes some getting used to. We'll think of something else," he said.

I figured this invitation would disappear as long as I didn't pursue it. So I shook his hand and quickly shrugged it off as a nice gesture. After all, if someone saved my life, I would do the same.

By the time Joey went to bed a cold drizzle started. My luck, that's when Bucky barked to go outside. I slipped on my jacket and went out the front door. But instead of wanting to go on a walk, the dog pulled me toward the back yard. I wasn't in the mood to play games, but he kept tugging at the leash, so I followed. He took me to the side of the garage and stopped. He was growling.

I saw the light on inside my Wagoneer. Bucky sniffed around the car and growled again. That was funny. I never left the light on. I looked in through the window and didn't see anything unusual. I know I had locked the garage door, so I went back to the house to get my key.

The lock was finicky, so I pulled on the handle before putting the key in. To my surprise, the handle turned and the door opened. Flipping the overhead light on and looking around, I saw that everything seemed in place, except for the driver's door; it was open. Now I knew something was wrong.

My briefcase was open on the passenger seat and several papers were on the floor. It looked like someone had rifled through it. I couldn't understand why. These were patient charts with nothing of interest to anyone. Or was there?

I ran my hands through my hair, angry both at myself for leaving my office papers in the car and at whomever had invaded my privacy. I was also scared. This was my house. Was someone still in the garage? I looked around, but only Bucky and I were there.

I picked up a flashlight from the workbench, went out the door, and looked around the backyard. When I saw nothing amiss, I went to the high fence at the back, left Bucky in the yard, and walked through the wooden gate into the alley. It creaked as it closed.

I peeked around the corner. At the edge of my neighbor's garage, a nondescript four-door sedan sat with the motor running. A light was on in the car with someone behind the wheel. I flicked off my flashlight and stayed in the shadow of the garage as I crept toward the vehicle. It was a Toyota Camry. I tried to make out the plate, but it was smudged with dirt.

I was almost at the rear end of the car when my foot hit a trash can lid. The sound must have alerted the driver, because he peeled off down the alley. I stood up trying to see any other markings, but between the darkness and the rain it was a futile effort.

I went back in the garage to check if anything else was missing. After fifteen minutes of rummaging, I satisfied myself that everything was in place. I decided to take one more look inside the car. This time I opened up the passenger door, put the briefcase on the floor, and flipped on the overhead light.

My eyes settled on something on the seat I hadn't seen before. It looked like a small sausage. I picked it up and stared at it. It felt rubbery. It took a few more moments before I recognized something hard on the surface. It was a fingernail. I quickly realized I had a human finger in my hand and immediately dropped it back on the seat.

I suddenly felt my pulse bounding in my neck as acid rose up to my throat and my mouth went dry. I realized it wasn't because of the finger. It was the spreadsheet. Someone thought I had it in my briefcase.

CHAPTER 15

I WENT INSIDE AND TOLD JORDAN WHAT HAPPENED. She stood in front of me with her legs planted wide.

"Ben, this has got to stop! Someone has broken into our garage, and the next place will be our house."

Jordan seldom lost her cool. That was enough for me. I picked up the phone and called Sennett. Jordan was next to me, so I put my cell on speakerphone. The lieutenant's first comment went to the core of the matter. "Whoever ransacked your briefcase is sending a message of intimidation."

"Why the finger?"

"Sandra Wells had her pinky cut off, didn't she? So did Cal Finney. We'll send this to the lab and see if it matches. If it does, I think you're right, someone thinks you had the spreadsheet. Did Calboy give you anything when I left the table?"

"When you left, Finney gave me a piece of paper with his name and phone number on it. Why?" I asked.

"I need to get clear on the sequence of events. Finney acted strange in the bar, like someone was watching him. He was probably right. When he shows me the spreadsheet, I asked him if I could make a copy. He gives me the paper and I leave. While I'm gone, he gave you the paper with his name and phone number. When I return I give him back the spreadsheet. He leaves and when we find him on the street, the spreadsheet is gone."

I ran my hands through my hair. "So why is whoever killed Finney after me?"

"Most likely because he gave you the paper with his name and phone number on it, but the killer doesn't know that. He probably thinks you have a copy of the spreadsheet."

I remained silent for a moment, trying to control my anger. "That's great. Forget the spreadsheet. This is about putting my family in danger."

"Once they think you have it, there isn't much we can do to change their mind. I'm on my way. Keep cool."

Sennett and his forensic team stayed at my home until midnight. They examined everything in the garage, dusted my car for prints, and even went in the alley looking for tire tracks. When they were done, Sennett said he was going back to the Long Ride in the morning to check out their surveillance tapes again.

Before he left he had an officer cover our house at night until, as he said, "This whole thing is cleared up." I thanked him, but it didn't do much to relieve the anxiety. Jordan and I didn't go to bed until two in the morning worrying if we should send Joey to her parents. We decided that no place was absolutely safe. We wanted him close to us.

The next morning the TV was alive with news regarding the possible connection between Franklin Robinson and the Sandra Wells. I watched on the set in the kitchen as the reporter claimed that leaks from "unknown sources" suggested that there were e-mails and texts between Robinson and Sandra Wells implying something more than a business relationship. The obvious implication was that the mayor's campaign fund was being used for personal reward. The District Attorney was being interviewed. With the election coming in three weeks, he said that it was imperative that Mayor Robinson receives due process. This set off a barrage of questions from the reporters in attendance. I wondered who these "unknown sources" were. More trials by the press.

No one loved a story like this better than the TV stations and print media. Campaign ads and TV spots suddenly popped up. For Turner Davidson, Mayor Robinson's opponent in the upcoming election, it was a chance to score points with the voters. For the media it was an opportunity to sell airtime and papers. Neither necessarily cared about the truth.

I read about Turner Davidson. According to the article in the Free Press, he was old-school Detroit. A former pastor of the Parkside Baptist Church, he was a flamboyant, hell-fire and brimstone orator with a view that represented Detroit as a statement of African American independence. In spite of the city's known economic problems, any suggestion of help from the outside, meaning the state government, was a jumping off point to rally his supporters. Either directly or by implication, Davidson never passed up a chance to criticize Robinson as a pawn in the hands of the governor.

The interviewer caught Davidson on the way to a political rally. The TV camera focused in on him, a large man with a white fedora, thick gold-rimmed sunglasses, and a three-piece white suit. The early morning sun glinted off his mirrored sunglasses as he walked from his black Cadillac Escalade. When the

TV interviewer approached him, he smiled engagingly. Asked what he thought about the accusations directed at Franklin Robinson, his response sounded as if he was reading from a prompter.

"We cannot have our public officials tainted by the blight of wrongdoing. This is especially true for minority groups, who have long taken the unfair brunt of criticism for political and financial corruption. If the accusations are true, this is an unfortunate smear on our people. If they are false, it is yet again, another attempt to disparage a single group on the basis of their color. I look forward to a quick and complete resolution of this problem. Thank you." With that he smiled and then walked resolutely away from the camera.

I cleaned the dishes and got up to go to the office. I had enough of the constant rehash of Sandra Wells' death. It almost seemed like a respite to go to work . . . that was until I got to the office. As soon as I walked in, Karen told me that I had an emergency, a patient with an ear problem. She said it must be someone important, because the mayor's office called.

When I walked in the room, I was surprised to see Tommy Holiday sitting in the examining chair. He appeared concerned, but not in pain. I wasn't particularly happy to see him. My overall opinion was that Holiday was a jerk, especially since I had seen him in the City Hospital board room. But this is medicine, and I try my best not to make it personal. Besides, after all the threats made on me at City Hospital, I was curious that he still came to see me. I asked him what his problem was.

"I lost my hearing last night in the right ear, and it's really bothering me," he said. "It came on suddenly. I must have wax in it."

"How did you happen to choose me?"

"Doc Farnsworth gave me three names. You were the only one who could see me."

Even though he was condescending, it didn't bother me. It just reaffirmed the paradigm. The three "A's" of success in medicine—availability, affability, and ability in that order.

I asked him if he had pain or was dizzy. He said no, so I picked up an otoscope and examined his ears. Both were totally normal. The next step was a hearing test. When I told him, he looked skeptical.

"How long will that take?"

"About twenty minutes."

He looked at his watch and then back at me. He gave me a hard smile. "I've got a meeting to go to. Can't you just clean my ears?"

"I would if wax was blocking the canal. It's your choice. In medicine if you do the right thing, you'll usually get the right answer."

The fact that he had to wait for the audiogram increased his irritation, but he reluctantly agreed. Fifteen minutes later he came back in the examining room. I had his hearing test in front of me.

"It turns out you have a fifty percent nerve hearing loss in your right ear." I went on to explain the two types of hearing loss. One is conductive loss, which is something that prevents the conduction of sound from the outer ear to the inner ear. This could be wax, a hole in the eardrum, fluid behind the ear, or something wrong with the small moveable bones in the ear. Most conductive hearing loss can be corrected. The other is nerve-hearing loss, which is imbedded in the hearing organ itself. Most nerve hearing loss cannot be corrected.

His eyes rolled. "That can't be, can it?"

"Well, you can believe me or not, that's your choice," I said, trying not to get angry with a patient who knows everything.

"This is bullshit. You examine me for five minutes, do a test, and come away with a serious problem. How does someone get this?"

I didn't get angry at his arrogance. I liked patients like Holiday. They challenged me to talk with them and get the message through without losing my cool. "Most doctors think it is due to a virus, but when docs start telling you it is a virus it usually means they really don't know."

He asked me if it could be treated. When I told him that a high dose of steroids is the best treatment, I could tell he was skeptical.

"The statistics show that under this treatment, 50% of patients get all their hearing back, 25% get some back, and 25% get no return. The trick is to get it treated in the first week. The longer it goes on, the less the chance of correcting the problem."

I could see him mulling over what I said. "I'm not sure about what you're recommending, but I don't want to take a chance."

I told him that if he was doubtful about the diagnosis to get a second opinion. I suggested that he not wait. I wrote down the name of a doctor at the university, gave him the prescription, and asked him to come back in two weeks. He was about to leave when he stopped at the door.

"How well did you know Sandra Wells?"

"I told you once before I can't talk about my patients without authorization. You can accept it or reject it, but that's a fact."

"Even a dead patient?"

"Yes, even a dead patient."

He thought for a moment. "Did she ever give you any information about City Hospital?"

"I'm going to ignore your question, because with your problem it's possible you didn't hear me the first time," I said slowly and forcefully. "I'm not in a position to divulge any information."

"How about I get a court order?"

He was pushing me hard and trying to get under my skin. I decided I'd had enough. "That's your choice. Now I've got other patients to see." With that I walked out of the room.

Holiday didn't say anything else. Not even a thank you. After he left, Karen came up to me and asked what happened with him. I told her there are always patients who think they know more than the doctor. It's usually futile to try and help them.

Her lips were pursed. "He was a total jerk."

I nodded my head. "Just remember, Karen, the last idiot hasn't been born."

AFTER HOLIDAY LEFT, I CALLED SENNETT. "The mayor's chief of staff was in the office today, still pumping me for information regarding Sandra Wells. What is his problem?"

"I always felt Tommy wanted more than just to be the mayor's boy," Sennett replied. "Maybe he has an interest in the new hospital that goes beyond sitting on the board of control. Big money is passing through a lot of hands, and no one is immune to getting a kickback, especially with the kind of dough that's being spent. Maybe Sandra Wells had something on him?"

"How loyal is Holiday to the mayor?" I asked.

"Before Sandra Wells died I would have said 100 percent, but if he was getting money, there's no telling what he would do. He is ruthless."

He explained that Holiday was a problem as a kid, shoplifting, fighting, and run-ins with the cops. Then one day one of the cops on the beat took a liking to him and tried to help him. He brought him downtown to the Kronk gym, home of some of the greatest boxers in America. A friend of his taught Tommy how to box; it turned out that he liked it. I guess you could say it saved his life.

He got himself squared away, graduated from college, and went to law school. After he passed the bar, he was a criminal defense lawyer. Hard work got him accolades from clients, and a reputation as one of most feared trial lawyers in the city, tough as nails and smart as a whip.

"What happened to his boxing career?

"Tommy boxed in the AAU and got an Olympic tryout, but he never went further than the amateur ranks. People tell me he can still hit the speed bag. Nobody messes with Tommy."

Sennett went on telling me how Robinson and Holiday knew each other since high school. "When Robinson got elected, Tommy was his first hire." Sennett hesitated for a moment. "The rumor on the street is that Tommy wants the mayor's job." I asked him what he thought about it. He said with everything that has happened he didn't know what to think.

I knew Sennett's feeling about Mayor Robinson and didn't want to fan the fires. So I changed the subject. "Do Sandra Wells' associates at work know anything about a relationship with the mayor?"

He shook his head. "They flat out said she would never do anything like that."

"What about the couple of hundred thousand dollars in her savings account?"

He said he didn't have an answer, but he was on it. Then he hesitated for a moment. "There is that card belonging to the insurance agent that they found in her safety deposit box. If a man sells or tries to sell a woman a life insurance policy at her age, and she has his picture in her safety deposit box, we should talk with him. Especially if she ends up murdered."

"Yeah, that's strange," I said. "Have you found him?"

"It took us a while, but we tracked him down. We're trying to find out where the policy is and who is the beneficiary. It's hard work, but in the meantime, we're going to pay Mr. Mark Crandall a visit."

I noticed he kept using the word "we." He knew, since the break-in at my house, I wouldn't sit idly by and watch things happen. Officially, I was now all in.

CHAPTER 16

THE FOLLOWING MORNING I RECEIVED A CALL from Sennett while I was in my car. He planned to meet with Mark Crandall that afternoon and wanted me with him.

When I arrived at Police Headquarters, Sennett was waiting for me and came out of the entrance as soon as I drove up. He got into my Wagoneer and sat down with a pained expression.

"What's the matter, George?"

"It's the spring in this seat that's pinching my butt. Doc, aren't you ever going to break down and get a new car?" he asked."

"Would you ever get rid of a person in your family?"

He looked at me for second as he slipped on his seatbelt. "Depends on whether or not you are talking about my cousin, Albert."

"I guess every family has a cousin Albert."

When I asked him where we were going, he said Corktown, the old Irish district of Detroit, the former home of old Tiger Stadium and some of the best sports bars in the city. That was then; now Tiger Stadium and its neighborhood's economic base vanished. Oddly, in its rebirth the area found hope as the site of an artistic resurgence in Detroit. Painters and sculptors occupied empty warehouses. Articles on Detroit's resurgent art scene filled newspapers like the *New York Times*. With this notoriety, new development started to arise, including modern condominiums. Mark Crandall owned one of them.

On the way over he told me Knudsen gave him a thumbnail sketch on Crandall. It sounded like a common story, graduating from high school and entering the military, where he learned computer skills in a base hospital. From there he worked in a Best Buy for a while, then took business classes at a community college followed by a business degree at Wayne State University in Detroit. After graduation he started selling insurance and earned a Certified Life Underwriter certification. In his mid-thirties, unmarried, with no family in the Detroit area, he worked as a contract employee for a large accounting firm, Sturgis and Martin.

By the time he finished telling me about Crandall, we turned off Trumbull and onto Brooklyn Avenue. I thought it was an odd name for a street near the vestiges of Tiger Stadium. Crandall's condo was on the 5200 block among a row of recently-built red brick condominiums.

I saw no parking places by his home, so I turned onto a side street and parked in front of a No Parking sign. Across the street were three teenagers dressed in tight jeans and black leather motorcycle jackets, trying to look tough in front of their dirt bikes. One of them was a miniature version of Rambo, short with long dark hair and bowed legs. He walked around my car like a big shot.

"What's up?" I asked the kid, as I got out of the car.

"Nothing, man," he replied, "just like to check out any new car in the neighborhood." His friends started laughing when he said it.

I gave them a stare, then shrugged it off. I didn't have time to deal with a couple of punks. Sennett and I walked the block back to Crandall's home. It was the third unit from the corner, unrecognizable from each of its cookie cutter neighbors. In front of the condo was a recent model black Ford Escape. We climbed the cement steps to the varnished wooden door replete with an ornate brass doorknocker, rang the doorbell, and waited patiently.

After two rings, the door cracked open and a trim, clean-shaven man appeared, wearing a V-neck gray wool sweater and a button-down white shirt open at the collar, exposing a silver cross. His neatly pressed dark blue wool trousers had just enough fold to cover the top of his black Prada Nevada Hikers. A mop of sandy-brown hair was carefully groomed and, except for a single crooked upper tooth, he had a pleasant face and an engaging smile.

"Are you Mark Crandall?" Sennett asked.

He stepped back from the door. "Yes. What can I do for you?"

Sennett showed him his badge and introduced me as his associate. A pleasant smile creased his face and he appeared relaxed. "A Sergeant Knudsen from your office called and said you might be coming over. He said it was about an investigation," he went on in a smooth, confident voice. As he spoke, he slowly opened the door and invited us inside.

I looked around. Just to the right of the entrance was the living room, and he motioned us to come in. If Mark Crandall was as fastidious at work as he was at home, you might easily call him a neat freak. A large leather couch sat under a bay window and two mission style chairs on either side were covered with a Native American red, gray, and black wool fabric. A freeform glass coffee table was in the middle of the room, topped with two large books resting near the edge. I looked at the one on the top. It said *A Day in the Life of America*. All in all the room felt comfortable.

I glanced at his study. On top of the desk were two home computers with large-screen monitors angled at each other. The screens were filled with Excel displays. Next to them was a Hewlett-Packard color printer with two piles of printed sheets. Six pens were lined up neatly on the desk, each in a different color.

Crandall seemed to get over his initial reserve and invited us to sit down in the living room. My gaze wandered back into his study and landed on some books on an adjacent shelf. One of them was the Merck Medical Manual; the other was the FAA Airplane Flying Handbook.

"Petty diverse interests, medicine and flying," I said.

He must have seen me looking at the books. "Those are mementos from the service. I keep medical books around. You know, selling life insurance, you've got to know your business."

"Makes sense to me," I replied. "How about these books on flying? Do you fly these kinds of planes?"

"While I was stationed at Elmendorf Air Force Base in Anchorage, I learned how to fly in my spare time. In the four years I was there I flew all over Alaska in small planes in all kinds of weather."

"Sounds exciting."

Crandall perked up at the mention of flying: His eyes lit up and he stood a little straighter. When I asked him what it was like flying into the wilderness, he said his most harrowing experience was landing on a small lake with near zero visibility. He said after he did that he knew he could fly anywhere.

Sennett listened while we spoke, then took over the conversation, explaining that he was there to interview Crandall regarding the death of his client, Sandra Wells. Crandall's eyes stared blankly at the news. "I wondered when I saw the news whether it was the same person."

Sennett explained that, because Wells was found semi-conscious in a burning building, they had to determine whether this was a homicide. His name was on a business card in her safety deposit box and Sennett wanted to follow-up every lead. Just a few questions. That seemed to satisfy Crandall, because he asked us if we wanted something to drink. Sennett said that would be nice and asked for a Coke.

Crandall went over to a small refrigerator at the wet bar in his study and pulled out two cans and two glasses with the initials "MC" on them. He carefully put two ice cubes in both glasses and then handed them to Sennett and me.

Sennett took a sip. "Do you remember anything specifically about Sandra

Wells?" I assumed from the soft tone in his voice that he was trying to take the threat out of this conversation.

Crandall seemed surprised at the question. "She was he youngest person I ever sold a policy. Sandra was a very nice person, very organized. She had her life planned out."

"Not to be offensive, but did you ever have a social relationship with her?"

Crandall shook his head. "No, I'm always professional with my clients. It was just business."

As he spoke, I set my glass on the coffee table. When I picked it up again, it left a ring. Crandall saw it and immediately got up to get a napkin. He wiped it several times to make sure the stain was gone. I apologized, but Crandall frowned in irritation.

"Did you ever know a policeman named Calbert Finney?" Sennett asked, as if the question was an afterthought.

Crandall blinked his eyes and the annoyance of my glass stain seemed to dissipate. "I never heard of him."

We were standing near a black end table next to the couch. I bent down to look at a photo of Crandall and two other men standing in front of a building. They were wearing civilian clothes. Crandall quickly changed the conversation.

"That picture was taken in Detroit with my two friends. It was just before we got inducted," Crandall said. "I tell you, some guys don't like the military, but it sure straightened me out."

I was going to say something when Sennett took out his notepad, studied it for a moment and then stood up. He said he appreciated Crandall's time and told him there wasn't much more he needed to ask him. As we walked to the door, I looked back. Crandall was examining his table. I think he was happy to see us go.

When we got outside, Sennett called his office and told Knudsen that we wanted to talk with Mark Crandall's employer, whose name was on the calling card in Sandra Wells's safety deposit box. He said the company was Sturgeon or something like that.

As we began walking back to the car, Sennett said, "We needed to find some specifics before we start pressing this guy."

When we were about a half a block away I stopped and stared at my car. I nudged Sennett with my elbow and pointed to to the tires. All four of them were flat.

"I've seen this movie before, George. Flat tires used to happen a lot in my old neighborhood when I was growing up. Do me a favor, call your station house and get a couple of squad cars over here."

Senett pulled out his cellphone and made a call. In the meantime I saw Rambo and his buddies laughing and high-fiving each other. I looked at them and then crossed the street.

"Okay, who's the smartass who flattened the tires?" I asked.

The three young men shrugged like I was talking a foreign language. At almost the same moment two Detroit Police cruisers came down the street, one in front of and one behind my car. When the officers got out, they had their hands on the top of their un-holstered guns.

I pulled out my badge. "You see this?" I asked. "You've got one of two choices: either you inflate these tires or my friends here are going to cuff you and take you down to the station." I grabbed Rambo by the jacket and dragged him over to my car.

"We didn't do nothin," he wailed.

"Okay, then that shouldn't be a problem. I'll get the forensic guys down here and take some prints off the tires. If we find yours or your friends, you're in big trouble. I'm talking juvenile detention." As I spoke, the policemen edged closer to the boys. Their eyes widened in terror. "Now what'll it be?"

I moved to the back of my car and opened the trunk, pulling out a bicycle pump and handing it to Rambo. "How about you start pumping?"

The terrified kid drooped his head and shuffled over to the car. He didn't look so tough any more. After fifteen minutes of pushing on the air pump, he was exhausted and the tire was barely inflated. Sennett invited the other two to join the fun with the same result.

"Come on, boys," Sennett encouraged them, trying as hard as he could not to laugh. "Put some muscle in it."

After half an hour the three boys asked for mercy and apologized. At that point I pulled out an electric pump from the trunk and plugged it into the car battery plug. I handed it to Rambo. "Is this what you were looking for?" I asked.

The boy and his friends pumped the tires. When they were done, they handed the pump back to me.

That's when Sennett took out a card from is pocket. "Call me at this number. I'll take you guys on a tour of the police headquarters. You never know, you may want to be a cop someday."

They took the card and rode off.

"Think it will work?" I asked.

"Reality bites. Who knows, maybe they'll think differently the next time. If I get a call, I'll know. By the way, how did you know that trick?"

"I said it happened in my neighborhood, but I didn't tell you who it happened to." I winked.

Sennett smiled. "Nothing like experience. It's the mother of invention. By the way, where did you learn to carry those pumps?"

I corrected him. "Necessity is the mother of invention. Experience is different. It taught me to carry a hand air pump when I go biking and an electric pump in case I get a flat."

We were about to get back in my car when Knudsen called. I watched as Sennett nodded his head and after a couple of minutes he clicked off.

Apparently, he had called Crandall's place of employment, but the CEO refused to talk to him. He said unless he was forced to, he wouldn't expose his company to the possibility of bad publicity. We'd have to talk to his lawyers, and unless we could show cause, that could take weeks.

From the look on Sennett's face I thought he was finished talking, so I shook my head in disgust. Instead, Sennett continued talking. Knudsen got a callback from Sturgis and Martin. This time it was from his secretary or receptionist. She said she needed to speak with someone from the police; it was important and personal.

"I can't go," Sennett said. "The mayor wants to meet with me about Sandra Wells. I don't know what this is about, but I need your help."

"Like I said, I'm all in," I replied, knowing full well I would do anything to protect my family. The problem was I didn't know what that really meant.

CHAPTER 17

THE OFFICES OF STURGIS AND MARTIN were in a high-rise building in Southfield, one of a variety of northern suburbs that abutted Detroit. In Southfield's case it was a potpourri of poor city planning and architecturally tastelessness, steel and glass buildings built by the dozens in the eighties to house the burgeoning office market. Demand outpaced building.

That was then. Now that rents dropped, "For Lease" signs ringed most buildings, and small businesses found refuge in attractive low budget lease rates. Still, companies like Sturgis and Martin were in need of large offices and big expressway visibility. Their offices were large enough for their name on the building, emblazoned like a giant billboard. It was a huge marketing ploy for a company that was trying to regroup after the Great Recession.

I entered the parking deck and walked to the elevator through a series of shops and restaurants. My ears popped twice by the time I walked onto the thirty-first floor and directly into the offices of Sturgis and Martin. My watch said one o'clock.

The receptionist who greeted me was a fifty-year-old woman with pulled-back gray hair, a white blouse and glasses. I read the name on her desk: Mildred Walters. Not a head turner, but very polite. I introduced myself as a physician and friend of Lieutenant Sennett.

She looked down at her desk, avoiding any eye contact. "I'm sorry, Doctor Dailey. I don't know who told you to come here, but this letter was left for you." She handed me a sealed white envelope.

I was pissed, particularly with her terse indifference. "Couldn't someone have had the courtesy to call me?" She remained silent.

Perplexed, I mumbled something, pocketed the envelope and walked out.

At the elevator I stopped and opened the note. It read: "Meet me in the bar in the lobby. I'll be right down." It was signed Mildred. When I finished reading it, I paused for a moment, wondering what this mysterious note meant. It didn't take much thought to realize I had no choice, so I pressed the down button.

By the time I reached the lobby the annoying clogging of my ears from the elevator ride returned. This time I squeezed my nose and forced air back into my ears. My hearing returned just in time to hear Smokey Robinson greet me with "Tracks of My Tears" as I entered the Motown Lounge.

I stopped for a moment and looked around. The place was filled with automobile memorabilia, including the hood of a '67 Mustang complete with the hood ornament, a pair of shiny exhaust pipes from a '75 Eldo convertible, and two side horns from a '36 Packard. It was actually kind of cool.

A waitress guided me to a corner table, with a view of the entrance. After sitting down I ordered a Coke, and wondered what Mildred Walters could want with me. It didn't take long to find out.

I looked to the left and saw her walking toward me. She glanced around to make sure no one followed her and then made her way to my table.

When Mildred got there, she smiled and stuck out her hand. Studying her face for a moment, I saw puffy cheeks, two deep frown lines above her nose, and some jowliness at the neckline, all of which said grandma. However, her eyes said something else. They stared intently at me, as if she had something important on her mind. In the end, her honest smile made any imperfection irrelevant.

She looked at my Coke and asked for an ice tea. I motioned the waitress over and ordered, figuring I would be the big spender.

"Why did you give me that note?" I asked.

"Thank you for seeing me. I'm sorry about the envelope. But I didn't want anyone in the office to think I was meeting with you. I overheard the police ask to speak to my boss, Mr. Fairmont, about Mark Crandall, and I heard him tell them he wouldn't discuss anything with them. I've been waiting a long time to talk with someone about Patsy Evans. This was my chance, and I didn't want to lose it."

"Who is Patsy Evans?" I asked, my voice barely clearing the background music.

"She's a young woman who came to the office six months ago—nice girl, young, kind of inexperienced and naïve. She was looking for Mark Crandall. When I told her he wasn't in, she acted distraught and asked for help. So I talked with her."

By this time, the waitress had returned with the iced tea. Mildred took two packages of artificial sweetener, opened them carefully, and spilled the contents into her drink. She deliberately put in a straw and slowly took a sip. The drink seemed to get her composed, and she began to talk again.

"Patsy was pretty vulnerable. It wasn't long before she was pouring her heart out about Mark Crandall. She said she met him at a bar. He told her he was an insurance agent and worked for Sturgis and Martin. She fell for him, and they had an affair, which is fine, except he took advantage of her."

When I asked her what she meant, she looked at the entrance to the bar again, checking to see if she knew anyone. She said that Patsy was one of those kids left behind in school. She was attractive, if she wanted to be, but she came from a small community in Michigan and lived on a farm. "I bet she never went on a date before she met this guy, Mark."

"Okay, a lot of girls get jilted. Why is this different?

Mildred hesitated for a moment, then said that even though she was giving up a confidence, she couldn't live with herself if didn't tell someone. I felt a hint of irritation in her voice.

She persisted, saying that Patsy Evans told her some of the things they did. Her face got red and she clasped her hands in front of her as she spoke.

"He took her back to his condo and gave her drugs. She woke up the next morning with her clothes off, knowing they had sex."

When I asked why Patsy didn't she go to the police, Mildred said she was naïve enough to think it wasn't rape. She was in love with him. It was her first time, and he was all over her. She couldn't believe someone wanted her. After that she said they dated regularly. He was very interested in everything about her, including her work.

On the surface, getting involved in a discussion about Crandall dating this girl seemed like a dead end. But Mildred seemed like a decent person, so I tried to humor her. "Why was he so interested in her? Was he looking for something she had or what she did at work?"

Mildred sighed and clenched her jaw. "Doctor, you don't understand. This isn't about business; this is about love. He dumped her after several months. She was devastated."

As she spoke, she reached into her handbag and handed me what looked like a small folder. In fact, it was a business brochure from Sturgis and Martin describing Mark Crandall. At the top of the folder was his picture.

"You see that face?" she asked. "That smug arrogance? He's just the kind of person that would prey on an innocent girl like Patsy."

I stared at the picture for a moment, then handed it back to her. She held up her hand and told me to keep it, so I politely put into my jacket pocket. I told her I understood what she meant, but this was a police investigation of a serious crime. If Mark Crandall was involved, we needed to find some kind of connection that could help us solve it. I asked her where Patsy Evans worked.

Mildred pinched her lips together. "From what I know she worked in some kind of cancer surveillance clinic at the medical center. She seemed very dedicated."

As far as Crandall was concerned, she said she had seen him a couple of times in the office. "He was one of those men who looked right though you, especially if you weren't important." Then she made a confession. "You hear things about people not saying something when they see trouble. I don't want to be that person."

"What do you mean?" I asked.

"I think she was suicidal."

I was taken aback by the comment. "That's terrible. I'm not sure what I personally could do to help Patsy, but I do know one thing—she needs psychiatric help. If you give me her address and phone number and I'll have someone from social services call her."

She took a piece of paper from her purse and handed me Patsy Evan's information. I immediately transferred it to my cellphone. When I finished, she seemed put off, as if she were expecting more from me. I felt bad, as a doctor I took an oath to help, but this situation was out of my expertise.

I tried to show my best doctor face and promised to call Patsy and try to help her. I hated giving out bullshit to this woman who was trying to do the right thing, but I was worried about some creep breaking into my garage, people getting killed, and a possible threat to my family. Nonetheless, I promised the police would try to find her and refer her to the right people. She seemed to perk up when I said it.

I thanked her, dropped a ten-dollar bill on the table, and got up. She was still sitting at the table sipping her drink and looking down at her placemat when I reached the entrance. Just as I was about to leave, Marvin Gaye sang out, "I Heard It Through The Grapevine."

It seemed prophetic, but I kept walking. I felt guilty and conflicted. My profession is based on helping people, but I have to understand my limits. I'm a doctor, not a social worker. What business did I have investigating Mark Crandall's social life?

CHAPTER 18

From my office the next morning I called Sennett about my conversation with Mildred Walters. I told him while I didn't understand the relationship between Crandall and Patsy Evans, it sounded like this girl needed help. After listening, he sounded just as puzzled as I was, but he said he would contact the police in Flint and try to find her. As I was hanging up, Karen gave me a message. It was from Sid Blanton, an old friend of mine. He had an earache and wanted to know if could make a house call.

Doctors usually don't see patients out of the office. It's just another chip in the gilded image of the family doc. Too many patients and not enough time. However, everyone has exceptions, and Sid Blanton was one of them.

Sid ran a jazz club on the Detroit Riverfront called the Pipeline. It was old-school, and I loved it—Oscar Peterson, Dave Brubeck, Miles Davis. They were my idols.

Any interest I have in music I blame on my mother. She wanted me to be educated, so I took piano lessons as a kid. To her great joy, she found I loved it. I played all my life, even through college. People couldn't figure me out, the jock who played music.

I was lucky I had the talent. After my lawsuit, I had nowhere to go, except my boat on Lake St. Clair. The Pipeline became my second home. I knew Sid, because I cured him of a cancer in his throat. When he found out I played, he invited me down one night to play a set with him. After we finished, he took me aside and offered me a job as the intermission man. For a loner like me it was a blessing.

Nowadays I didn't get down there as much as I used to, so, any excuse to go down to the Pipeline was fine with me. Sid's ear problem was as good an excuse as any.

It was around two in the afternoon when I parked my car in front of the modest redbrick building a block and half from the river. It was a single story structure located on the grounds of a torn-down, old tire plant that blighted the most beautiful part of the city. Unfortunately, the decline in the economy and the collapse of the city government left large tracts of land void of anything except weeds and drifting garbage.

A cool, fresh breeze moving south from Lake St. Clair brushed against my face as I got out of the car. I paused a moment and wistfully looked at the swift current of the Detroit River. For a moment I wished I was on my boat, broad reaching to Harsten's Island.

I walked into the club and was immediately surrounded by the mellow sound of a trumpet echoing through the dimly lit club. I knew the song in an instant, "So What." I turned and looked at the stage. Instead of Miles Davis, I saw a medium-sized, balding African American in front of a drummer and a base player. The trumpet player was wearing a pink silk shirt and grey pants. He had brown Gucci loafers without socks. Sid Blanton was pure cool.

I looked up at his face. His cheeks puffed and his lips pursed on the mouth-piece of his shiny Calicchio trumpet. The sound from the horn poured a muted energy into the room.

As I listened, I glanced around the place. Charlie was behind the bar. To the river side of the room two men in suits sat at a table. The muted light from the window sparkled on their beer glasses, making them look like candles. In front of the men lay open folders and a couple of briefcases.

When Sid saw me, he motioned to the boys to take a break and put his horn into the case behind him.

"I feel special, having my doctor making a house call," the man said in a voice as rough as gravel.

"You are special, Sid. Only you and Miles Davis could make that song sound that good. I would have sworn his ghost was in the room."

"Well, if you don't fix my damn ear, I might just be one."

I took out an otoscope from my bag and slipped on a clean speculum. I looked inside and saw some swelling and redness on the outside of the ear canal. When I pulled on his ear lobe, it hurt. "You have an infection in your ear canal, Sid."

I pulled out a bottle of eardrops from my bag, handed it to him, and then admonished him to quit messing with his ears with Q-tips. He asked me how I knew. "This isn't my first rodeo. You must have been sleeping the day your mother said nothing smaller than your elbow in your ear."

"No way, doc, my mother never let me sleep. She always had some chore for me. Why do you think I played the trumpet? I was always so busy playing my horn, she could never get mad at me. Got out of a lot of chores too. Best scam ever."

We both started laughing. When we stopped, Sid looked at me for a moment and then snapped his fingers. "I almost forgot. There's a young lady waiting over by the bar for you." The way he smiled when he said "young lady" made me wonder who it was. It was a lascivious look, the one he reserved for the ladies of the night that frequented his place.

I looked across the dimly lit room and in the far corner near the bar was a woman with long, curly blonde hair and dark sunglasses. At a distance I couldn't get a good look at her, so I went over to the opposite corner where Charlie, the bartender, was washing some glasses. He was an ex-Navy Seal with a Silver Star and a memory of Kabul that made him happy to be out of the mainstream. When he saw me, he nodded toward the girl at the table.

I started toward her. In the muted light she looked like she was in her late teens or early twenties. She wore a maize and blue sweatshirt and gray sweatpants with pink Nikes. Her head was bent down as if she was staring at the small purse lying in front of her.

The woman looked up as I approached the table and took off her glasses. I studied her face for a moment. Her bleached blond hair was pulled back into a ponytail, adding lifelessness to her pallid skin. I almost thought she looked dissipated except for a splattering of youthful freckles and a sensuous mouth that even without lipstick contrasted against her straight white teeth.

The entire effect could have been appealing had it not been for her eyes. It wasn't just their color. No question they were a beautiful, piercing dark blue shade that shone from beneath her lids, but It was the way they darted from side to side that made me hesitate. She looked worried. Her face seemed oddly familiar.

I pulled up a chair and sat across from her. It took me a moment, but I realized where we met. "Tell me if I'm wrong, but don't you work at the Cabana?" I used the word "work" to soften the real meaning."

She nodded. "I was there with Queenie." Her voice was small, echoing the fear in her eyes. "I guess you have a pretty bad opinion of me, don't you?" The way she spoke, stragely seemed educated.

I stared at her for a moment, trying to figure out why she was here. I must have scared her, because she started fidgeting with the napkin in front of her. "Look," I said, "I'm a doctor, not a cop. I deal with people every day. No matter who they are or what they do, they all need some type of respect. My opinion of you doesn't matter. It's your opinion of yourself that does."

When I said it, the words must have struck home, because her eyes moistened. She sniffed a moment, shook her head, as if to erase the memory of something, and then sat silently looking down at the table.

"How did you know I would be here?"

Sitting there in her sweatpants, she lost her sex kitten appearance and her "street" speech. "I kind of lied," she said sheepishly. "I told your receptionist that Lieutenant Sennett asked me to deliver a document to you. As soon as I mentioned his name, she told me you were going to the Pipeline."

"That was clever. I'll have to remember that trick."

Then I stopped for a moment and changed the subject. I told her I already saw something in her that was worthwhile. When she asked me what it was, I said that she was wearing my alma mater's colors. Then, for reasons I never quite understand about myself, I asked her if she attended college. As soon as I said it, I regretted my question. After all, she was a hooker. But to my surprise, she smiled for a moment, then her raised her voice and responded sadly that she was a music major at Ann Arbor for two years.

I was going to ask her how a nice girl like her got into place like this, but I realized that wasn't going to get me anywhere. She had a problem, and I wasn't a social worker. Besides, she didn't just trundle down to the Pipeline to talk about college life. Instead I asked her why she had come to see me.

Fear lit up her eyes again. "Cal Finney," she said.

I remembered her at the Long Ride with Finney, the afternoon that he was murdered and then at the Cabana Motel. "You're Carrie or Carine or something like that. Isn't that right?"

"Carina Knowlton is my name," she said with an edge of embarrassment. "Cal told me about you."

I asked her why she came down here to talk about Finney, and she responded by fiddling with the paper napkin in front of her. In the background I heard the trio start the Johnny Hodges's version of "Loveless Blues."

She shifted on her chair trying to get comfortable. "He was on to something. He told me he had some information that was important, something medical, involving the mayor's office and City Hospital. Cal wasn't smart enough to understand it, but he said it was something big,"

By this time she had a small pile of shredded napkin in front of her. It still didn't make any sense, so I repeated why me. Carina said that Cal looked scared the last time she saw him, like something might happen. "He told me you were the best damn detective in the city, and if anything happened to him, I was to give you this envelope." When she finished, she reached inside her purse and pulled out a white envelope. Her hand shook as she handed me the paper.

I took the envelope and opened it up. Inside was the spreadsheet I saw at the Long Ride. I thought of the dead body of Cal Finney lying in the street and quivered, realizing that his demise was connected to this piece of paper. Life couldn't be that meaningless. I pulled out the spreadsheet and looked at it for a moment, but it still seemed like a bunch of random numbers. Holding this paper, I felt an inexplicable sense of evil and thought to give it back to her. Instead, I stuffed it into my pocket.

Carina picked up another napkin and began folding it in half. "Now he's dead. I'm so scared I'll be next."

"Why do you say that?"

"When you work like I do you get vibes, you know what I mean? Guys say something, things happen. All of sudden somebody disappears."

"Not to get personal, but were you and Cal more than just friends?"

"Not at all. He treated me like family. He was a great guy."

Her job finished, she quickly closed her purse and put on her jacket. Before she left, I asked her if she had told anyone about this. She didn't respond. Instead, she looked furtively around the bar as one of the two men near the window got up to go to the restroom.

"Maybe once I said something to my pimp. He went through my purse and saw the paper. Then he asked me what it was. I told him I didn't know."

"What's his name?"

"Aurelious Jones. They call him Snake," she responded. As she did, she casually swung her head toward the man walking toward them. Suddenly, her face paled and her hands again began to shake. She turned with her back to the window. In the dim light I couldn't recognize the men.

"I've got to get out of here," she said, making a break for the exit.

Before I could reply, she was out the door. I turned around, stupefied at what had just happened. Charlie must have been watching the conversation from behind the bar, because he came up to me.

"Hey, doc, when did you start hanging with hookers?" He smiled.

"First of all, I'm not hanging out with her. Second, since she was wearing sweatpants and a college T-shirt, how did you know she was a hooker?"

"If you've seen what I've seen, you know a hooker."

The man who scared Carina returned to his friend. I vaguely recognized one of them. The other man I had seen on television. I tried again to see their faces, but they were turned toward the window, engrossed in conversation.

"Charlie, who are those two guys over there?" I nodded my head toward the window.

"One of them works for the mayor. I don't know what he does, but he comes down here regularly. The people he meets are usually sports guys or politicos. I heard one of them call him Tommy. I think the other guy is Turner Davidson. He's running for Mayor."

I looked again. It was Tommy Holiday. He was too busy talking to notice me.

"Why do you ask?"

"That girl I was with saw them. It was like she saw a ghost. She got up and almost ran out of here."

"Hookers are funny. They like to take a guy's money and play the sex game, but they don't want anyone to see them dressed as regular people."

"Assuming that you're right, if a hooker told you that someone was after her, would you believe her?"

"Like I believed my sergeant when he said if I didn't move faster, he was gonna put me in the plunger."

"The plunger? What's that?"

"The cold water plunge into ice water. Trust me, no one wants the plunger." I checked my jacket to make sure I had the envelope. No plunger for me.

I was going to say hello to Holiday but thought better of it. Nothing to gain, so I got up from the table and walked out. I looked back at him, as I hit the exit. He was still engrossed in his conversation. I was totally confused. Why was the Mayor's Chief of Staff having an amicable conversation with his boss's biggest rival?

Chapter 19

I LEFT THE PIPELINE PUZZLED AND CONCERNED. It wasn't until I my hand brushed against the bulk of the spreadsheet in my pocket that I realized the reason why. Someone had died for this piece of paper, and I wanted to get rid of it. That's when I called Jordan and told her about my meeting with Carina Knowlton, but she didn't seem fazed. For her it was business as usual. When I mentioned how Carina bolted from the bar when she saw Holiday, the tone of her voice quickly changed.

"I need you to come down to my office now, Ben, and make sure to bring Sennett with you. We need to talk."

"Are you sure you want to get involved?"

"At one point you might have been right. The moment someone broke into the garage everything changed. This is no longer business. Now it's personal."

It was hard to argue with her logic, so I called Sennett, and at four o'clock we entered her seventh floor office in the McNamara Federal Building on Michigan Avenue. I have to admit I felt a little more secure with Sennett next to me.

The twenty-seven-story building was named after former Senator Patrick McNamara. I liked the place, mainly because it was where I met Jordan. I didn't go down there very often, but every time I passed the front door my first response was the morbid feeling of hopelessness that comes with being down and out. Fortunately, my brief anxiety always evaporated with the knowledge that pushing that door open was the beginning of a miracle. Broke from alimony payments and bereft of my medical practice, I took a one-time job establishing the validity of an insurance claim on a Federal employee. It took me to the office of a Federal attorney. Little did I know that I was walking into the office of my future wife.

When her secretary showed us in, Jordan was engrossed behind her desk, reading a document. On her right were several large file cabinets. To the left was a dark wooden bookcase filled with volumes of legal treatises.

I looked at the books for a moment and then cleared my throat. She looked up quickly and apologized for not seeing us.

"No problem," I said, pointing to two books, one entitled *Le Bon Usage* and next to it the *Oxford Spanish Dictionary*. Next to them was a book on *Food, Farming, and Sustainability Readings in Agricultural Law."*

"Why the language textbooks?'"

"I minored in languages in college and spent a year abroad in Paris. Sometimes it comes in handy with cases."

"Okay, I can understand that, but Farming Law? Come on."

She laughed. "That is to impress visitors like you."

As we folded into in the soft leather chairs that faced her desk, I had an instant remembrance of when we first met. It was business, but I couldn't ignore that first look, that exquisite smile. Love at first sight, maybe, or was it my abject loneliness? Regardless, it was electric. Strange how things happen; this time the smile on her face was genuine and the pictures on the credenza behind her were of Joey and me.

Sennett interrupted my daydreaming. "The office looks the same, except the pictures have changed,"

"They better have or we'd be seeing a different kind of lawyer," she said with a faint smile. Then her face turned solemn, as she started thumbing though a folder on her desk. "I'm concerned by this spreadsheet that Ben mentioned."

"So I am I," Sennett replied. "The more I investigate Sandra Wells' death, the more I believe she was murdered because of it." He picked up a number two pencil from her desk and rolled it between his fingers. He always did this when he was frustrated.

"I want to help," she said. "Just in case, my boss gave me the okay."

She went on to explain that Federal grants were being used to fund City Hospital. After all of the previous corruption in Detroit, the Justice Department had a standing directive to police the construction contracts.

"Somebody wanted Finney dead," Sennett said. "It probably had to do with the spreadsheet. Finney must have known he was a target, which explains why he was so nervous when we met with him."

At that point I pulled out the envelope with the spreadsheet from my coat and showed it to them. I felt a sense of relief when I set everything on the desk, like I had rid myself of something very toxic. Jordan and Sennett studied the fifty columns of eight number sequences. After a few minutes they put the paper down in frustration. When Jordan asked me if I had any idea what the numbers meant, I shook my head and held my hands up in surrender.

"I'm going to make a copy and give it to our team," Jordan said. Instead of making a paper copy, she scanned it, and put it in a file on her computer. She then sent an e-mail copy to Sennett. When she finished, she seemed distracted as she got up from he desk, distracted enough to spill the two-foot pile of documents onto the floor with her elbow.

Her eyes glared. "Shit!"

I was taken back. I rarely saw Jordan lose her composure on something like this. I quickly got out of my chair and helped her recover the documents from the floor. When I gazed at her face, I saw a strange look of anger in her eyes.

More engrossed in the spreadsheet, Sennett ignored the toppled documents.

"I'm not sure what that piece of paper represents, but I do know this," Sennett said. "We're playing in a different league, a league where killing people is the norm." The pencil was now lodged under his middle finger. His knuckles were white from clutching it harder.

"Great," I said. "I feel like I'm carrying the Ebola virus."

"Carina Knowlton say anything else?" he asked.

I told him that she mentioned her pimp's name. It was something like Snake." When I said the name, I saw Sennett's raise his eyebrows.

For her part, Jordan seemed to be trying to remain on her task. "As a Federal attorney, I've got to stay focused," Jordan said. "Laws have been broken and the perpetrators must be brought to justice." This time her voice trembled. She stopped for a moment and stared out her window again. When she turned around, her eyes were watering. "But there's another reason I need to be involved. As a mother and a wife, I'm really scared. Someone already burglarized our garage looking for something and left an amputated finger on the seat of Ben's car. This is serious business. I'm not going to stand by as a passive observer. We have to stop this before something else happens to our family."

I got up from my chair and stood behind the desk with my hands on her shoulders. She rested her face on the back of my hand for a moment. Then shook her head and wiped her eyes.

"I'll be okay. Just be careful."

"We will. Our only connection is the spreadsheet and Carina Knowlton. We need to find her." Sennett replied firmly. Suddenly I was startled by a loud cracking sound. Sennett had snapped the pencil in two. Apparently he was also getting jumpy.

CHAPTER 20

IT TOOK MOST OF THE NIGHT TO CLEAR MY HEAD; still, I woke up early, anxious to go with Sennett to visit another contact. He was waiting for me by Cobo Hall, parked at one of the outside lots. Cobo Hall was Detroit's answer to McCormick Place or the Jacob Javits Center. Its biggest claim to fame was the annual Detroit Auto Show, an extravaganza of machinery that for two weeks erased the dismal image of the Motor City.

When he got into my car, he was frowning, apparently concentrating on something on his cellphone.

"You look like you're stumped on a Jeopardy question," I remarked.

"Nah, just confused about what happened to you and this Knowlton girl."

He explained that he had Knudsen run a police record on her. "It turns out that she is the daughter of a rich industrialist from Bloomfield Hills. She was a straight "A" student in high school and then went to the University of Michigan. Something happened in her sophomore year."

I put the car in gear. "What was it?" I asked.

"Maybe drugs, no one knew exactly. She had an arrest for prostitution. It was a first offense, so they went through the social worker. It was the usual story, got in the wrong crowd, parents divorced, away at school with no supervision. Throughout it all, one common theme ran through the family: too much me and not enough we." He pointed to turn east at Jefferson and then continued.

"When the auto business started to crash, her father started drinking more and messing with women. When that happened, the wife left and then suddenly died of heart attack a couple of months later."

I suggested that the girl blamed her father, but he didn't seem sure, saying, "nobody knows what goes on behind closed doors." As I weaved through traffic, he suggested that the father had his own financial problems and probably lost track of his daughter's needs. When I asked whether he got his life together, he replied, "If that means financially, he succeeded. He owns a jet, plays golf at the fanciest clubs, and bought a beachfront home in Cabo."

"Why didn't the daughter go back to her father?"

"Interesting question. She wouldn't tell the social worker. Just said she didn't want to see her father again."

"Poor little rich girl, huh?"

"Messed up little rich girl would be a better description. Now all we have to do is find her."

I drove down Jefferson Avenue, following Sennett's instructions. After a few minutes, the route seemed familiar. Then I realized where we were going—back to the Cabana Motel.

The temperature dropped and a light rain began. With it the leaves swirled around and dropped off the trees. Beautiful Fall had turned into dreary November.

It didn't take us long to reach the Cabana Motel, but Sennett told me to drive past it. I looked at the parking lot, three-quarters full at ten in the morning.

A mile south of the Cabana, Sennett pointed to a flashing neon sign on the street corner to the left. I turned onto the side street and stopped in front of a respectable-looking bar. The sign read "The Sly Trap."

"Looks like we're upscaling our eating establishments."

"Not what you think. Sylvester Monroe runs the main business office for every pimp in town."

I parked close to the corner and locked the door. My car wasn't much, but those kids going after my ride made me a little nervous.

We walked up to an ornate heavy wooden front door, carved with a black and red spider in a web. Opening the door and stepping inside, it took a moment for my eyes to adjust to the dimly lit interior. In the background I heard the drumbeat of some hip-hop rapper, yelling "motherfucker" faster than the ratty-tat-tat of a full clip assault rifle. Slowly, my eyes made out three or four occupied booths where loud voices tried to shout over the music.

Sennett pointed the way to the back of the bar. Standing in front of a long mirror was a huge African American with his eyes shielded by dark Dolce and Gabbana sunglasses. Around his neck were three heavy gold chains that hung down below the open collar of his turquoise blue shirt. The biggest of the chains had a black onyx stone set in diamonds in the shape of an eye,

"Yo, Lieutenant?" the man asked with a wary tone to his voice. "Why you be comin' down here to mess with my shit?'

George Sennett made a career out of busting the toughest and meanest crooks the city had to offer. Dealing with them was part of his job. But that didn't mean he had to be like them to exercise his authority. It was his habit to avoid speaking the ragged language of the ghetto in order to make them sweat with fear. I'd seen George Sennett in action. They were right to be afraid of him.

"Sly, nobody's messing with you. I need to find the pimp down here handling a girl named Carina. You know anything?"

Sly Monroe probably knew plenty, considering the people that were frequenting his bar at ten in the morning. I also knew that Sennett had his sources in the city. He left them alone like a savings account in a bank, pulling out a chit of information every now and then. Sly Monroe was no dummy. He knew this too. Sennett was there to make a withdrawal.

"First table on the left by the rear door. His name is Aurelious Jones. Everyone here calls him Snake. Be careful. He's one mean dude."

We walked to the back of the bar and there, near the rear exit, sat a thin black man with a closely shaved head and a goatee made of two long braids tied at he ends. The sleeves of his low cut cotton sweater were rolled up. His elbows rested on the table and his hands gripped a pencil as he added up a column of figures. Last night's take, I guessed.

As I came close to his table, I got a good look at his sinewy arms. On the inside of both forearms were two cobra heads tattooed with fangs dripping blood. Under them were a couple of Chinese symbols that I was sure didn't say peace and love. I imagined if Aurelius Jones lost his temper both of those serpents would dart out of his arms.

Sennett wasn't impressed. He slid onto the seat opposite Jones, while I continued to stand to the side of the table. Jones seemed to ignore both of us and then raised his head slowly. His eyes were narrow and his nostrils flared, like an animal sniffing his prey.

Sennett didn't say anything, just showed him his badge. Jones leered at it. "Last time I checked, I didn't invite no motherfucking pig to sit at my table." His voice was deep and his eyes looked at Sennett without fear. I saw him reach for an object next to him on the seat.

Sennett didn't see this movement as he put the badge back in his pocket. I had no choice. I whipped my hand across the table and grabbed the two braids hanging from Jones's chin. As soon as I latched on, I pulled his head sideways across the table.

He erupted with a cry of pain fit to wake the dead as he tried to break loose. It was to no avail; my grip was too strong and the pain too intense. By this time the man's face was writhing in agony.

"Now, Mr. Motherfucker," I said calmly, "you are going to have a nice, polite conversation with the lieutenant."

By this time Sennett jumped to the side of Jones and pulled out a 6" switchblade from a seat next to the pimp.

Sennett was mad. "What is this?" He held up the knife. "You go around cutting people up with this? Maybe you cut fingers off, huh?"

Jones shook his head, his eyes watering with pain. I let go as Sennett lifted his head up and threw him back into his seat. The anger had left Jones's eyes. All that remained was fear.

"I don't know nothin' about cutting fingers."

"We'll see. I'm taking this knife down to the station. We'll see if they can find anything interesting on it."

Sennett methodically wrapped the knife in a napkin and put it in his coat pocket. When he was done, he asked Jones if he knew Carina Knowlton. Jones didn't respond. "Do you want to go another round with Dr. Dailey?" As he waited for a response, I opened and tightly closed my fingers just below Snake's chin. All he could do was shake his head.

"I'm not good at head shakes, Aurelius. I need words."

"I ain't seen the bitch for three days," he mumbled. "She got three days of my money. If I catch her, I'm going to make her pay." The voice lost its resonance, and the words came out in a squeaky pitch.

"Are you good at beating up women?" Sennett asked casually.

"You got to beat 'em up, otherwise they don't fear you," he said looking for some place to escape.

"I get it, but it's hardly a fair fight, is it?"

"What is fair got to do with it? Bitch has my money, I want it back."

Sennett ignored the comment. "Where do you think she is? Who does she hang with?"

"She got a place down in the New Center with a couple of other girls, but don't bother going down there; I already checked."

Sennett asked for the address. After Jones gave it to him, he asked a couple of more questions about Carina's customers. Jones drew a blank. It was clear that Sennett wasn't going to get any more information, so he stood up wordlessly and extricated himself from the booth.

I walked ahead of him. The place had gone silent; even the rap music was off. I felt like every eye in the place was staring at us. Sennett nodded to Sly and then opened the door. From this side, the spider seemed to be smiling. When we got outside and into the sunlight, I breathed a sigh of relief.

"You really think Jones cut off the victim's fingers?"

Sennett smiled. "I doubt it, but I don't want to take any chances. I'll take the knife in and have forensics look it over. What I really want is for him to feel fear. Fear makes people do strange things. You never know what a guy like Jones might do." He paused for a moment, then smiled. "Where the hell did you learn that beard trick?" he asked as we walked to my car.

"No trick. My coach taught it to me. When you're in the pile and you want the ball, grab anything you can get a hold of."

He nodded. "I'm going to add it to my encyclopedia of personal safety." When we were at the car I asked him where we were going. He mumbled something about the New Center. I didn't bother to reply. I was too busy adding Aurelius Jones to the list of people I pissed off.

CHAPTER 21

HEADING WEST INTO THE CITY, SENNETT GOT A CALL. It was Knudsen. I watched him as he listened. The longer the conversation continued, the closer his eyebrows came together. He spoke very little and clicked off after a couple of minutes.

"That Knudsen is an odd fellow. Whenever he has something important to say, his voice rises a little higher. It makes him sound like he's nervous."

"Maybe you have something to do with that," I said.

Sennett started laughing. "You may be right. Anyway, one of the detectives interviewed Sandra Wells's attorney. She actually had a last will and testament."

"Did he indicate what it said?" I asked.

"The attorney claims he is under instructions to not disclose anything for at least six weeks after her death. That suggests that Sandra Wells knew she was in trouble."

"What about her cousin?"

As he spoke, I exited the ramp at the New Center. "From what Knudsen said, Wells and her cousin in Windsor were close. Her name is Charmayne Phillips."

We drove past the Fisher Building, new home of the city government. Its calling card was a brilliant, glittering golden dome that shone like a beacon for miles in the bright sunlight. When we got to Second Avenue, I made a left and passed Hit City USA, a tribute to the vibrant sounds of black musicians coming out of the projects and tenement houses of Detroit. As we did, Sennett sang a few bars of "Ain't No Mountain High Enough." I told him not to quit his day job.

At Pallister I knew we were close to the number we were looking for. As I drove by a couple of beat-up row houses across the street, Sennett pointed to the second one on the left.

I parked the car and walked with him up the cracked sidewalk and onto a wooden porch in serious need of a paint job. It was eleven in the morning, and most people were at work. But if you were a prostitute, I guessed you probably had the night shift.

Sennett rang the worn brass button next to the paneled wooden door and waited. Nothing happened. He rang again and then knocked hard against the peeling door jamb. It took a moment, but we heard someone shouting from inside.

The curtain on the sidelight next to the door was drawn back for a moment. Then someone from inside shouted: "Go away. We don't need anything."

Undeterred, Sennett shouted back. "Detroit Police. We need to talk to you." With that he pulled out his badge. The curtain inched to the side and a Tigers baseball cap poked around the edge of the window. A couple of moments later we heard the lock unfastening; then the door opened slowly.

We were both surprised when from behind the entrance stepped Queenie, dressed in a V-neck Detroit Tigers shirt, thong underwear, and flip-flops. Her tight sleeveless shirt pushed her chest forward, showing off her substantial cleavage. In case anyone thought she was advertising, her drooping eyelids told me we had woken her from a deep sleep.

As she rubbed her eyes slowly, I looked inside. A couple of old pizza boxes littered a coffee table in the living room. Next to the table were two leather re-cliners and a flat screen TV on a wire stand.

Her lips edged downward and her head tilted away. "C'mon, Lieutenant. What do the police want with me at this hour of the day?"

Sennett asked if we could come in. She nodded and turned her back to us. I watched as she walked down the hallway, wiggling her ass. It wasn't by accident. She bent over to pick up a cotton jacket that was on the floor. The only item that left anything to the imagination was the tiny string from her thong stuck up her rear. She put her arms through the sleeves. As she did, she brushed her breasts across the sleeve of his jacket.

"Did you and your friend have something personal on your mind to come here on off hours? Maybe we all could have some quiet time together," she said, the sleep now gone from her eyes. As she spoke she began massaging her breasts.

I had heard that Sennett attracted women, but I didn't figure this encounter had anything to do with his masculine appeal. Neither did Sennett.

He checked her license and then coolly looked at her. "Look, Queenie, that shit may work with some of the guys on the beat, but I'm not here to check out your coochie. I want to know about Carina. She's your roommate, isn't she?"

The moment he mentioned Carina's name, a mask came over Queenie's face. "I don't know nothin' about nothin'. Who sent you over here anyway?"

"Don't you worry about who sent me over, just worry about you soliciting an officer of the court." He paused for a moment. "And don't forget, you did it in front of a witness. Jail time isn't pretty."

Experience is a hard teacher. A look of resignation spread over her face. "I haven't seen her for three or four days. Last time she was here she was real upset. She had a big bruise on her arm. I think it had something to do with her pimp."

"Did she tell you where she was going?"

"Carina and me never talked much. She wasn't like the rest of us. She spoke nice and seemed smart, like she went to college or something. I could never figure out why she was doing this."

"Did she have any friends?"

Queenie shifted her weight from one leg to the other. It seemed odd to have a serious conversation with a half-naked woman in the doorway of her house. I think she thought so too. "The only time I ever heard her talk about anyone was a few months ago. It was about some guy she knew in Ann Arbor."

"Boyfriend?"

"No, I don't think so. It was about some painting or shit like that."

"Where's her room?"

Queenie pointed up the stairs. "Second door on the right. But don't be expecting to find anything. Someone was here last night and threw the place up for grabs."

When Sennett asked if she knew who did it, she shook her head as if she had been asked to explain the theory of relativity. "You figure it out. It was probably one of her johns. Or maybe it was her pimp." She said she didn't ask, just stayed in her room and kept quiet.

"Was she here last night?" Sennett asked.

"If she was, I never seen her. That's probably why they tore her place up."

"What do you mean?" Sennett asked again.

She said a thickset white guy in an open collar shirt came in. He had short sleeves with big-man muscles and looked like he was used to getting his way. When she told him Carina wasn't there, he got angry. She thought he might be going to do something to her, but he didn't. The man just turned around and left."

"Why was he so angry?

"Man's got a hard on, he needs to put it somewhere. Can't get what he wants; he get upset."

It was hard to argue with simple logic, so we turned and started walking up the narrow stairs. The banister was rickety and the paint was flaking off the plaster walls. On the second floor we turned right past the bathroom. I glanced inside and saw a dirty towel on the floor and a Formica countertop displaying an endless disarray of cosmetics.

At the end of the hall Carina's door was shut. Sennett opened it and looked inside. Queenie was right; the place was a mess. Clothes lay on the floor in random piles. The sheets were off the bed and the mattress was upside down resting against the bedspring. The one thing that caught my eye was her teddy bear, looking forlorn in the corner.

Sennett searched for something else. He opened the closet, rummaged around for a couple of minutes, and then shut it. Then he poked around under the bed and took the cushions off the battered rattan chair in the corner.

By the time he made his way to the worn wooden nightstand next to the bed and opened the drawer, he was sweating and grumbling. After rummaging inside and finding nothing, he slammed the drawer closed and glanced at her bright-red cosmetic bag next to a small plastic lamp. The bag was empty and the contents were spilled on the bed. Frustrated, he combed though a variety of lipsticks, mascara wands, and packages of condoms and came up empty, leaving a pile on the bedspring.

From my position across the bed, I thought I saw a matchbook sticking out of the cosmetic bag. While he moved toward the door, I picked up the plastic pouch and turned it upside down. As I did, the matchbook floated onto the bed. I picked it up and studied it for a moment. There was a number on it.

"What is it?" he asked

"It's a number with a 734 area code, maybe Ann Arbor."

At that moment Sennett's phone rang. It was Knudsen. Sennett listened and nodded his head, then asked me about the phone number on the matchbook. I gave it to him. After writing it down in his notebook, he asked Knudsen to find out whom it belonged to. It took him a couple of minutes to locate it. When he finished, he wrote down the address and moved to the door.

"Where are we going?"

"Not we. I gotta get back to my office. The mayor wants to talk with me."

"What about Carina?"

"She'll have to wait. When the mayor calls, I gotta be there."

I wondered where that left me.

CHAPTER 22

I DROVE SENNETT BACK TO POLICE HEADQUARTERS. On the way I asked him what the address was in Ann Arbor, and without thinking he gave it to me. He said the phone number belonged to a Sean Richardson on 231 Maple Street off Huron Avenue in Ann Arbor. I think Sennett realized he made a mistake, because he told me to let him take care of it. I casually nodded my head and by the time I dropped him off he seemed to have forgotten about it.

My agreement with him ended when he left the car, because I knew two things. First, no way was I not going to Ann Arbor. I was involved in this mess whether I liked it or not. Someone was snooping around my family and that made me involved. Second, having been married for a while, I knew no woman consciously leaves the house without taking her makeup bag. Carina Knowlton was either in a hurry or in big trouble. Whatever it was, it couldn't wait until Sennett got done with the mayor.

It took twenty minutes on I-94 until I was past Metro Airport and another twenty before I exited on State Street. I drove north into the city on Stadium Avenue with the brick colonnades of Michigan Stadium on my right. Another ten minutes and I was on Huron Avenue.

After a couple of passes I finally found Maple, a dead end street with five or six tumbledown 1960s bungalows. Like many other houses in the college town, these rental dwellings were the only viable student housing option, the end result of the city's no growth policy. If someone moved out, it wasn't long before it was re-rented. And it wasn't cheap.

When I reached 231, I parked the Wagoneer and then studied the surroundings. The last of the oak and maple trees were blazing with brilliant intermingled red and yellow leaves. The flickering late afternoon haze lit up only the edge of the street. The rest of the dwelling was hidden in a deep shade that added to the structure's drab, decrepit exterior.

Maple Street was empty, no cars and no people. The students were probably in the library studying for mid-term exams. As I looked at the house, I detected a similarity between Queenie's home and this one, both about the same size and both in sore need of repair. Funny how environment and perception can change value and desirability; one was a ramshackle hovel in a decaying city and the other was shabby-chic campus housing.

I got out of the car and approached the house. The overhanging shade of the eaves, the silent, empty street, and the damp smell of leaves increased the building's gloom in the fading afternoon light. I walked up the stairs and onto the large front porch. To my left were a couple of dilapidated wooden Adirondack chairs and a hibachi next to a porch railing. No lights were on, and the creeping darkness made it impossible to see clearly.

A feeling of dread washed over me, and I chastised myself for taking on this fool's errand and not listening to Sennett. I almost turned around to leave but decided that, having come this far, I should at least knock on the door. While I waited, a few rays of the lingering sun managed to penetrate into the house. When I looked through the front window, I saw that a couple of chairs were on their side and the couch had been pushed on its back.

Then, suddenly, I thought I heard something. It sounded like a strangled cry for help. I waited until I heard it again. Without thinking I turned the door handle. It twisted but didn't open. I knew I couldn't wait for an invitation to go in. There was only one way. I took off my coat, wrapped it around my arm up to the elbow, and gave a hard snap against the glass pane on the door.

The glass exploded. I cleared out the remnants and reached in to unlock the door. After I put my coat back on, I walked inside and snapped on the hall light. It was worse than I expected.

Bookcases were toppled over, and the contents lay everywhere. The threadbare couch lay upside down on the worn wood floor, like a dead horse. The only sound I heard was the steady sound of water running in the back of the house. The only light came through a partially open kitchen door.

My pulse quickened as I once again heard the moaning of a person in trouble. Expecting danger, I inched around the corner to the kitchen and moved toward the sound as the muscles in my back tightened.

I stood at the side of the kitchen door and slowly pushed it open. At first all I saw were pots and pans helter-skelter on the floor and broken dishes. Then gradually my eyes began to focus on the figure lying in a pool of blood near the back door. His eyes were shut and dark bruises covered his face. It took a moment to realize it was a man, probably in his mid-twenties. Sean Richardson?

I rushed to his side. The first thing I felt for was his pulse. It was still beating.

Quickly, I started looking for a site of the bleeding. The bright red color meant it was probably from an artery. It took me a moment, but I found the source, a slash on his left arm just above the elbow. Alone and fighting back panic, I knew I needed something to stem the flow. It took me a few moments until I looked on the counter and saw a couple of dishtowels and a wooden spoon. No more fear; I knew what I had to do.

I reached for the dishtowel and tore it in half. As quickly as I could, I tied half the cloth tightly around his muscular upper arm in a tight square knot. But the bleeding continued. I quickly realized that a simple cloth tie placed around an arm of that size wouldn't work. I needed a winch.

I took the second piece of the towel and tied it below the first. I then laid the handle of the spoon across the first knot and twisted it until the blood stopped flowing from his arm. I secured it with a second knot. Once the bleeding had ceased, I finished the second half of the winch with a second square knot to hold the spoon handle in place.

Once that was attended to, I checked his arm. This time there was no bleeding. However, the pulse in his other arm was barely beating. I looked at him lying semiconscious on the floor. His mane of blond curly hair was now soaked red by his blood. The skin on his face was a waxy, cadaveric color made more horrific by a combination of fear and pain that contorted his features. In spite of the blood loss, he was still jerking his body, as if to escape. I needed to get him out of there.

"Try not to fight me," I said. "I need to get your blood to flow toward your heart. I'm going to pick your feet up." I lifted the man's legs and rested them on a chair, trying to force as much blood upward as possible.

I checked his chest. He was still breathing but that was about all. That's when I pulled out my cell and punched 911.

"I need EMS now!" I commanded to the voice that answered. "I've got a Caucasian male with a lacerated brachial artery." I gave the lady on the other end the address.

As she spoke, I heard something like a chair knocked over from outside the house. It couldn't be the EMS. I assumed it was trouble. "Send the police, too!" I clicked off and then took his feet off the chair. I had to get him out of the house.

Bending down, I grabbed the victim's shirt and pulled him toward the back door. I was just about to reach up to the door handle when I decided it might be too risky. Instead I got down on all fours and crept toward the door. When I reached the knob, I turned it and at the same time opened the door slightly. As soon as it opened, three loud explosions from outside echoed above my head. Bullets struck the cabinet next to the sink and a dozen plates came crashing onto the floor. I was in a trap. The feeling of panic returned. I was unarmed and there was a killer outside.

I needed something to hide behind. My gaze passed back to the kitchen and stopped at a can of charcoal lighter fluid on the counter. I pulled down the other dishtowel from the counter and ripped them into three pieces. I soaked two of them with water and put them on the floor next to me. Then I opened the charcoal lighter fluid and poured it on the other piece in the sink.

The man on the floor was semi-conscious, but I spoke to him anyway. "We're going out the front door. We have to stay low to the floor. That's where the oxygen is. I'm going to put this towel over your face and then drag you out."

Without waiting I took a newspaper off the counter, rolled it tightly and then turned on the gas stove. I lit the end of the paper and then ignited the charcoal-fluid-drenched towel in the sink. It immediately started spewing out a cloud of dark smoke that started to fill the kitchen.

I put one water-soaked towel over my face like a bandana and then went back to the young man lying on the floor, and placed the other towel over his mouth. Slipping my hands under his arms, I pulled him toward the front door. The wet towels protected our faces, but I figured the smell and the smoke would divert whoever was in the back.

Smoke was beginning to fill the living room, but I could faintly see the streetlight. Painfully, I inched toward the flow of air from the open front door. I could hear the distant wailing of a fire truck as I dragged the victim out the front door. I crawled along the porch until I reached the Adirondack chair. We were both shielded behind the chair and the porch rail. I could only hope that the assailant was chased away by the smoke. But what if he wasn't? I couldn't stay there if the house went up in flames.

Waiting for the police was not an option. I had to know if the killer was out in front of us. I picked up a watering can lying on the porch next to me and threw it over the railing about fifteen feet. As I did, I heard two shots ring out above our heads, and then heard nothing except the sound of sirens as the fire trucks and police got closer. I felt the fear of a trapped animal on the porch, unsure if help would arrive in time. It only took a couple of minutes, but it felt like an hour until the police and fire engines arrived. Guns drawn, several officers circled the house.

"I'm a doctor," I yelled. "This man needs help." I held up my badge as they neared me. "We have a shooter in the area. The house is on fire. I've got a severely injured man on the porch. He needs help immediately."

The police took no chances. They circled the house and when it was clear, they rushed onto the porch. The first officer checked my badge, and I gave one of the others Sennett's phone number. While they called, the fire department brought out their hoses and entered the house under the cover of the police. At the same time two EMTs rushed onto the porch.

"He has a lacerated brachial artery and needs help immediately," I said.

"Are you a doc?" one of the policemen said.

"Yes, but this isn't a time for credentials," I said, my voice hoarse from the fumes.

The techs pulled out their IV equipment and quickly had a line started with lactated Ringers solution in the right arm. Then they examined his arm. "We have a pulse." One of the EMTs pulled out his two-way, calling into the Emergency Room. "We need to get this patient to University Hospital now!"

I could hear the entire conversation. They gave him clear instructions and said they would be ready. As they were about to put the man on a stretcher and leave for the hospital, the EMT's asked: "You put on this tourniquet, huh?" I nodded.

"Nice job."

I didn't respond. Instead, I turned around and looked inside the house. The firemen entered the living room, and within ten minutes they had the fire in the kitchen controlled. When I looked back at the victim, they already had him on the stretcher and were quickly moving to the ambulance. As I watched, I took out my cell and called Sennett. When he heard the sirens, I don't think he was happy that I went by myself.

"Boy, it's pretty dangerous to know Carina Knowlton," he said. "Cutting people up with a knife like that."

"What do you mean?"

"Carina Knowlton must have something that someone wants back."

"Maybe they thought she still had a copy of the spreadsheet," I rasped, choking out the words.

Sennett agreed. He continued telling me he had just got off the phone with Jordan. So far as the Feds were concerned, Wells had been in the process of putting together information, but it wasn't complete: Some information had been missing from her files. The thought that Sandra Wells's death was planned now seemed certain.

"Something is seriously wrong here. Who is going after a prostitute with a hitman?" Sennett paused for a moment. "We need to find Carina Knowlton, and we need to find her soon."

I spent half an hour with the police, and after speaking with Sennett, they said I could leave. I got back in my Jeep and sat behind the wheel for a moment. As the realization of what just happened began to sink in, my hands began to shake hard enough on the steering wheel that I had to wait a few minutes until I was breathing regularly.

Before I left Ann Arbor I needed to make one more stop. Pulling out on the highway, I headed for University Hospital. I spoke to Sennett while I drove.

They identified the victim as Sean Richardson. Sennett already checked him out. He was clean. Twenty-three years old from Elk Rapids, Michigan, a small town on Grand Traverse Bay. I had been there once or twice with my boat. It reminded me of Amity in the movie, "Jaws," charming and remote.

Richardson was in his first year of medical school. He had no police record, and the potentially one bad thing he had ever done was to be friends with Carina Knowlton.

When I arrived, Richardson was in the operating room. The EMS unit had gotten him there just in time. No one knew who I was and the only person I spoke with was a police sergeant, who was waiting in the emergency room. The cop's details were sketchy, and the medical personnel involved in his case were with him in surgery. I knew I was no longer needed, so I thanked the officer, then stopped at a vending machine. I picked up a couple of granola bars, washed them down with a Coke and walked back to my car in front of the Taubman Center.

I drove out of the hospital complex. It didn't take long for my eyes to start drooping and the muscles in my neck to sag. I was beat. It was an easy decision to stop for a moment at a park along the Huron River to clear my head. When I got there, I pulled into a parking space and watched the swiftly moving river. With the Wagoneer in neutral, I closed my eyes and started breathing slowly through my nose. Sennett told me about it: He called it yoga breathing, and I decided it couldn't hurt me. The next thing I knew it was fifteen minutes later and my cellphone was ringing. It was Jordan. Sennett had called her.

I told her what happened, including the injury to Sean Richardson and the encounter with the killer inside Richardson's house. "Were you in danger?"

"I stayed out of harm's way."

This seemed to satisfy her for the time being, but knowing Jordan, she was going to grind out the details from Sennett.

I told her that Carina Knowlton was on the loose. No one knew where she was. At the mention of Carina, she immediately started discussing the spreadsheet I had given her. "The Fed analysts reviewed it. They said it looked like a pattern used in a hospital, but, so far, it was only numbers. It doesn't look promising."

"Why should anything about this case be easy?"

CHAPTER 23

I SPENT ANOTHER SLEEPLESS NIGHT. My adrenaline was still high as I tossed and turned, thinking over the events in Ann Arbor. I finally got up about five in the morning, went down to the kitchen and turned on the lights. It wasn't long before Bucky was at my feet. Always loyal, he looked up at me with anticipation.

I read where dogs can tell when their master is upset. In Bucky's case I think he intuitively knew something was wrong, because as soon as I came in he rubbed his head on the side of my leg waiting to be patted. I scratched him behind his ears and after a few minutes my head felt clearer. I think he knew it too, because he got up and lay on his spot near the door.

After I made a pot of coffee I sat down I sat down at the kitchen table and stared out the window into the darkness. I felt afraid, and, while it didn't help that I had saved a young man's life under a barrage of bullets, my fear was not about me. It was about my family. What was worse was that I knew my family, meaning Jordan, was afraid, too.

As I sipped the hot liquid, I happen to glance at myself in the floor length mirror in the hallway. I had a mopey, defeated look that pissed me off. I'm not a handwringer. I had to find a clue, something to solve this problem. Right now, only two things were tangible. One was the spreadsheet that no one could decipher, and the other was a mixed-up prostitute, who was somewhere in the city. I was determined to find her. The problem was, where was she?

It was too early to call Sennett but not too early to get moving. I went upstairs, showered, and got dressed. I must have made some noise, because Jordan awoke and asked me why I was leaving so early. I told her I had some things to do at the office. I kissed her cheek and told her I loved her. I didn't wait to hear her say "Be careful." On the way out I peeked in Joey's room. He was sound asleep.

Before I left, I took Bucky out in a cold ground fog that obscured the street-lights. I was disoriented for a moment until I saw our night policeman in his unmarked car across the street, so I went over and chatted with him for a few minutes. When I finished, I went to get my Jeep and pulled out of the garage. I felt my confidence restored as I realized that I was not going to play the victim.

It was seven thirty when I rolled into the office. I went through some mail on my desk and then looked up Sandra Wells' chart again, checking once more to see if I missed anything. I didn't. At eight o'clock Karen rushed into my office. She pushed her hair back from her reddened face and suddenly began talking.

"I just got a call from a woman named Queenie. She sounded panicked, almost hysterical. It was a bad connection." When I asked *her* what she want-ed, Karen replied that her friend, Carina, called her. "Apparently, Carina said you know her. I think she said something about being in a trap. She said one other thing." Karen pulled out a piece of paper from her pocket and opened it. Then she showed it to me. "Carina said if anything happened to her to call Herbert Knowlton."

"Get Lieutenant Sennett on the phone for me, right away. Then tell anyone who calls that I've got an emergency." When I said that, the sting of fear flashed over Karen's face; she had seen me call Sennett like this before. I felt bad using the most overused excuse in the medical business, but it wasn't a lie, I thought. Just not the right kind of emergency.

While she called, I went back to my office. As I put on my coat, Karen came back and told me Sennett was waiting on the phone. I picked up the phone and quickly explained Carina's call. When I finished, he asked to call Queenie back and get Carina's cell number.

Sennett said he was ten minutes from my office and would pick me up. As soon as Karen called Queenie and got the number, I rushed out of my office and down the stairs. I went to my car first, unlocked the door, and looked in the glove compartment for some kind of protection. The only thing I could find was a screwdriver. I put the pathetic weapon back in the glove compartment, wondering what the hell I was doing.

Sennett's unmarked car pulled up to the front of my office with his light flashing. I jumped into the passenger seat, and he sped out of the parking lot. One of my patients saw me as I got into Sennett's car, and I guessed she was wondering what the hell kind of emergency I was going to.

I gave Sennett Carina's number, and he called Knudsen to trace it. As soon as Sennett got the information, he swung onto the highway. Two minutes later Sennett's phone rang. He answered, then looked at me and said, "They located Carina's phone at the Sly Trap."

Chapter 24

Low clouds had moved in and a light rain began falling on the relatively warm ground, creating an oppressive dreariness. By the time Sennett drove down Harper, the ground fog hampered our visibility. Nearing the Sly Trap, he pulled up to a Burger King across the street. Two squad cars were waiting. After doing a drive-by, they decided to put one car in the alley and the other on the drive coming out of the parking lot. Sennett, in the meantime, was talking to Knudsen, trying to find out everything he could get on Herbert Knowlton.

This time we didn't go inside. Sennett had spoken with Sly Monroe and asked him if Jones was there with anyone. He said no. Sly was smart enough to keep his mouth shut.

We waited until the other two units were in position at either end of the bar. The parking lot was small with one ineffective light to illuminate it. At eight o'clock Sennett nudged me on the shoulder and pointed to the rear entrance of the bar. I saw a crack of light on the parking lot as the door opened and then closed.

"Do we go in now?" I asked.

"No. We have to catch Jones leaving with her."

We waited another fifteen minutes. Suddenly a thin bar of light shone out again from the rear door of the bar. This time it remained opened. A large man emerged, dragging a motionless person on the pavement toward a black Escalade. From a distance the man resembled a Sumo wrestler with a glistening shaved head, a triple ripple neck, and arms that looked like they could crush a refrigerator.

When the big guy reached the back of the vehicle, he opened the rear hatch, effortlessly lifted the body over the edge like it was a small bag of trash and then pushed the legs inside. After closing the tailgate, he looked around, satisfied he was alone, and walked back to the rear entrance of the bar.

Sennett called the two backups and told them to hold their position at the front of the bar. "This is it, Ben," he said calmly. "Don't stay in the car. Move to the back for cover."

Sennett put the car in gear and pulled up to the side of the Escalade, just as the sumo wrestler was about to open the passenger side door. Sennett pulled his gun out, opened the door, and stepped outside. I hurried out of the car on the other side.

"Stop and put your hands in the air!" Sennett commanded, keeping the door to his car between him and the man.

The man saw Sennett. He immediately put his hands up. At the same time, he shifted his weight from side to side, moving toward the left front fender of the squad car.

"You gotta name?" the man responded. His voice was deep and unafraid.

"Yeah, it's Lieutenant Sennett, Detroit Police."

By this time the man was closer to Sennett. When he was about four feet away, he turned suddenly. With an unexpected agility for a man his size, he jumped in the air and slammed his foot against the door.

The blow knocked Sennett down and his drawn gun clattered on the asphalt. The man then sized me up. He must not have seen much, because he walked nonchalantly toward me with his arms swinging loosely at his side. I had nowhere to turn, especially with Sennett on the ground. The brute was ten feet from me. My stomach turned rock hard, and I gulped for air to stay quiet. I had no choice.

As he took a step forward, I sprung from a crouch, lowered my shoulder, and chop blocked the side of his knee. A cracking sound came from his leg, followed by his scream as he fell to the pavement like a felled tree. In football it would have been a fifteen-yard penalty and automatic ejection from the game. In the real world, it saved my life.

By this time Sennett was back on his feet and brushing himself off. He called one of the backup units. The other stayed in the front of the bar. Sennett retrieved his gun and cuffed the assailant.

"Check the rear of the car," he said. "I think the girl is in there."

I went to the back of the Escalade and jerked open the hatch. Inside I saw Carina Knowlton barely breathing on the rubber mat. I glanced at her swollen face and neck. Her eyes were barely visible.

For the second time in two days I needed EMS. As Sennett tapped out 911, I pulled Carina down from the rear of the SUV and onto the asphalt with the aid of the two officers. She was unconscious but still had a pulse. From the light inside the car, I could see her neck had a dusky color, and her breathing was in short gasps. My thought was strangulation, and the only treatment I could give her was mouth-to-mouth breathing.

I put my mouth on hers and started forcing air into her lungs. Slowly her color started to return, but she still hadn't regained consciousness. In the distance I could hear the wail of the EMS unit.

Out of the corner of my eye I saw another ray of light coming from the rear door of the Sly Trap. A man stepped out from the door. From his beard and ragged hair, I could see it was Aurelious Jones.

"Lamont, what the fuck you doing?" he shouted.

"What I'm doing is about to arrest you for trying to murder this girl. Now get up against the wall," Sennett commanded.

Snake looked back at him, his mouth twisted into a cruel smile. "You ain't got shit, Lootenant." Those were the last words he ever uttered. Two flashes erupted from the side of the building near the street, and he went down, blood pouring from his neck.

"Get down!" Sennett shouted. We all dropped to the ground. Sennett motioned to the other officers and they slowly fanned out from the car, guns drawn. One of them crept to the front of the building, then gestured to the others to follow, leaving Sennett and me at the car. Using the Escalade as protection, he inched his way to Snake. He was motionless. Judging by the large pool of blood on the ground, I knew he must be dead.

I was about to get up from Carina and see if he had a pulse. Suddenly, I heard Sennett yell. "You want to die?" he asked? This is an active crime scene."

I crouched low and waited. When the four officers were sure the shooter was gone, they motioned for us to come out. I quickly checked Jones. I was right; he was dead. Looking at him lying on the dirty asphalt of a mean pickup bar, I was stunned that a human life had come to this sad end.

That compassionate reaction lasted only for a short moment. I quickly went back to Carina Knowlton just as the EMS team arrived. One of the techs gave her oxygen through an ambu bag and the other started an IV. Within a couple of minutes she was breathing on her own. As I started examining her neck, for the third time in two weeks somebody asked me who the hell I was. "He's a doc, now lay off and let him work," Sennett said angrily.

Her breathing was shallow but not stridorous, and I noted no free air in her neck. The absence of free air meant that the injury to her neck had not perforated her windpipe. The EMS tech had a pulse oximeter on her finger that read 90% saturation. At that level they wanted to intubate her, but I told them with the possibility of a crushed airway from strangulation, putting a tube in her airway might cause more problems than it solved. "As long as she moves air on her own, I would give her intravenous steroids and continue to bag her with oxygen. If she needed something done to control her airway, it would be a tracheotomy." I felt her pulse; it was now full. Then I looked at her head, and noticed she was starting to move.

"Who shot Jones?" I asked.

Sennett's stared coldly at the dead body of Snake. "Don't know," he said.

It didn't take long before six more police cars buzzed around the Sly Trap. Sennett got in one of them and barked out directions on the radio. From the look on his face I think he knew it was too late to catch whoever shot Jones. Regardless, they cordoned off the scene and looked for evidence. Four of the cars edged into the surrounding neighborhood, and fifteen minutes later I heard the whirring sound of a police chopper scouring the area.

I waited for Sennett to come back to the car. When he did, he slouched down behind the wheel.

"That was close," I said sheepishly.

Sennett shrugged it off. "They say never go to a gun fight with a knife, but I have to admit that was a pretty good chop block. In reality, even if you had a gun, it wouldn't necessarily save you. You know how long it took me to use mine?"

I shook my head.

"It wasn't until I had the same near death experience after two years on the beat. My partner saved my life because I couldn't pull the Goddamn thing out of my holster. I vowed I would never let that happen again. Being a cop is 40% luck and the rest is good fortune."

We watched the EMS unit bundle Jones up and take him to the morgue, while the cops cuffed Lamont and put him in a squad car. Life and death and more business for Alan Davis. I looked over at Sennett. In spite of his escape from a close call, he looked irritated.

"You should be happy, lieutenant. We just got our asses saved."

"I am happy. Happy that I'm breathing, happy that you're breathing, and happy that Aurelius Jones isn't. My problem lies in the fact that this whole investigation is in jeopardy. I thought we had something going with Carina Knowlton, but now our only clue to this mess is on the way to the hospital. Who knows if she will live."

I eyed him steadily. As he was talking, his gaze was focused on the pavement. "Are you okay, George?" I asked.

"Yeah, just depressed. I get that way every time I see another one of my people dead on the street."

"Kind of the way I feel when I lose a patient," I said sympathetically.

"Maybe, but this is something different. Aurelious Jones was a bum, and maybe he deserved to die like he did. But there's more to it. When you lose a patient, they go into the obituary column and that's that. When Aurelious Jones dies, it's on the front page of the paper and all the TV newscasts. It sells TV time and newspapers and perpetuates stereotypes. But nobody sees the good things, only the bad."

Realizing I had been callous to the emptiness of Jones's death, I told George I was sorry. Sennett shrugged. Then he recounted his conversation with Sly—see no evil, speak no evil. It was the same with the rest of those other jokers in the bar. No help from anybody. Just another day at the Sly Trap protecting the public.

"If it was that easy, anyone could do it."

"Yeah, but the public doesn't know what we do. All they can do is criticize," Sennett muttered."

"As long as I am your public, you're safe."

When Sennett lifted his head, he opened the door to his squad car, got behind the wheel, and started the engine. His business face was back, stern, focused, and determined.

"Where we are we going?"

"University Hospital," he said, "to speak with Sean Richardson." I went to the opposite side and got in.

As we drove off, I thought about Aurelius Jones. He was a despicable man, but it was hard as a doctor to justify anyone dying such a violent death. As far as Lamont was concerned, where he was going he probably wished he was with Snake. Then I looked over at Sennett. His jaw was set and his hands were firmly gripped on the wheel as we spun out onto the main highway. Jones may have been just another dead man, but the Motor City's obituary was not being written anytime soon.

CHAPTER 25

O N THE WAY TO UNIVERSITY HOSPITAL, Sennett gave me some more information on Richardson's background. He was an All American kid—great athlete and student. Good enough to be a Rhodes Scholar, who studied medical economics in Bangladesh. Now he was a fourth year medical student, planning to go into sports medicine. He asked me what I thought Richardson's chance for recovery was.

"We'll know when we see his arm."

When we arrived, Sennett showed his badge to the valet and parked in the "No Parking" area. From the look on his face I think the attendant was pissed, but what could he do? It was a long walk to the elevators and then to Richardson's floor. A weary RN at the nurse's desk directed us to a room on the north side of the hospital.

It was a modern, small private room with a large window that made it look commodious. Richardson was in a chair looking out the window with his back to the door and his injured arm elevated. From a distance I saw no duskiness in his extremity, just large muscles with sinuous veins crisscrossing his forearm. The closer we got, the better the arm looked.

Richardson heard us enter and turned around. It was clear from the alarmed look on his face that he didn't know who we were. Sennett introduced himself and then pointed to me. "This is the doctor who saved your life."

Richardson's eyes were soft and filled with an inner glow. "I don't know how to thank you."

"I'm betting you would do the same thing for me when you're a doc."

"The doctors said I would make a full recovery."

I first looked at his left hand. His little finger was untouched. Then I looked

at the rippling muscles in his biceps. "With arms like that I bet you'll be an or-
thopod. They're all big guys with muscles."

Sennett changed the subject and asked him how long he knew Carina
Knowlton. He said they'd been friends for a long time and that she had lived
across the hall from him freshman year in the dorm. As he spoke, his mind
seemed to wander to a different place for a moment. "Thank God she left my
house just before I was stabbed."

I could tell that rehashing the events was hard for Richardson. He looked
wistfully out the window at the Huron River, as it swept toward Lake Erie. After
a long pause he replied in a soft voice choked with emotion and told us what
happened. "Shortly after she left, a man with a heavy accent broke in through
the back door of the house and threatened me with a knife. He wanted to know
where Carina was, and when I said I didn't know, he cut me with the knife. I
didn't remember much after that."

Then, almost as if he was afraid to ask, he wondered if anything happened
to Carina. I told him that someone attacked her and she was rescued. When I
said I thought she would be okay, he seemed relieved. True or not, I didn't think
this wasn't the time to go into details.

Sennett questioned whether he and Carina were more than friends. As soon
as he asked, a shade of anxiety came over Richardson's face. He said he always
had a thing for Carina. Best looking girl on campus, funny, energetic, smart—
the whole package. She loved school, especially art and music. He thought their
relationship might go somewhere. Then something happened.

Richardson thought it was due to a family problem at the beginning of her
sophomore year. She never told him the details. Two weeks after school started
she dropped out. He said it was something she didn't want to talk about, as if
she was ashamed.

After that, he saw her every month or so. When she came up to campus,
they hung out, went to Hill Auditorium to see a concert, or took in a game at
Crisler Arena. Richardson's face flushed. That's as far as it would go. They became just friends.

"The day of the attack she had come up to see me. I had never seen her
that scared before, like she was running away from something very evil. She
was trembling all over and could hardly breathe. She said she was afraid she
was being followed by someone and didn't know whom to turn to. I said I
would take her to the police for protection, but the moment I said that, she
panicked and ran out of the house. The man who attacked me came in about
ten minutes later."

Sennett inquired if he knew what Carina did in Detroit, where she went,
that kind of thing. All Richardson could recall was that she worked for a public
relations company. Clever spin, I thought, for being a prostitute.

Sennett asked him about her friends, fishing for anything. I could see Richardson was getting tired from the emotional and physical distress he had endured. He struggled to remember what she said, finally recalling a cop, named Cowboy or something like that, who worked undercover on corruption in the city, something about a business scheme. When the name Sandra Wells came up, he shook his head.

The IV must have been bothering Richardson, because he started fidgeting with the tubing. I rang the nurse for him. While we waited, Sennett queried him about Carina's home life.

The mention of her family suddenly animated his face. "I don't know much about her home life. She said her mother died and her father lived alone. When I asked her more, she said she was going to take me to her house. It was almost as if she wanted me to make my own decision about her family."

"What happened?" Sennett asked.

"We went to her house once. It was big with a pool in the backyard, a couple of fancy cars in the garage and expensive-looking paintings everywhere. Her father was there, Herbert Knowlton. As far as I'm concerned, he was a complete jerk, bragging about everything—his cars, his homes, and his business, some weird investment called the Full Coverage Fund."

"What about Carina?"

"He only mentioned Carina when he said how good-looking his daughter was, like she was an object. It was almost a sexual comment. If I didn't know better, I would have said he was either drinking or high on something. I couldn't wait to get out of there. You know, nice house, nobody home."

Sennett nodded. "What did Carina say?"

"She didn't say anything. She didn't have to. Her father said it all."

Richardson started to fidget with his IV again. "This thing is starting to bother me."

As he said it, the nurse came in. She turned out to be a freckled-faced woman with short hair, who looked like she was fifteen. That was the only thing about her that spoke of inexperience. She immediately turned off the IV and unwrapped the saline-soaked bandage. Richardson remained silent as she removed the Kerlix dressing. Underneath the cotton wrap was a pad of Telfa, covering the incision. I stared at the wound for a moment. It had an unusual zig-zag appearance.

"Looks like a pretty nice job, Sean. They did a z-plasty repair."

"Yeah, the surgeon came in this morning and explained it to me. I guess it was a deep, ragged slash. The artery was cut but not severed. Fortunately, he sewed it back together." As he spoke, I could see the pain in his face as he remembered what had happened. "He told me he had never seen a wound like that before."

"Did the surgeon think that was an unusual place to stab someone?"

Richardson nodded. Apparently, that was exactly what the surgeon said, adding that maybe the attacker wanted his victim to die a slow death. To him it didn't matter, he was thankful he was alive. Then he smiled at me. "The doc that put the tourniquet on ruined that plan."

The nurse came back, re-started the IV, and re-dressed the wound. Then she turned to Sennett and me. She might have looked young, but I heard no meekness in her voice. "You guys have had enough time with my patient. He needs some rest," she said with the voice of authority.

We were about to leave, when Richardson held up his hand. "I remember one other thing. I don't know what it means, but she told me that someone named Tommy Holiday was a problem. I asked her what it meant. She said Cowboy told her about him. He said it was important and not to forget it. That's all she knew."

I saw Sennett write the statement down in the small notepad he kept in his pocket. Then he looked up at Richardson.

"We better do what the nurse said, Ben."

With that we said goodbye and made our way into the corridor. As we walked out, I glanced at Richardson. He was the unsuspecting victim of someone else's problem. All he wanted was a relationship. All he got was a near miss with death.

Sennett was silent as we entered the elevator and walked to the front of the hospital. His car was parked where he left it in a No Parking zone. As expected, a ticket was stuck under his windshield wiper. I saw him take the ticket and rip it up. Sennett missed the smile on the attendant's face. He was probably too busy thinking about Richardson.

When we were inside the car, I asked him how often he had seen people killed with a knife. He said it happened once in a while, but the statistics showed that murder by guns was roughly five times more common than knives. In his mind, all murders were terrible, but with the open wound, the body disfigurement, and the amount of blood loss, there was no question which one was more gruesome.

"Speaking of gruesome, why do you think the attacker didn't cut off his finger?"

"My guess is you broke into the house before he had a chance."

I stared out of the window, realizing just how close Richardson was to dying a horrible death. Then I felt my shoulders tighten as I realized it could have been me. "I guess you'd have to be one sick son of a bitch to kill someone with a knife," I said.

Sennett started the car, looked out the window, and nodded his head solemnly. "You're right, boss."

CHAPTER 26

I LOVE THE KITCHEN IN OUR HOUSE. It's bright and airy with large windows overlooking a patio, shaded by a couple of century oak trees. The eating area was adjacent to a family room with a large screen TV and my favorite couch. On Sundays, Joey and I camped out watching football. He peppered me with endless questions about the game, while Jordan sat in her chair reading the *New York Times*. But don't think Jordan was left out. She loved the game too. Her problem was she was a Miami Dolphins fan. When you root for the Lions, you have to put up with a lot.

Jordan was in the kitchen when I came home that night from Ann Arbor. We all had dinner, but I waited until I put Joey to bed before I told her what happened. When I came downstairs, the last glass was in the dishwasher. She seemed calm as I explained my visit to Ann Arbor. Then I got to the part about Carina Knowlton. After I finished I waited for a response, but I knew it wouldn't be quick.

Instead of discussing it, she wiped her hands with a towel and changed the subject to Sandra Wells. She said no one knew how Wells got two hundred thousand dollars. However, they did find the name of the beneficiary.

"The policy beneficiary was a man named Edward Ford. That's where it stops. Mr. Ford and the policy seem untraceable. It's irritating, but I'm sure within the next month or two someone is going to appear to collect it."

I went over to the counter to help her finish with the dishes. When I looked down, I noticed a small carving knife next to the sink and held it up, staring at the sharp tip. When she asked me if I was planning on using it, I told her about Sennett's comment about the pathologic killer that was on the loose.

As I put the knife down, I could see that Jordan seemed distracted. "You know, Ben, some people are destined to find trouble," she said. "I don't think that's you. I think trouble finds you. That's a whole lot different."

I nodded, helpless to describe anything that I could have done to avoid my brush with a killer. Neither could I deny that my life wouldn't change. She said that I had a reputation for solving crimes. People sought me out for help, not dissimilar to seeing me as a doctor.

She put the knife in the rack and closed the dishwasher. "With that comes the fact that sometimes you are not going to be able to control every situation. If that's the way it's going to be, then I think you have to accept the fact that you need to be able to protect yourself. Be smart. Learn what you need to and maybe even go through some training."

"What kind of training?"

"I hope I'm not going regret asking you this."

"What's that?"

"Are you carrying?"

"No," I replied self-consciously. I was taken aback by my lame answer. I always thought I was mentally and physically tough. Sure, I had plenty of fights growing up. They were usually settled by fists in back of the gymnasium or by contact on the football field. But shooting another human being is not some kind of teenage right of passage. It's controlling life and death at the squeeze of a trigger. Besides, I'm a doctor. I took an oath to save lives, not take them.

"I thought Frank checked you out on the range," she said.

Frank Arsinegas was my instructor at the police academy. "He did. That was a couple of years ago."

"You mentioned something he called 'The Arcinegas Rules' when he was teaching you how to use a weapon. Do you remember it?"

I nodded. "He made me memorize it. Never carry a gun unless you are prepared to use it. The trick is to understand when to pull the trigger. You need to engrave this paradigm in your brain: The best advice is avoidance. Be prepared, avoid dangerous situations; and, if you can't, try to de-escalate—calm the attacker with tone and body language. If you can't and you feel you or people around you are in immediate danger, use your weapon. And that, my friend, requires practice."

"Sounds like you were a good listener."

"He meant what he said. I had to recite that every time we met. We spent hours at the range, assembling, disassembling, and firing a Sig Sauer 9 mm."

"As I recall, you bought a gun. What happened to it?"

"When I was done, I got a concealed weapons permit and then bought a Sig Sauer 328. As soon as I bought it, I brought it home and put it away in a locked box on the top shelf of in the basement storage closet, hoping I would never have to use it. Do you think I should take it out?"

I knew Jordan was having a hard time with this conversation. Although she agreed with the second amendment as the law of the land, she never agreed with the proliferation of handguns and the lack of careful vetting of handgun owners. But here she was, encouraging me to carry a weapon.

"I'm not sure. It's a worry, and to carry or not goes both ways." She didn't say anything else.

We watched TV for a while and then Jordan went to bed. I was still running on the adrenaline of what happened that day. As I sat on the couch, I thought about what she said. In many ways it was disturbing, not only the stress on her, but the danger I had put my family in. I realized I had a tremendous feeling of guilt, because I knew what she said was true and, in some odd way, I embraced it.

CHAPTER 27

I WOKE UP THE NEXT MORNING, went downstairs to the basement closet, and pulled down my gun. When I left the house, I took it with me, carefully putting the box on the backseat and the gun in the glove box. The whole process left me feeling very uneasy. From a rational standpoint, I knew why. Life and death situations were part of my profession as a doctor. I also saw people die from violence and the harm that evil can do. From an emotional standpoint, I was ambivalent. I took an oath to save lives and now, at the moment of truth, I would have to deal with the conflict. My mental gymnastics ended with the ring of my cellphone. Sennett wanted me to meet him in Birmingham and go to Herbert Knowlton's house.

I met him at a shopping mall at Telegraph and Maple Road where Sennett's car was sitting near the entrance. I got in, but didn't realize until we were near the house that I had left my gun in my car.

Herbert Knowlton lived on Yarmouth, a fancy address in the northern suburbs near Birmingham. We drove north on Cranbrook Road until we found his neighborhood, one of the wealthiest in Bloomfield Hills. Mostly car guys lived around here; and, if they weren't auto execs, they were bankers who serviced the auto industry. Sennett had called but there was no answer.

As we neared Knowlton's house, a white Ford Focus zipped through a stop sign and nearly hit us before turning on to Cranbrook Road. Sennett shrugged his shoulders, as if to say he was used to this in the city but didn't expect it in the burbs.

We turned right onto Yarmouth and passed several large houses until we came to a Cotswold Tudor. Close cropped and edged Kentucky blue grass surrounded the blue slate walk that led up to the porch. The brass carriage lights were on as we made our way up the path to the ornate wooden door. It seemed unusual for them to be on at this time of the day. Before we got out of the car Sennett pulled out his notepad and wrote something down.

Sennett climbed the steps and knocked on the door but got no answer. I followed him as he went around to the back of the house and looked in the garage. Knowlton's Lincoln MKZ was inside.

He then went to the back deck, which looked out over an oval pool covered with a black tarp. We stepped up on the deck, peered in the window of the kitchen, and saw no one. Sennett banged on the back door, but again, no response.

The morning sun was low in the sky and the angled rays barely filtered their way through the overhanging branches of several large evergreens. Something caught Sennett's eye as he looked downward at the pool, and he pointed out the spot he was looking at. It was a glistening red speck shining up from the deck. He followed a trail of specks toward the pool. When I saw the ominous path, I felt my stomach knot.

This wasn't a time to get a search warrant, so he pulled the elastic bands that held down the pool cover. As he did, the thick rubber tarp sprung back, exposing the half-filled pool below. He looked under the tarp and then jumped to his feet.

"Help me get this thing off the pool!" he yelled.

We pulled the tarp back and looked down at a thick, dark red stain that discolored the water. When we pulled the cover back further, a body in an Adidas tracksuit appeared floating face down. It looked like an adult male.

Sennett pointed to a pole at the end of the pool. "Get that hook and we'll pull him to the shallow end."

We dragged the body until it was at the low end of the pool, grabbed him by his tracksuit, hauled him up on the concrete, and turned him over. I was sickened looking at the limp body and the contorted, lifeless face of what I assumed was Herbert Knowlton, or what was left of him. My gaze moved from his bloated face to a deep gash in the front of his neck. I could feel my skin tighten when I saw a wound from a bullet hole in the side of his left temple. Whoever killed him was taking no chances.

When I looked up, I saw Sennett on his cellphone, talking to the police. He pulled something out of his pocket and gave them a number. After a couple of minutes he clicked off the phone.

"Don't tell me you were giving them the license number of that car that pulled out in front of us?"

"Sure, it's what I was trained to do."

By that time I could hear the wail of sirens coming up Cranbrook Road.

WE STUCK AROUND THE YARD FOR ANOTHER HOUR as the police questioned us and then entered the house. In the front hall stood an antique brass umbrella holder resting on an ornate Persian rug. The rug led to the end of the hall where a mirror in a wrought iron frame reflected into the open door of a study.

It was what one would expect in this neighborhood. What wasn't expected was the blood. It was smeared and spattered everywhere. I assumed the murder took place in the study, next to the bedroom. From the appearance of the tracks, the killer dragged Knowlton across the white wool Berber carpet to the outside through a sliding door in the kitchen. There must have been a struggle, because blood was blotted over much of the floral wallpaper in the hallway.

Sennett watched as the police meticulously examined papers and letters on Knowlton's desk, looking for any lead. They opened the drawers but found nothing. Whoever killed Knowlton removed every clue. Even his computer was missing its hard drive.

I looked around the room and saw some old photographs of Knowlton on a shelf and a desk. None with Carina. I assumed he was with his rich buddies on golf and fishing outings. The pictures chronicled a Who's Who of almost every politician, sports figure, or famous businessman in the city. Knowlton was certainly well connected.

One of the photographs was knocked over on his desk, probably from the struggle. The glass was broken. I picked up the photo and noticed something odd as I stared at Knowlton and a young man in a Tigers baseball cap standing in front of a cement brick building. In the background were some trees and a length of weed-covered railroad tracks. Knowlton was wearing a blue blazer, gray pants, and a wide-brimmed hat. He was shaking hands with the young man and smiling.

I studied the photo of Knowlton for a while. He was a corpulent man with thick, full lips, a red face, and a crooked smile that made him look angry even when he was having fun. I visualized him on the 19th hole with his cronies at some fancy club downing his third martini and regaling all who would listen about the last woman he had conquered. I realized what Sean Richardson meant.

Something in that picture was familiar. I looked at it again and then I realized what caught my notice. In the background on the building was a number. I remembered that number from somewhere. Then it came to me: It was the number written on the floor of the burnt out house where Sandra Wells was found. I was about to say something when one of the forensic guys came over, and I lost the thought.

"Hey, Lieutenant," he said. "You've got to see this." He was a big man with a large abdomen pushing against the buttons of a long, light-blue lab coat. On his hands were plastic gloves, and a protective mask hung at his neck. He had a reddish beard and gloomy eyes that said he had seen almost everything.

Sennett turned toward him as he walked across the patio. "What have you got?"

"I think you better look for yourself."

We walked over to Knowlton's body, which was stretched out on a plastic body bag. The officer bent over, lifted Knowlton's left arm, and held out his hand. The baby finger was missing.

"What do you make of this?" he asked.

Sennett shook his head. "There's a killer on the loose. We have to find him before he does this again."

"What's our next move?"

"Old style hard work, follow the leads."

The officer nodded knowingly. It was the kind of thing only a policeman accrues, seeing life at its basest level. I understood how a constant barrage of crime affects the mentality of those who commit their lives to protect society. In some ways it's not unlike being a doctor only protecting people from harming each other requires a special devotion.

As I walked out of the house, my shoulders felt heavy and my stride was short. It didn't take me long to realize that my response was from an intense feeling of sadness over the death of Herbert Knowlton. Not for the victim; it was for his daughter. How did a young woman, surrounded with this kind of opulence, get into the dangerous life she was living? I hoped she lived, so we could find out and help her.

CHAPTER 28

SENNETT WALKED BACK TO HIS CAR, opened the door, and slouched in the seat. Both of our pants were still damp from hauling Knowlton from the pool. After staring aimlessly out the window for a few moments he started the engine and backed down the driveway. This time, as we passed the expansive homes of Bloomfield Hills, the neighborhood didn't seem so fancy. We were both silent on the way to my car. Dragging a corpse out of a pool will do that to you.

I was about to get out when Sennett's phone rang. He answered and then stopped and listened. As I opened the door, he held his hand up. I waited until he was finished. "The net of this investigation has just expanded into Canada." I must have looked at him as if Martians had landed in Royal Oak, because he started laughing. "Sandra Wells's cousin contacted the local police authorities in Windsor, across the Detroit River."

He explained it wasn't by accident he had received the call. When he found out that Sandra Wells had a cousin, named Charmayne Phillips, he called a friend of his in the Police Department and made him aware of the connection. Apparently, Phillips contacted Sennett's friend.

It turned out the cousin didn't have a serious problem. Somebody had stolen her computer. But Sennett's friend, Brian MacGregor, didn't take a chance. Neither did George; he wanted me to go with him.

We stopped at his office to drop off my car and then left for Windsor. On the way I asked Sennett if he had found anything on the Full Coverage Fund. He said that they went to the address of the place of business, but no one was there. "It turned out to be a building that rents out small spaces on short term leases. No one ever saw anyone come in the office." Sennett added that payment was a cashier's check received from a closed post office address with no forwarding information.

Once on Jefferson Avenue, Sennett turned on the exit next to the GM building and into the entrance of the Detroit-Windsor Tunnel, a well traveled crossing between the United States and Canada, second only to the nearby Ambassador Bridge.

Personally, I always liked the bridge better than the tunnel. I felt uneasy about the grimy narrow tunnel with old sweaty tile walls and the acrid smell of engine exhaust. I had an unreasonable feeling of claustrophobia, a sense that at any moment those old walls would break.

It took about fifteen minutes to make the crossing. As we exited, the custom agents gave us a thorough grilling: Carrying a concealed weapon into Canada was frowned upon. It was fortunate that Sennett called MacGregor ahead of time. The Police Headquarters in Windsor was on Goyeau Street, just after the tunnel exit. After our inspection we turned left and soon reached the nondescript multi-story gray building on the left side of the street.

It was a strange structure, a glass block facade on the first floor and imposing colonnades facing the street. On the upper stories were small windows. If the entire effect was to create a small prison, the architect achieved his purpose. If it wasn't, the city needed an inquiry on how the project passed architectural review.

Sennett parked the car, and we walked in the main entrance, where a guard stopped us. The explanation for Sennett's gun lasted long enough for another phone call to MacGregor. Once past the inspection point, we followed directions to his office on the fourth floor.

MacGregor's office had an outer waiting room. After announcing ourselves to the officer at the desk, we sat down in a couple of uncomfortable plastic chairs. I picked out a brochure on a rack next to the chair and started reading. It was a copy of an article written in The Windsor Star, discussing the increased safety of living in Windsor as compared to Detroit. It was clear from the report that the citizenry valued their well-being.

After a few minutes the desk officer brought us into MacGregor's office. A large, blond oak desk sat in front of the window that looked onto the unimpressive storefront street. While the office may not have looked friendly, the man at the end of the table did. He was beefy but not fat with a trimmed reddish mustache and an open, friendly face that spoke of the outdoors rather than the sallow fluorescent lights of the police station.

He got up immediately and shook hands. Sennett introduced me.

MacGregor's face crinkled with a wide grin. "Traveling with your doc, huh? You're not sick, are you?"

Sennett laughed. "No, I just keep the doc around in case I might need an emergency tracheotomy."

MacGregor smiled, then his face turned business serious. "Charmayne Phillips is in the conference room."

He led us into a small meeting room on the third floor. In the middle of the drab gray-carpeted room was a Formica conference table with aluminum legs and six uncomfortable looking chairs. Sitting with her back straight in one of them was an agreeable-looking woman in her late twenties or early thirties. She had a pudgy, round face with pageboy cut sandy brown hair and short bangs hanging over a freckled forehead. She stood up when we walked in and extended her hand. Her smile was engaging and her handshake was firm.

MacGregor made the introduction, but it didn't take long for Charmayne to start talking. She was clearly upset with Wells' death and the way she died. She said she never guessed her cousin would be found in a burnt-out house in the inner city. In her words Wells was dedicated, industrious, and proud of contributing to the city government.

When Sennett asked her if she had some premonition that something was wrong, Charmayne said that at a dinner with her a couple of months ago she seemed uneasy. "When I asked Sandy why, she thought it had something to do with her job of overseeing the legalities of the construction of the new city hospital, saying that she felt like an undercover agent." Sennett asked her if her cousin ever spoke of any direct threats. Phillips replied that it was only a feeling.

Sennett then asked her about her cousin's social life. "Sandy's mindset was always in the future, getting married, having a family. She even put some money away in a life insurance policy. It was kind of weird, but Sandy said she wanted to make sure if anything ever happened to her that the money went to fund any children she might have."

When asked her if she was dating anyone, Phillips pushed the bangs away from her forehead and straightened herself in the seat, as if she was telling a confidence. "Sandy told me she thought she had met the man she wanted to be her child's father."

Sennett asked if she gave her a name. She shook her head, saying that her cousin seemed very evasive. One thing she new for sure: Whatever her cousin set her mind to, she would succeed. A moment of silence passed until MacGregor spoke. "Did your cousin warn you to be careful?"

Phillips nodded. "That's why I called about my computer. Sandy said to watch my back. Report anything you think is suspicious. I have to tell you, I was scared after talking to her. Now that she is dead, I am . . . terrified."

MacGregor took it personally. His face got red and he focused intently on the young woman. "Ms. Phillips, this is Canadian turf. We will protect our citizens. You can depend on my word."

Charmayne eased in the chair and bowed her head in relief. "Thank you."

"Now, what could someone possibly want with your computer?" MacGregor asked.

"Honestly, I don't know. Certainly I have nothing related to Sandy or any of our conversations. That's when I got scared."

MacGregor looked concerned. "We never take things like this lightly, especially when Lieutenant Sennett is involved. Maybe you misplaced it or they didn't find what they wanted. Miss Phillips, to the best of our ability, I promise they won't bother you anymore. Regardless, we'll watch your residence for the next couple of weeks."

MacGregor's voice sounded louder and his words were precise. The mere fact that a crime, possibly associated with the murder of Sandra Wells, happened in Windsor rankled him.

Charmayne got up and thanked him. I could sense from the way she responded that she felt relieved.

After she left, MacGregor led us back to his office and sat down behind his desk. He picked up a pad of paper from his desk and wrote something, then set the pad back on his desk. "I'll get back to you, George," he replied with a tinge of frustration in his voice. I bet that MacGregor railed against anything that could possibly tarnish the reputation of his low-crime city.

Sennett understood too, because he waited for a moment and then changed the discussion to the Red Wings, inviting MacGregor to a game. That lightened up the inspector, who was apparently a diehard Maple Leaf fan. He and Sennett talked about hockey, and then made an arrangement to go to a game. We were walking out the door when MacGregor stopped.

"George, if I find a crime, you can be damn well sure I'll find the bastard who did it."

"I'm sure you will," Sennett replied.

It was obvious that neither Sennett nor MacGregor liked unfinished business.

When we reached the car, Sennett decided to make a stop at the Tunnel Barbeque. We spent the next half hour devouring a plate of ribs and avoiding any discussion about Sandra Wells.

When all that was left on our plates were a bunch of bones, he put his napkin down and looked up. "Knudsen gave me this paper this morning." Sennett pulled out a piece of paper from his coat and showed me a composite sketch of a man. "I told him to check out that missing finger business on Knowlton to see if that was a signature of any known criminal. Believe it or not, he made a match, a hit man named Rene LeBeque. Apparently, that's his given name. On his rap sheet he is known as Pinky."

I looked at the rat-like features of the man. He had a deep widow's peak, a scar on his right cheek, and bushy eyebrows that made his eyes appear like small, lifeless cavities in his face. "And this is him?"

Sennett nodded. "This is a police drawing based on a photo from a correctional facility he was in when he was a teenager. No one has a recent photo."

Sennett looked at the papers as he talked. "LeBeque grew up in a small town in Quebec called Chicoutimi. It's a quiet place along the Saguenay River north of Quebec City. According to Knudsen, not much happens there, except watching the whales in the Saguenay River. LeBeque got in trouble early—shoplifting, purse snatching, and other petty crimes. His weapon of choice was a switchblade. Apparently, the local authorities weren't unhappy when he was sent to a youth correctional facility in the big city."

Sennett said that lasted for a couple of years. "When he got out, he sought bigger things. He joined a gang in Montreal called the Frères de Sang, or Blood Brothers. As part of the initiation, in addition to getting tattooed with "FDS," they had to show how macho they were. Apparently Lebeque took out his switchblade and cut off the tip of his pinky finger."

Sennett hesitated as he read from the paper. "Hence the name 'Petit Doigt' or Pinky. Over the next couple of years, the paper reported four gang-related murders. Each victim had his pinky finger cut off. The RCMP thought LeBeque was involved, but nothing was proven. Then he disappeared."

Sennett waited for a moment as if he was trying to remember something. "Oh, and by the way, two other things."

"I can't wait."

"Guess who his boss is?" When I gave him the blank stare and shrugged, he replied, "The Canadian Mafia."

"And the other thing?" I asked.

"The bullet that killed Knowlton matched the one that killed Cal Finney."

I stopped for a moment. "George, who is the only person who has a connection with the four dead people?"

Sennett thought for a moment. "Carina Knowlton."

CHAPTER 29

I LEFT THE HOUSE AT SEVEN THE FOLLOWING MORNING to see Carina Knowlton. When I reached City Hospital I chose once again to go in through the emergency entrance. This time the cranes seemed completely harmless and the cops a lot friendlier.

As I walked through the door, I remarked to myself how much hospitals are the same, even the smell. It's a peculiar disinfectant odor, and it permeates throughout the building. Thankfully, it doesn't go home with you.

Then there are the people that work there. It was always the same janitors mopping the floors, the same orderlies moving patients on gurneys, and the same faceless line of patients seeking care—or so it seemed to me. In the middle of it all were nurses and doctors, sipping Styrofoam cups of coffee and talking. Some laughing about an incident last night, some trying to pass information to the next shift, and the rest relieved that the stress of their job was over for twenty-four hours.

This time, as I turned to enter the main lobby, it all changed. Five or six blue-clad policemen were gathered near the main entrance to the hospital. As I tried to go past them, one large cop came up to me, as if he were guarding against invading Huns. He had his hand on his baton as he looked steadily at me—the hunter and the prey.

"What can I do for you?" he asked, more as a command rather than a question.

I don't usually fuss with people like this. There's no advantage. First, they have a gun and second, they represent the law.

"I came to see a patient."

"Do you have something in writing? If you don't, you'll have to come back another day."

This was getting irritating. That's when I reached into the inside pocket of my jacket. The moment I did, his hand changed position from the baton to his gun. I smiled at him and took out my badge. It was the last thing he was expecting. I could see his chest sag slightly as he reached for the badge. He examined it closely. "So you're Dailey, huh?" he said in a milder tone of voice.

"Yep, that's me." He asked for my driver's license. After he examined it closely, he gave it back to me. "Sorry," he said. "We had a robbery in the hospital earlier this morning."

"Robbery?" I said. "I've never heard of such a thing in a hospital."

"Yeah, it was in the medical records department. Somebody was hacking some files. They think it was one of those anti-Planned Parenthood groups."

"Wow," I said, "that's strange. Did they get anything?

"As far as we can see, nothing was touched. That's why we shut things down. Don't worry. That computer system is solid."

I repeated my request to visit a patient. He took my badge and license, then left to speak with his sergeant. After a couple of minutes he came back and handed my identification back to me. "You're all set," he said, smiling.

Nice guy, I thought as I walked to the elevator. I just wouldn't want to be on the other side of the law if I met him again. I went up to the fourth floor and looked for Carina Knowlton.

I found her room at the end of the hall farthest from the nurse's station. A couple of cops in suits stood in the corridor, guarding the entrance. They were near a mobile storage rack filled with gowns, gloves, masks, and paper shoe covers. Over the entrance to the door was a sign warning "Infection Precautions." When they saw I was trying to go into the room, they closed in on me from either side of the door. From the way they glared at me, I didn't think they were going to ask me who was going to win the Super Bowl.

Just about the time I was going to pull out my badge again, Sennett brushed by them. He was dressed in a protective gown, hat, gloves, and facemask, cradling a folder in his left arm. When he saw me, he told the cops, "Guys, relax. He's okay."

I pointed to the folder. "What are you doing, making rounds?"

"Very funny," he replied. "I got some pictures I wanted to show Carina, but I had to get dressed up first."

I looked back at the two policemen. "When did you decide to put guards on her room?"

"The moment I found out that the bullet that killed Snake was the same kind that killed Calboy."

Sennett went to the metal cabinet and handed me a mask, cap, gown, and then gloves. He said the doctors were worried about some type of infection and mentioned ARDS—acute respiratory distress syndrome, one of the worst hospital-borne infections.

"You know, George," I said, "I saw the way you handled the gown and gloves. It was very professional. How did you learn it?"

"Terrorism training. We all have to do it."

I put the paper gown on, covering my body from neck to knee. As I tied the strings on the facemask, I asked him what his next move would be. He said if Finney and Snake were killed with the same gun and Richardson was stabbed in the manner of a Mafia hit, we had to follow the evidence. "Knudsen told me they ran some profiles and they all fit this guy LeBeque."

I went back to the cart and looked for a pair of protective shoe covers. They invariably didn't have ones for people with big feet. After looking at the selection I finally found a larger size, and, while I sat down to put them on, I asked Sennett about the Canadian Mafia. He said it was tied to the mob in the States but not as active as the Seven Families. "Mostly into numbers, prostitution, some drugs. They even tried smuggling cigarettes into Canada." He said the RCMP caught them trying to launder the money.

I got up, and we both walked into Carina's room. When we entered, she was sitting upright in bed. With the IV still in her arm and an oxygen cannula in her nose, she appeared vacant and disoriented. As soon as she saw us, a flash of recognition crossed her eyes and she smiled.

"The nurses told me I was in bad shape when I reached the hospital. I understand you saved my life," she said with a rasping, breathy voice.

"I think the EMS guys did all the work."

"Regardless, I'm glad to be alive. How is Sean?"

I told her about finding him on the floor and applying the tourniquet. "He reached University Hospital in time to save his arm. As far as I know, he's going to be okay."

She pressed the palms of her hands to her eyes. "Thank you."

After a few moments she went on to describe what happened. She went to Ann Arbor to tell Sean she was running away. He begged her to stay, but she said she was dragging him into something he didn't need to be part of. When she went out the back way, she saw a man coming toward the house. She ducked behind a chair before he saw her.

Carina described the man as being medium built with a receding hairline and a scar running down his left cheek and into his lip. The next thing she knew there was some shouting, a loud scream, and the words "Adieux, mon ami." When she heard the commotion, she ran from the house and hid in the bushes. Distraught and without protection, she decided to go back to Snake and plead for mercy.

"Are you okay?"

She didn't reply, only looked at me with downturned mouth and a vacant stare.

"At least you won't have to worry about Snake any more," Sennett said.

"He's dead?" she asked. When I nodded, her lips parted and she pressed her hands to her eyes again for a few moments. She said he wanted his money. When she told him she didn't have it, he beat her up and then choked her. She pretended to pass out. He must have thought she was unconscious, because he didn't bother to search her coat, where her cellphone was. When he left the room, she called Queenie. After that, she didn't remember anything until she was in the EMS truck.

Sennett looked pensive, as if he was debating something in his mind. "I hate to tell you this after all you've been through, but we found your father dead at his house." He didn't tell her how he died. Then he added: "Carina, Did your father know Snake?"

She nodded.

"How do you know?"

"My father is a con man and Snake is a pimp. It's a match made in heaven." Her voice was barely a whisper, probably the result of the attempted strangulation. It made it difficult to understand her speech.

"In what way?" I asked.

For moment she remained silent, then slowly, she began to softly choke out the words. I knew from experience that sometimes it's easier to tell someone you don't know about your problems.

"He sold me, my own father. He used his daughter to make money."

"What do you mean?"

She described her father's alcoholism and the exorbitant life he led after he inherited the family auto parts business. Booze, wild spending, fancy cars, sleazy women, country clubs—apparently, he did it all until he was broke.

Sennett asked her about her mother. She said, beside Sean, her mom was her best friend and the only reliable person in her life. When she was in college, her mother left her husband and shortly thereafter died suddenly of a heart attack. Then it was just she and her father.

Carina added that her mother managed to keep him under some kind of restraint, but when she died, his life began to spiral out of control. With creditors constantly threatening him, he declared bankruptcy. Apparently, he even mortgaged the house and defaulted.

"Then one day a man came over to the house," she said haltingly. "He was in his late thirties. Nice looking, dark complexion. I was in the kitchen doing some homework. I saw him go into the study with my father. When he came out, he walked into the kitchen."

Her eyes began to widen with terror as she spoke. She said her father introduced him as Mr. Forrester, a business associate. He said he was over to discuss business with him, but his car had broken down and he asked me to drive him back to his house. It was only a mile away.

"I told him I would. We got into my car, and I drove him to his home in Royal Oak. We talked on the way over. He seemed nice enough. When we got to the townhouse, he said he had a package inside for my father and asked if I would come in to get it. I walked inside the house with him. As soon as he closed the front door, he attacked me."

Somehow she remained calm, describing everything, as if she had been waiting to share her pain with someone. "Fighting him off was hopeless. He overpowered me and then dragged me into the bedroom and tied me to the bed and raped me again and again. At a certain point I couldn't remember anything except the pain and the bleeding. It was my first time."

It was early in the morning when he dropped her off at her house. She staggered inside and collapsed on the carpet in the foyer. By the time she finished the story she seemed numb, as if she were describing someone else's life.

"What did your father do?"

"Do? You think he did anything? He said—and I'll never forget this as long as I live—'It's just one night. And what he is giving us in return is priceless.'"

"What did you do?'

"Are you kidding? I was a whore. My father saw to that. It wasn't the only time. The man—his name was Jack, or something like that—came back for more. Each time my father let him have me."

"Why didn't you go to the police? Say something to someone?"

"Who would believe me? My father would say I was crazy. No one ever saw it happen. How could I prove it? I was ashamed."

"How long did this go on?"

"Three or four months, until I ran away from the house. I had nowhere to go, no money. The only skill I had was to fuck somebody, so I became the whore they made me into."

Even with all that she had been through with her father, tears still gathered at the corners of her eyes. "At one time he was the best father I could have had. Something happened to him that I will never know, but I can never forgive what he did to me. Right now he's the least of my problems."

As she began to realize her situation, the fear of the hunted returned to her eyes. Gazing wildly around the hospital room, she became more agitated. She even stared at the closet as if she expected some hidden person to appear.

Sennett asked her if she felt up to looking at a couple of pictures. After a few moments she nodded, so he proceeded to take the cellphone out of his coat and showed her the downloaded police drawing of Pinky LeBeque.

Carina looked at LeBeque's face and identified him as the man she had seen on the porch. Then Sennett showed her a photograph of Tommy Holiday. She said she had met him at one of the downtown bars when she was with Finney. She thought he was pretty full of himself and condescending to Cal.

While she studied Holiday's photo, I reached in my pocket for some gum. When I did, I felt the brochure of Mark Crandall from Sturgis and Martin still in my jacket. I pulled it out and looked at Mark Crandall's photograph. On the spur of the moment I decided to show her Crandall's photo.

"Have you ever seen this man before?" I asked, opening the brochure so she could see it.

Her eyes bulged and air moved out of her body in raspy breaths. Her words sounded like the groan of a wounded animal. "Not him!"

The noise must have startled the guards, because they burst into the room, guns drawn. Sennett held up his hand and they quickly holstered their pieces and walked out the door.

"How do you know him?" Sennett asked softly.

"He's Mr. Forrester, the man my father sent me with." She was now shaking with fear. "Please take it away!" she begged, her hands shaking in terror, her eyes with fear.

I put the brochure back in my jacket and rested my hand on her shoulder. "Don't worry, Carina. You're safe here." When I said it, her face transformed into a blank mask, an escape to another place. She remained silent, staring at something far from the confines of her hospital room. At that point the nurse walked in, and Sennett and I both knew the conversation was over.

We walked slowly out of the room and made our way outside to Sennett's car. Silently I sat looking out the window, trying to make sense of what Carina had told us. The sky was steel gray and the cold wind from the North made the swirling leaves rise from the street like ghosts.

Sennett asked me how I happened to have that photo. I told him about Mildred Waters. Then he wondered why I showed it to Carina. I had no answer.

Sennett sat silently behind the wheel, eyes adrift, looking for something neither of us could find. Finally, he straightened his back in the seat, reached for his keys, and turned on the ignition.

"We need to find that son of a bitch."

CHAPTER 30

WHEN I WALKED OUT OF THE HOUSE the following morning, I saw our policeman driving off from his night watch. It was comforting to have him there, but a fear of the unknown still haunted me. Just to be sure, I walked around the backyard.

Everything looked unchanged. The garage door and the gate to the alley were both closed. The football was in its place. Then I looked for the key to the house. At first I didn't see it, but after searching I saw the plastic rock a couple of feet from its usual place in the flowerbed next to the patio. I picked it up and looked inside. The key was there. I reminded myself to tell Joey to quit playing with it. I could feel myself getting jumpy, as if I had been binging on caffeine.

When I finished, I went into the garage, got into my car and opened the garage door. Just as I started the engine, the phone rang. It was Sennett.

He told me he had some interesting news from MacGregor. Charmayne Phillips found her computer on the front seat of her car. When I asked him if anything was missing, he said nothing was wrong, except for black paint that had rubbed onto the computer cover.

"What was that all about?"

"Must have been dropped or something. They tested the paint. It turns out the particular paint on the computer was used on a Ford Escape."

When I said I thought it was a bit much to test the paint smudge on her computer, Sennett reminded me that MacGregor was a fanatic about crime in his city. The mere thought of a murder sent him into a frenzy. He tested for prints and anything else he could find. The computer was clean.

Sennett knew I wasn't impressed, so he asked: "Who do we know that has a black Ford Escape?"

I hesitated but he didn't wait for a reply. "Mark Crandall."

"First of all, how do you remember that?"

He explained that he wrote it down in his book when we were at Crandall's house in Corktown. It seemed a little far-fetched to me, pin something on Mark Crandall when thousands of black Ford Escapes were on the road. "What is his motivation?"

"Nothing, except the two hundred thousand dollars Sandra Wells had in her bank account. Remember the card with his name on it in her safety deposit box?"

I was skeptical, but he was insistent that we pay Crandall another visit. I met him at his office, and we made the fifteen-minute drive to Crandall's condominium. This time we found a place to park. A squad car was in front of his condo, but no trace of the Escape.

The cops went up to the front door and knocked. After several bangs on the doorknocker without an answer, we went to the adjacent condo and rapped on his neighbor's door. The door opened and a middle-aged woman peered out. We asked if she saw Crandall recently. She said she usually saw him going to work in the morning, but not for the past couple of days.

The uniformed cops were having no luck getting in the house. I heard Sennett tell them to forget a locksmith. In a case like this, where there may have been a crime, the locksmith was usually a policeman with a sledgehammer.

Sennett gave the order to the officers and the front door was broken in two raps of the two-man door buster. A room-to-room search began. At first glance it looked as if Crandall had left the condo without a trace.

Ten minutes later the crime scene truck had arrived. At Sennett's order, two specialists went immediately to his computer. One was a string bean, with thick oily hair, bushy eyebrows, and a sallow complexion, reminding me of Dracula. The other was a Laurel and Hardy, roly-poly stump of a man.

They seemed to know what they were doing by the way they went through the computer. After a few minutes they had the computer working. The e-mail box was empty, no files, and no contacts. Then, the thin man raised his hand.

"What is it?" Sennett asked.

"I looked on his calendar for today," the thin man responded.

"What is it?" I asked

"It says Delta Flight 72." Sennett pulled out his cell and called Knudsen. After two minutes of waiting he nodded his head and hung up. "Delta Flight 72 landed in London last night. He's long gone."

THE NET FOR MARK CRANDALL STRETCHED OUT QUICKLY, including radio, TV, and police in multiple countries. Sennett assured me that they would catch him, that it was only a matter of time.

In the meantime, the officers continued to comb through Crandall's house with organized precision. The upstairs had two bedrooms, like the living room, nothing was out of place. Even his closets were organized: ties on a rack, laundered shirts separated by color on hangers, and twelve pairs of shoes neatly arranged on slanted shelves. I looked at the names on the shoes—Gucci, Prada, Ferragamo. Crandall had the same expensive taste in his suits and jackets—Canali, Armani, and Zegna.

When I came downstairs, two other policemen had already torn the study apart. Nothing turned up except for some accounting books and magazines, a couple of unused tickets to an upcoming Lions game, and his checkbook. I thought the checkbook was strange for an accountant who was used to computerized bills. After looking at the check register, I didn't see a smoking gun, only utility and cable bills and his mortgage payment.

I stopped for a moment and surveyed the study. It was no longer the neatly arranged room I had first seen. Books and magazines lay scattered everywhere. The furniture had been moved around, as the police looked for evidence. Even the drapes were pulled down.

Standing next to his desk, I happened to look at the near-empty bookshelves and again noticed the Merck Manual. Out of curiosity I thumbed through it. Inside, the front page had a folded corner. I opened the page and found some written notations on survival rates for a number of diseases, mostly cancer. Some numbers were written down, all between twenty and thirty. The Merck Manual seemed strange, but when I thought of his business as a life insurance agent, it made some sense.

Sennett thought the yield on this search would be low, and he was right. After two hours, nothing turned up. It was scrubbed clean. As a precaution they took some hair samples from a pillow for DNA. Now all we could hope for was a break. At two in the afternoon we got it. Someone spotted a black SUV half-submerged in a stagnant pond just off the Detroit River near Grosse Isle. The car was registered to Mark Crandall. Before we left, Sennett gave instructions to forensics to run the DNA sample as soon as it got to the lab. With the siren on, it took us about half hour to get there.

As the name implied, Grosse Isle was a big island in the middle of the Detroit River. For people who lived in this downriver area of Detroit, this was their exclusive neighborhood. Large homes, a boat club, golf courses, and big boats anchored in slips that backed up to the houses. A bridge united the island with the mainland. The residents made sure crime wasn't part of their daily life.

By the time we arrived, the fire department had pulled the vehicle out of the water. Sennett showed his badge to a fireman next to the car, a young guy in his twenties, short hair, clean-shaven, looking as if he had spent time in the military.

"Anything in there?"

"There's a lot of blood on the seat."

"Don't touch anything," Sennett said. "I'll have the lab guys come down and take a look."

Sennett got out and inspected the car. It was still early, but with daylight savings time gone, the hazy sunshine was fading quickly. After a few minutes of scrutiny, Sennett stopped at the right side of the car. He motioned me over.

There, on the passenger door was a dent with a black streak. "Looks like Mr. Crandall had an accident. Maybe it was with a computer." Sennett motioned to the officers and pointed out the dent.

While they inspected it, Sennett walked around the car, carefully avoiding touching anything until the forensic team came. He took out a small Maglite from his coat, bent down, and looked under the car. Nothing.

Sennett was about to open the car's hood, when one of the firemen yelled at us. "Hey! You guys better come down here."

We turned and scrambled down the embankment to the firefighter, who stood near the edge of the river. As I got a little closer, I stopped and looked at two objects on the shore. When I realized it was a pair of black boots, sticking out of the mud, I pointed them out to Sennett.

He bent down, removed the boots with a handkerchief, and, when he reached dry ground, set them down. On the bottom of the boot was a bright red stripe. Sennett looked inside to read the label. "Prada," he said.

He was about to walk further along the shore, when he stopped. "Well look what the dog just brought home," he said.

I went over and looked at three round, shiny metal cylinders. "What are they?"

"Shell casings. From the way they've mushroomed they look like hollow points. You get hit by one of these and you better hope the shooter had cataracts."

We both stared at the shoes and the empty cartridges. All I saw was death. Sennett left them for forensics and started walking up the embankment. At the top, one of the crime scene officers saw us and yelled down for Sennett to come over. When we reached the car, the officer was standing by the front door, holding an object in his rubber-gloved hand.

"I found this under the front seat." He held up a blackish-purple, round object that looked like a piece of a small hot dog.

"Looks like a piece of finger," Sennett said, looking at the object. It was startling at first, but since I had picked one up from the seat of my Jeep, I looked at it more clinically.

That wasn't the case with the policeman. He was stroking his throat and grimacing. "Really?" he croaked.

"Yeah, really. Make sure you get a DNA on it. Do it right now."

Sennett spent a few more minutes, giving the investigators instructions on the boots we found by the pond. When he finished, he walked slowly back to his car. "What do you think happened?" I asked.

The lieutenant shook his head and muttered something to himself. I knew when to leave him alone.

After leaving Sennett, I called Jordan, told her about Crandall's car, and said I was on my way to her office. What I got in return was a quick veto. She needed to get out of the office. This case was getting to her. That's when she suggested the Pipeline.

I didn't need any encouragement. While I was no stranger to stress, I found ruminating on unsolvable problems usually made them worse. Chewing gum wasn't doing it for me either. Paying a visit to Sid and playing a set with the boys might.

I told her I'd meet her in an hour, but got to the Pipeline early and played a couple of numbers, including "A-Train" with Sid playing the opening sax solo. I finished just as Jordan walked in.

When Sid saw her, his eyes sparkled and his fingers tapped silently on the side of his trumpet. Suddenly he put his lips on the mouthpiece and burst out with the opening bars of the Hayden trumpet concerto. When he finished, everyone at the bar clapped in amazement.

"Where did you dig that one up from?" I asked.

"I always save something for a pretty woman," he said with a laugh. Jordan came over and kissed him on the cheek. That made him smile even more. "I'm going to play that riff more often."

We both laughed and then walked to a table by the window. Charlie took our order for a Diet Coke and a Labatt Blue. He chatted with Jordan and me for a few moments and then went back to the bar. I sensed he knew we had something to talk about.

When Charlie left, Jordan put her drink down. Her shoulders slumped slightly and her head bowed to her chest. "Ben, I don't want to adopt. I think it is too big a risk. I want to carry my own child. If I can't, I've come to the realization that I can accept it."

There were no tears, only a long exhale of relief. I knew she had gone over everything in detail. When she made up her mind, it was final.

"Did you call Tom Brownley?"

"Not until we spoke," she said, firmly. I knew the conversation of adoption was over. I took her hand and held it mine and told her I would support any decision she made.

She squeezed my hand and a slow smile of relief creased her lips. We sat silently for a few moments, then, suddenly, she shook her head and straightened her shoulders. She had something else on her mind. "I had a conversation with an FBI special agent that morning," she said in a low and steady voice. "Apparently Wells had told him she thought there might be a problem with the contracts for the new City Hospital. When he pressed her for facts, Wells said that it was complicated and might be related to patient care in the hospital. She thought it might involve Tommy Holiday."

I took a long, thoughtful draw from the bottle. "Why wasn't something done?"

"Not enough facts was the agent's opinion," Jordan said. "He confirmed what others said, Wells was particular about being perfect. Now the only thing she left as evidence is the spreadsheet which was given to you, and no one knows what it means."

"Aren't crimes like this always about money?" I asked.

She studied her Coke on the table as if some genie would emerge with an answer in a puff of smoke. "You're right," she nodded. "From what Carina told you, the relationship between Carina and her father had something to do with making Herbert Knowlton rich."

"The irony is," I said, "that as much as Carina wanted nothing to do with her father, unwittingly, she was drawn into his death and the deaths of three other people. What about the money in her safety deposit box?"

"Sandra Wells was smart, but she had to have been an investment genius to put away that kind of money. Just the way she told her cousin it was 'for her family' is strange. We need to follow that angle."

I agreed. The "family" or "future family" left me stymied. What family? Was this for a future investment or was there another purpose?

Jordan twirled the straw in her glass, then put it down. "With no heir, the money probably goes to probate. That's strange investment planning for a person as organized as Sandra Wells. Someone that detail-oriented must have had that eventuality covered." As she was talking, my cellphone rang; it was Sennett. I listened carefully, asked him a question, and told him I would call him back.

"I think we're modifying our theory," I told Jordan. "Make the number of dead people five."

"Why?" Jordan asked.

"The police found Crandall's clothes washed up on the shore south of Grosse Isle, his name stitched on the inside of his coat. They found three bullet holes through the coat. And the shell casings that were found at the scene turned out to be identical to the bullets that killed Cal Finney."

"Okay," she said, "but we still need a body."

I explained to her that I asked Sennett the same question. He said that due to the number of cables under the river, if someone was shot, that body could sink and be trapped in a nest of lines and cables. I explained it was not unusual for police divers to find bodies.

"The crime guys found a partial on the floor of Crandall's car. When they took it to Allan Davis he confirmed it was the fifth digit of a hand. The DNA sampling on the finger was a match for a sample of Crandall's hair. He also said the aging of the specimen was a few days old. The only thing they didn't have was a body."

The real question was why he was killed. LeBeque was a Mafia hitman. Somebody was paying him to do this. Why else would he be after Crandall?

I called Sennett back. He was on another line, and while I waited, the boys were playing Sonny Rollins's version of "St. Thomas." I was thinking about how nice a cruise to Punta Gorda would be.

The Lieutenant sounded aggravated when he returned to the phone. "Ben, go over that meeting you had with the woman at Sturgis and Martin. Her name was Mildred something."

I told him her name was Mildred Walters and then rehashed my visit with her. "It was really strange. The whole conversation focused on this girl who got jilted by Crandall. Her name was Patsy Evans."

"Give me that name again," he interrupted.

"Patsy Evans. Why are you suddenly interested in her?" I replied.

"Crandall is dead, and he knew Patsy Evans. We need to find out more about that girl."

Jordan and I hung around for another half an hour and listened to the boys playing. It didn't do any good. I had the feeling I was suffocating.

CHAPTER 31

Fortunately or unfortunately, the "we" in Sennett's "we need to find out more" turned out to be me. The investigation of the Mayor in what was now being called the Sandra Wells Incident was heating up. Because of this, Sennett said he was tied up again with the Mayor for the rest of the day, asked if I could go to the Evans's home in his place. When I asked him if that met the standard of the department, he said I had a badge. "Plus, you know the case better than anyone else in the department."

Without hesitation, I agreed to see her. Ordinarily, I would refuse, because I'm a doc and not a policeman. But this was about my family. I couldn't stand still on this and wait. If I didn't do something proactive to protect them, I could never live with myself. I think Sennett knew this too, and that's why he gave me the go-ahead.

I sent him Patsy Evans's number from my cellphone, and he called the family. Within in a few minutes he phoned back. He said he spoke to Patsy's mother. The girl wasn't there, but Mom seemed concerned and wanted to talk.

The address for Patsy Evans was in Owosso, Michigan, a small town north of Detroit, near Flint. I got in my car, plugged the location into my Garmin, and headed north from Detroit on I-75.

After thirty minutes, I saw the I-69 exit to Flint. When I saw the sign, I couldn't help but remember an article I read about Flint in Forbes magazine. It was listed it as the #2 most miserable city in America. The focus of the piece was about using lead-contaminated drinking water for the inhabitants of the city. I wondered how the government could be so neglectful as to deny safe drinking water? The response from the state officials was that it was too expensive to fix the problem for both the inhabitants of the city and the industrial areas that supported the economy, so the government chose the economy and exposed the people to a nightmare of serious risks from polluted water.

It took an hour until I passed Flint and saw the exit to Owosso. I turned down Main Street for a mile and then turned north on M-52. Well-kept houses and the stubble of harvested cornfields flanked both sides of the road. The sign that read 'Evans Farm' was one of them.

When I saw the sign, I turned down a long driveway and drove up to a friendly looking white farmhouse. It had fresh paint and a neatly trimmed lawn and shrubs. The large maple tree in front of the house was leafless.

I parked my Wagoneer on the gravel drive in front of the house. It was cold outside and the wind was blowing hard from the northwest. I stepped out of my car, turned up the collar of my jacket, and walked up the gray steps to the front porch.

Shortly after pressing on the doorbell, a woman in her late fifties greeted me. She had full red cheeks and light gray hair cut short. A patterned knit sweater with multicolored leaves on it rested above gray wool pants and white sneakers. From a distance, the only thing I could think of was Betty Crocker.

I showed her my badge, but I don't think she even looked at it. Instead she said hello, invited me in, and then stared vacantly down the driveway. She walked slowly as she brought me into the front entrance hall. I noticed that her arms clutched her body as if to hold it together. When we reached the end of the hall, I caught the smell of cookies baking in the oven.

We passed into a cozy living room with white shutters. A large couch sat in front of the window with a colorful quilt resting on the back. On either side next to it were two large red plaid easy chairs, one of which had an ottoman. In the corner of the room was a television and on the other side a rocking chair with a knitting bag next to it.

She motioned me to sit down. I took one of the easy chairs. She sat across from me in her rocker.

"Mrs. Evans, thank you for seeing me. I understand your daughter is not at home."

She put her hands in her lap and fingered her wedding ring. "I told the police lieutenant that, but when he said they were investigating something to do with Mark Crandall, I said I would like to meet with them anyway." She stopped for a moment, her face scowling with anger. "Why do you want to speak with me?"

I asked if she knew her daughter had a relationship with a man named Mark Crandall. "Yes, she had a relationship with that man, and he almost killed her," she said. I told her I was there because Mark Crandall had died. Her voice, which had been angry, was now tinged with fear.

I went on to recount what Mildred had told me in the Motown Lounge, but, mercifully, none of the explicit details. I could understand a mother being mad at someone who had rejected her daughter; but the emotional effect on Patsy seemed excessive. I think in some way her mom felt guilty.

She must have understood this, because she started to explain what happened. She said Patsy never had a boyfriend before. She was a shy girl who kept to herself. Mrs. Evans blamed herself because she didn't encourage Patsy enough to go out with her friends, but that's not what her daughter wanted. She spent most of her college life wrapped up in business school and accounting. Although she was an outstanding student, her main drive in life was to help people; that's why she took a job at the medical center.

Things were fine for a year or so, then, suddenly, she changed. Her mother said she acted so unlike the daughter she knew, different clothes and a snippy attitude. Sometimes she wouldn't come home until early in the morning. "I told Patsy that I noticed a difference in her, shortly after she said she met this wonderful guy, Mark Crandall. Mr. Evans and I were a little alarmed about her transformation, but we thought it was ultimately for her good, you know, a sign she was socially active."

I asked her if she knew what Crandall did for a living. Mrs. Evans said Patsy told her he was a very successful insurance agent who worked with some of the top people in the city. When I asked if she remembered any names, she mentioned that he was a good friend with the mayor's chief of staff, a man named Holiday.

"What happened to their relationship?

She shook her head. "One day without an explanation he stopped seeing her. She didn't know why, but suddenly Patsy changed. She stopped talking to us. Every time I asked about her relationship with Crandall, she became defensive. Then a couple of months ago they got a call from her doctor, who had admitted her to the hospital for treatment on the psychiatric ward. He said she was depressed and possibly suicidal."

As she told the story, Mrs. Evans started to weep. She took out a tissue from the table next to her chair and dabbed her eyes, and then picked up a half-finished scarf. She started knitting, as if doing that would remove the memory. I suspected this wasn't the first time this occurred.

She waited until she composed herself and then put down her unfinished scarf. "Patsy didn't tell anyone what transpired, but the people at her job wanted to know where she was. We had to notify Patsy's work place that she was sick and wouldn't be back for a while. We didn't want to damage her work record, so we told them she had a serious infection. A while turned into several months until finally, Patsy got a termination letter."

I asked how she was doing and if I could speak with her. Mrs. Evans said she just came home last week, and her psychiatrist said she was still pretty fragile.

I wasn't in a position to push it any harder, so I changed the subject. "What about her job? What work did she do?"

"Patsy was hired after college to work at the medical center as a data analyst in the medical records department. She must have been smart, because the supervisor asked her to work on a project in the Cancer Institute, collecting research data. After a year on the job she was given a full time position as a data coordinator in the cancer surveillance building, collecting information on cancer survivors." When I pushed her for more detailed information, she said she didn't know.

I watched Mrs. Evans carefully as we talked. She picked up a knitting needle again and started to work on the scarf. Clearly, she was on the edge, and at this point, I knew I had nothing to gain in trying to convince her to let us see Patsy.

I apologized for bothering her and asked, if possible, to see Patsy at a later date. Mrs. Evans suggested that I call back in a couple of weeks. Then she excused herself for couple of minutes. I sat waiting looking out the living room window at the occasional car driving down the highway. She came back with a plastic bag filled with warm oatmeal raisin cookies. I thanked her, put on my coat, and left the house with the cookies. The brisk, cold wind stung my face as my boots crunched on the gravel driveway.

When I got in the car, I started the engine and waited for the warm air to kick in. I couldn't resist the intoxicating smell of the cookies and tried one. As I sat in the car eating, I was puzzled. Mark Crandall didn't seem like the kind of guy who would be dating a girl from a farm in Owosso. The puzzle must have made me hungry, because I ate two more before I forced myself to put them away.

After a couple of minutes of silence, I put the car in gear and drove down the long driveway. When I was back on the expressway, I called Sennett and spent ten minutes telling him about my visit.

"You know what, Doc?" Sennett responded. "Mildred Walters said Crandall was a calculating guy that was always looking for something he could get. The only thing that Patsy Evans could give him was sex or something at her work. It didn't sound like sex was a problem for Crandall, so we need to check out her job."

He was about to say something else, when he was interrupted. After a couple of minutes he came back to the phone.

"I know I'm keeping you busy with these interviews, but you're into this deep and probably the only person I can depend on. The Captain just called. He wants to see me about the Sandra Wells case. Something about Tommy Holiday asking some questions. Can you go to the cancer surveillance center?"

"Don't worry about me. This isn't about doing you a favor. I have to do this." I thought about what I just said. "You know, George, I'm beginning to feel I like I have another job," I told him.

"Maybe you do, Doc."

CHAPTER 32

WHEN I GOT HOME, I WAITED until dinner was over and Joey was asleep. Then I told Jordan about Patsy Evans. As I spoke, I could tell by her nervous movements and anxious voice that she had realized, as I did, that this investigation was snowballing out of control. But we both knew it didn't matter. I had to follow this case to the end.

I knew one other thing. I couldn't hold two jobs. Managing patients' problems with this business on my mind was impossible. I called Melvin Dean, a colleague of mine, the next morning. When I told him I had an out of town family emergency and needed coverage, he said he had plenty of eager young guys in his group who would be happy to cover. I hated to do it, but I had no choice.

Then I called the office and told Karen to shut things down without a return date. She said that wouldn't work with my patients, so I told her to tell them a couple of weeks. I did one other thing. Before I left, I put my gun in my jacket pocket.

When I got to police headquarters, I ran into two cops I played against in high school, Bill Stacey and Don Trent. Both of them were State fans. We always kidded around during the season.

"What did you think of that interference call in the State game last weekend?" Bill asked.

"To me it looked like it was contact," I said with a smile, as I started emptying my pockets.

"I knew you'd say that, especially because your team won," Stacey said

"Does that mean you forgot that offside call last year that cost us the game?" As I spoke, I took out my gun from my coat pocket.

"Whoa, you're carrying, Doc?"

I nodded. Suddenly their faces turned serious, as they examined the gun. They looked it over and gave me the "be careful" pat on the shoulder as I put it back in my coat.

I left them and made my way up to Sennett's office. When I walked in, I saw Knudsen's head peeking out above two piles of charts on his desk. "What the hell?" I asked, gesturing toward the paper fortress.

He shrugged. "It's all Patsy Evans' stuff."

While Knudsen spent the rest of the day going through the papers, Sennett was up to his ears in fending off the constant inquiries from the press along with dealing with Patsy Evans' mother. Apparently, she called the department and reported that her daughter didn't come home last night. She wondered if it was related to my visit.

"Dammit, now I'm involved in organizing the search," he said with a heavy sigh. "When I called the local police, they said that they already knew about her, but that was all. That's all I need is another mystery." I agreed.

Sennett's frustration gained momentum, as he paced back and forth in his office, teeth grinding and hands clenched. People dying and no answers. I figured it was a good time to leave, so I got up. Sennett looked at me as I walked to the door.

"Ben, you were right."

"What do you mean?"

"This is a job; and on this job you've got to be aware of everything. Don't take any chances."

My "I won't" didn't seem to sit well with him. "Maybe you should take some more time at the range?"

I was startled; then I thought about the people that had died in this case. I had to admit that I questioned whether I could actually shoot someone, but the more I thought about it, the more I believed it was my inexperience at work, not my doctorly compassion that might hold me back.

"You think I should?"

"Actually, it was Jordan's idea. She called me. You need practice with that gun you're carrying. Arcinegas is at the range and is waiting for you. Spend an hour with him, just getting used to firing your gun again. Everyone needs a little practice." He said it casually, but he couldn't hide the fact that he was worried too: He kept smoothing and re-smoothing the front of his jacket, although it wasn't wrinkled.

No argument from me. I took the elevator down to the gun range. When I got there, Arcinegas asked me what I wanted to shoot with. I pulled out my little Sig, and he laughed.

"Doc, you ain't gonna hit shit with that peashooter." Better be real close when you use it. Otherwise, try one of these." He handed me a police issue Glock, but I shook my head.

"This is about all I can carry. Otherwise, my patients might get a little nervous."

I quickly went into the locker room and changed into police sweats. When I came out, Arcinegas handed me a set of earmuffs. He seemed happy to see me, but made no chit chat. This was business.

The range was about seventy-five feet long with individual cubicles. The targets were full body figures at about thirty feet. He set my Sig and his Glock on the counter.

"Doc, show me a couple of shots and then we'll see how you're doing,"

I took the gun and held it with two hands pointed at a target. I put three shots into the target's right hip, and felt proud that I had hit the target at all. I don't think my instructor felt the same.

"That was good, but could be better. Now don't lean forward," he said, "The gun does not have that much of a recoil. And always keep moving to create distance or simulate moving to cover. Remember, if you're going to shoot, set yourself properly. " He picked up his Glock, set himself, and squeezed off three quick shots into the heart of the target. "What did you notice from my shooting?"

"The shots seemed effortless."

"That's right." He set me up in a more upright stance, knees slightly bent. "Now I want you to remember this: front sight, front sight, squeeze. That means always look through the front sight of the gun, use two hands, and squeeze the trigger with smooth pressure on your shooting finger. If you mash the trigger with your finger, the bullet will go wide."

This time when I fired I put three shots in the target's chest.

"That's good. Now let's put in some work."

We spent about an hour practicing and repeating the same shots over and over. He then had me work on moving targets for another hour. It was the no-nonsense type of football practice my position coach had worked on with me in college. Repetition. By the time I was done I was drenched in sweat. I looked up at the targets I had shot at; most of them were struck in the heart. I quickly realized this wasn't practice for a game.

"You're okay, Doc," Arcinegas said, as we walked out of the shooting range. "Not perfect, but pretty damn good. Being perfect comes with experience. Remember these two rules: Never take a gun unless you are willing to use it, and assume every firearm is loaded. Every man and woman I've trained had that fear-of-firing situation. Let's hope it never happens to you. But if it does, be prepared to act."

When I got dressed and was outside the locker room, I was surprised to see Sennett waiting for me. "I saw you shoot. Not bad."

I told him that, after playing on the practice squad in college, I knew the comment was reserved to avoid discouraging someone, but I didn't take it personally. He looked embarrassed for a moment and then got to the real reason he stopped by.

"I've arranged for you to go to the Surveillance Center this afternoon. The director has a letter from the office and from Jordan."

I told him I had cleared my office appointments and was about to leave when I remembered I didn't have a copy of the spreadsheet. I picked up a copy of *Australian Yoga* off Sennett's desk and thumbed through it while I waited. Studying the contorted poses of the incredibly limber people on the pages reaffirmed my opinion that there are some things in life I will never do.

Fifteen minutes later Knudsen handed me the spreadsheet. After focusing my eyes on the numbers for a moment, I folded the paper and put it in my coat pocket. But unlike the first time I carried this document, my muscles relaxed and my breath came easily. I had a mission: to unravel the mystery of these random numbers.

THAT AFTERNOON I ARRIVED AT THE OFFICES of The Medical Center Cancer Surveillance office. I knew about this organization. They followed up on cancer survival rates in southeast Michigan. It was an important service, since it showed the effectiveness of certain treatments and the survival rates of a variety of malignancies from different hospitals in the city.

I parked my Wagoneer in the visitors' lot of an old brick building on John R Street near the main hospital. Before I went inside, I reached into my pocket to make sure I had the spreadsheet. After locking the car door, I walked up the cracked cement sidewalk and into the entrance of an old, unimposing three-story red brick building. Once inside I checked the directory for the office of Virginia Gates, Director of The Michigan Cancer Surveillance Center. It was on the first floor.

The building had no fancy marble floors, padded leather chairs, or well-dressed receptionists. Instead, the entrance had basic hospital decorating—enameled block walls, dull tile floors, and glaring overhead fluorescent fixtures that buzzed like angry bees. I found Virginia Gates's office at the end of the corridor.

When I knocked on the door, a loud, high-pitched voice beckoned me in. Inside was a middle-aged African-American woman with a thin face and black glasses sitting behind a gray metal desk. With no makeup and her straightened black hair pulled back in a ponytail, she could have been mistaken for a librarian. The sign on her desk read: Virginia Gates, Director Cancer Surveillance Center.

She sat behind a vase of fresh mini-carnations and a large screen desktop with a neatly stored pullout keyboard. In contrast, the rest of her office was filled with files piled up on the floor. In spite of the fact that Sennett had told her I was coming, she seemed startled. I suspected she didn't get many visitors.

"Don't worry, m'am," I said softly, "I'm just here to ask a few questions. I guarantee you it won't take long."

She sighed heavily, and spoke with a firm voice. "Are you the doctor that the police department called me about?"

I nodded and then explained that I wanted to talk to her about Patsy Evans. She asked me for identification, so I showed her my Michigan State Medical License and my badge. She put the license next to a search warrant that Knudsen had faxed to her. When she saw they matched, she handed my license back.

She cocked her head to one side and shook it slightly. "You know, Patsy doesn't work here any more. She left without notice over a year ago. Her mother called and said she was sick. When we didn't hear from her, we had no choice but to . . . terminate her."

"Patsy is missing."

She looked surprised when I said it, replying that she was last person she would ever suspect to be involved with the police. "No one has accused Patsy of anything," I said. "The police are concerned that someone she knew might have done something wrong."

Gates's face paled as she cupped her hand to her mouth. "I'm so sorry for Patsy and her family. I loved working with her. She was devoted to her job. I was angry when she left, but I still kept her desk, hoping she would return."

I asked if I could see the desk and computer where she worked. She got up and moved a couple of chairs with files on them. "I'm sorry," she said. "We're understaffed. Just not enough time to put everything away."

She turned toward the door and led me into the back office. It was a cramped space with ten or fifteen desks, five employees, and two-dozen metal storage racks. On each side of the room were unwashed windows looking out onto a partially full parking lot. As in Gates's office, files and metal cabinets were everywhere.

She pointed to a corner of the room and explained that when an employee left they would put the contents of their desks into a designated rack. It didn't happen often, because of dedicated employees and a low turnover. But she kept the items anyway. Sometimes they returned.

Gates took me over to an unused desk in the corner of the office and pulled out a laptop computer from the metal shelf. On the cover a tag read: Patsy Evans. I noticed that next to her computer stood a vase of artificial flowers and a small book of poems by William Butler Yeats with a bookmark in place. Curious, I picked it up and looked at the page. It was "The Isle of Innisfree."

Gates plugged in the computer and seemed surprised when it booted up without a problem. After a couple of taps on the keyboard Patsy's files appeared as unrecognizable columns of numbers. Gates explained that most of the files were data entry of patients with some type of cancer. Each individual was grouped into categories, depending on their diagnosis. The staged cancers and their treatments were in the columns.

I asked her how the follow-up with the Center worked. She said that the main source of information came from the patients' physicians. The Center sent out yearly inquiries to their doctors asking if the individuals were alive, free of disease, or were undergoing treatment. The computer program managed information such as gender, disease, age, etc. and turned it into spreadsheets. Analyzing the spreadsheets produced information of survival, treatment programs, and complications. Since, thousands of people had cancer in Southeast Michigan, the only way to track of them was to continually contact their doctors.

I asked Gates to show me on the computer the spreadsheets they used. She seemed proud of her system and was happy to comply. When the computer screen came up, I asked her to print up a copy for me. After the printer quickly spat out a sample page, I studied it for a moment and then reached in my coat pocket for the spreadsheet that Carina Knowlton had given me.

I wasn't sure, but I detected a similarity, so I asked Gates to see if the entries on my sheet matched any of Patsy Evans's records. When I compared the pages, it was obvious that some of the numbers corresponded. I glanced over at Gates; she nodded. In spite of trying to maintain a poker face, I could feel my pulse race with excitement at the possibility of an answer.

She took each page to the copy machine and printed out sheets with names and demographic information. After about twenty minutes, she handed me forty-two printed pages.

"Your spreadsheet matched our records," she said. "These are all patients who are under surveillance. How did you get it?"

When I told her I couldn't divulge that information because it was part of an active investigation, she didn't seem pleased with answer. But when I asked her if, by looking at these names, there was anything particularly special about these individuals, she looked at them more carefully.

"Nothing that I can see on the surface. Seems like a random selection from all over the area. But I did notice a number of them have passed away."

I asked her if I could take the copies. She nodded and handed them to me.

"That was a legitimate search warrant, wasn't it?" she asked with a smile.

"Cross my heart and hope to die."

I thanked her and told her that she had helped us immensely. I was half way to the door when she called after me. I turned around and came back.

"Here's one thing I remembered. I don't know if it means anything, but I had a couple of people inquire about Patsy. One was a man who came here about two months ago. He said he was a policeman and showed me a warrant like yours to examine Patsy's computer. I have to say he was pretty rude. That's why I remember him. I opened up the computer and found the files he was looking for. I thought it was kind of strange, but he had the credentials."

"Weren't you suspicious?"

"I sure was. Before I opened up anything I called the Mayor's office. They said he was legitimate."

"Who was the other person?"

"Oh, that was about six months ago. Real nice gal. She was here asking for some information on some patients in Patsy's computer. It was something related to Medicaid payments for cancer treatments. She showed me a letter from the State of Michigan Department of Human Services. I printed up some information for her."

"What was the information?"

"Come to think of it, it was similar to the spreadsheet you showed me, but in much more detail."

I asked her if she remembered her name. She paused for moment, then told me she thought she had saved her card. Gates went to look for it and after a couple of minutes returned with a smile on her face. "People say I save too many things, but you never know."

She handed me the card. As I studied it, I felt my mouth go dry. It said Sandra Wells.

Gates took the card back and looked at it. "Sandra Wells, now that I think about it, that name seems familiar to me," she said. "Didn't I read something about her in the newspaper?"

"Maybe," I responded. "Do you recall the man's name?"

"Not really. All I remember was his name was something to do with vacations or holidays, something like that. Other than that, I really can't say." I thanked her and was just about to leave, when she stopped me. "I hope Patsy is okay."

INSTEAD OF GOING BACK TO THE OFFICE, I pulled out my cellphone and called Sennett to tell him what happened. He was so elated I thought he would jump out of the phone. When I finished, I called Jordan, told her what I found, and said Sennett and I we were coming over.

It took us fifteen minutes to get to her office. When we walked in, I noticed Jordan's desk was devoid of paper. "What happened? No more cases?"

"No, when George told me he wanted me to look at something, I knew you guys were going drop something big on my desk. What have you got?"

I put the files from Virginia Gates' office on her desk. Jordan looked at the pages and started to separate them out, first into men, women, and age groups. Then she opened up her computer and started entering in data.

Jordan put each name in a column, noting sex, diagnosis, marital status, and current location. She noted that most of the patients were in their seventies, with an almost even number of men and women, and they were all single. Her fingers flew over the keys of her computer. After fifteen minutes of entering data, she stopped.

"Ninety per cent of these people are dead," Jordan exclaimed. "They all died in the last three years."

At first I was taken aback; it sounded suspicious. Then I looked at their diagnoses. "All of them had had been cancer survivors for over ten years, but none had been cancer-free."

"Ben, you're going to have to help me with these diagnoses."

"Cancer of the breast, prostate cancer, chronic lymphocytic leukemia—they're all long-term survival cases." I remembered the notation in the Merck Manual at Crandall's home.

I mentioned it to Jordan, but Sennett interrupted. "Let's assume Patsy Evans had something Mark Crandall wanted, and let's assume it was something to do with her job. The two known facts are that the spreadsheet came from the Cancer Surveillance Center, and that Mark Crandall had a relationship with Patsy Evans, who worked there. I don't believe in coincidence. There must be a reason."

"No reason, unless he was going to make money or find a cure for cancer," I said.

When Jordan asked what kind of money could he make, I shrugged my shoulders.

None of us could figure it out. Crandall was in the life insurance business, but who would sell life insurance to people with incurable diseases? It didn't make sense.

"Maybe he was getting them to participate in some kind of study or investing in some new kind of drug," I suggested.

Sennett said we needed to check out each of these individuals on Patsy Evans's list and see what they had that enticed Mark Crandall to want their names. The look of determination in his face said this wasn't going to be easy.

CHAPTER 33

SENNETT WAS RIGHT ABOUT ONE THING. It was hard work. Each one of the individuals on the list needed to be contacted. To make it harder, none of them had a family member or friend listed as a contact. They were all single, widowed, or without relatives.

Jordan suggested that we see if they had accounts with Mark Crandall at Sturgis and Martin. Sennett called Fairmont and once again got the cold shoulder. This time the lieutenant had a court order, and it took another call from Knudsen to find out that none of the names were clients of his firm.

Sennett looked for an official document, like an insurance policy, that connected Mark Crandall and the individuals on the list. On the surface it seemed simple, but dealing with dead people wasn't. The only official papers we did find were death certificates. This was accomplished by checking with the counties where they died. None of the documents mentioned next of kin.

"It's like these people didn't exist," Jordan said.

"Everybody knows somebody," Sennett said.

"I don't mean to sound stupid," I interrupted, "but how do you get a death certificate?"

"Didn't they teach you that in medical school?" Sennett asked.

When I shook my head, he proceeded to tell me that most dead bodies are taken to funeral homes. "The person there fills out the certificate. The information on the certificate includes name, address, next of kin, social security number, that kind of thing. A doctor, coroner or medical examiner then signs off with the cause of death."

I looked through all the certificates. In each case the name of the physician was scribbled on the death certificate. None of them had autopsies. None of them owned a house. The cause of death for each of them was the chronic diseases noted at the surveillance center.

Sennett said it was not unusual for the certificate to not have all of the patient's diagnoses, indicating that all the state wants is the immediate cause of death. While we talked, Jordan kept adding information to her spreadsheet. She studied the columns for a moment. "Every one of these people lived in a rural area," she said, "and most were buried in a private cemetery. It takes money for a burial—cemetery plot, funeral home, and maintenance. I want to know where they got the money."

Sennett scratched his head. "That seems a little way out, Jordan."

"Maybe, but look at this one, Reginald Stone. He lived in a poor area of Lenawee County and was buried at St. Regis in the Hills. That's a fancy neighborhood. I'm sure membership in the church or being a relative of a member is a prerequisite."

"Okay," Sennett said. "I'll call Knudsen and have him poke into it."

It took Knudsen half an hour to get the information. In the meantime Jordan had entered data on all of the other names. She finished the last column when Knudsen called back. Sennett listened intently on his cellphone, and after five minutes of nodding, he clicked off.

"Knudsen said that the secretary for the parish remembered Reginald Stone. He came in one day, saying he wanted to make a contribution to the church. The way she spoke of him sounded like he was the least likely person to come into a fancy neighborhood and drop money on them. Shabbily dressed, unkempt and carrying a large, over-stuffed shopping bag is the way she described him. She said she was a little scared when he put the bag on her desk. By the time he had emptied it she counted fifty thousand dollars."

I asked what she did with the money. The secretary replied that he wanted to join the congregation so he could get a burial plot in the cemetery.

"I assume that's where he was buried."

"Yes. No one came to the internment. Kind of sad, don't you think?"

"Sad for him and sad for us. We're no further ahead."

Jordan continued through the list. After another half hour she put the cover down on her computer. "Every one of the people on this list was like a person without an identity. It's almost as if they didn't exist."

"The pattern of these people was that they were all loners living in a rural area with serious, long-term diseases that were ultimately fatal," Sennett said after going over the patients. "We need to go back to the cancer center and go through their patient list to see if any other patients like this are still alive."

I was back at the Surveillance Center when they opened at nine o'clock the next morning, only this time Sennett and Jordan came with me. Sennett looked unhappy: Patsy Evans was still missing. Virginia Gates looked equally unhappy to see that we had returned. I think the idea that something criminal was happening in her surveillance center was unnerving. Frankly, I didn't blame her.

Sennett was apologetic, telling her that something in the spreadsheet that came out of Patsy Evans' computer was important and he needed her help. Once Sennett explained what he wanted, Gates became much more cooperative. She sat down at Patsy's computer to re-examine the files. This time she pushed a couple of keys on the computer, but nothing happened.

She immediately checked the back of the computer. "Look!" Her face was a mixture of anger and disgust. "Someone removed the hard drive!" When Jordan wondered about a backup, Gates said it might take a few days to come up with it.

"Is there a main server accessible?" Jordan asked.

It took half an hour to locate Wilber Grant, from IT. Sennett wasn't good at waiting. He kept pacing the room. Finally, the phone rang and Grant came on the line. Virginia explained to him what had happened, then handed the phone to Jordan. In a couple of minutes she described what she needed. He said he would get back to us in an hour.

I agreed with Sennett: Waiting was the worst. When a life is hanging on the line, every second feels like an hour. I sat in a chair and tried to stay calm. Sennett, on the other hand, was still pacing.

"George, you're going to wear a hole in the floor," I said.

"Can't help it. I'm not made for waiting."

He was just about to say something else when Gates' phone rang, and she picked it up. It was Grant. She quickly took her pen and began writing. When she finished, she thanked him.

"Wilbert ran a search through the files with three diagnoses—breast cancer, chronic lymphocytic leukemia, and prostate cancer. Then he narrowed it down to southeastern Michigan. Once he got that, he narrowed it down to unmarried, divorced, or widowed, preferably living in rural areas. He came up with 255 names."

Jordan showed us the list that had just popped out of Gates' printer. All of the demographics were there. Without wasting time, Jordan took out her cell and started calling names on the list. On the third call she made a hit. The man, Freddie Jackson, lived in a senior living facility in the city of Wyandotte south of Detroit. She gave Sennett and me the paper and said she had to prepare a brief.

Most people in Detroit refer to Wyandotte as being downriver, in reference to the fact that it lies south of Detroit next to the Detroit River as it empties into Lake Erie. The city was home to several industries, including the country's largest toy pistol manufacturer, a large shipbuilding plant, and Wyandotte Chemical, which became part of the BASF Corporation. The community boasts such noted residents as Lucille Ball, Lee Majors (The Six Million Dollar Man), and Connie Creskie, the 1969 Playmate of the Year. I thought it was an odd mixture for such a small community.

Wyandotte is easy to get around in, since most of the north-south streets are numbered 1-20 and the east to west streets are named after trees. Freddie Jackson lived at Wyandotte Senior Living Housing on Sycamore Street, near the river.

The building was a non-descript eleven-story orange brick structure near a busy highway. We parked the car and walked into an entrance lobby that had threadbare, muted green, patterned carpeting. There was a damp, moldy smell in the air that an air freshener had failed to hide. In the background every now and then a speaker squawked out an announcement.

On one side of the lobby alternating rust and yellow colored leather chairs rested near the window. On the other was a reception area with a blonde oak desk. Behind it was a girl with purple highlighted hair and a couple of tattoos on her forearms, who looked to be in her mid-twenties, reading a copy of US Magazine. As we approached the desk, she gazed upward with a bored look.

Sennett asked for Freddie Jackson. Seemingly irritated by the interruption, she nodded and pointed to the outside patio near the main dining room. She said that when the weather was good, he spent most of the day outside reading books. We followed her directions and made our way through a glass double door to the large cement area that she had referred to as the patio. Several wrought iron tables with cushioned chairs surrounded the concrete slab. At the one farthest from the dining hall sat a man in a plaid cotton shirt and khaki pants with a book in his hands.

We walked to his chair, but he didn't bother to look up. Sennett coughed slightly and then said hello. The man who glanced up from his book was short and thin with a weather-beaten face, bushy eyebrows, and chapped lips. I would have guessed he was no stranger to alcohol or tobacco. From the sour expression on his face, he looked annoyed.

"Are you Freddie Jackson?" Sennett asked.

"What if I am?" was the challenge from the man at the table. His voice was deeper than I anticipated from someone of his size.

Sennett introduced himself and me, but the man didn't seem fazed. "What do the police want with an old coot like me?" he asked.

Sennett went on to explain that we were investigating a crime that might have involved individuals with insurance policies. He said that Jackson's name came up in some material they had reviewed. At the word "insurance" Jackson raised his head and looked at Sennett closely.

"What kind of insurance? I ain't done nothing wrong," he said with a Kentucky drawl.

When Sennett replied life insurance, Jackson snapped his finger. "I knew some day someone would come around and ask me about life insurance."

"Why?" Sennett asked.

"Because I ain't no dummy. I spent two years in Jackson Prison for smokin' pot. That gave me an education neither of you boys will ever get."

"In what way?" Sennett asked.

"You know a scam when you see it. This fancy dude came and seen me out of the clear blue. Said he wondered if I was interested in getting money for my life insurance policy. I said I got chronic lymphocytic leukemia. I told him I had a policy and that no insurance company in the world was going to give me anything until I die. The man said he had a way of getting me some money from it."

"What way was that, Freddie?" Sennett asked.

"This boy was smart. He didn't spill the beans on what he was doing. Just said he could do it."

I pulled out my photo of Crandall and showed it to him.

"That's him. Look at his eyes. He thinks I'm some kind of dumbass hillbilly. I've seen those shifty eyes before. I ain't never goin' to do business with a guy like that."

When Sennett asked him if the man gave any hint of how he would get the money, Jackson became animated. "He said he knew someone who could do it and gave me a card with the guy's name on it. He'll fix it up. His words," Jackson said.

"Did you ever call?"

"Naw, I told him to go fuck himself. I said I ain't got no time for some slick-willy shithead like him trying to con an old man."

Sennett asked him how the guy responded. Jackson was laughing and said he must have scared last night's dinner out of him, because he picked up his briefcase and hustled out of there faster than Maury Wills could steal third base. As he said it, he slapped his hand on his trousers.

"You a baseball guy, Freddie?" I asked.

"Sure am. Been to the '68 and '84 series. Used to usher down at the old Tiger Stadium. I got me one of Willie Horton's bats."

"I'm a fan too, but I like Miguel Cabrera."

"Boy is good, real good, but too many calypso kids are in the bigs now. Lot of youngsters won't play the game. It's too slow. They want basketball or football."

You couldn't help but like Freddie Jackson, but I could tell it was time to move on. I slid my chair back, making a scraping sound on the cement. Sennett knew it too, because he got up and thanked him for his time. We started walking away. About halfway to the door to the patio, Jackson called out to us.

"Say, Lieutenant, I just thought of something. I still got that card that gyp-ster gave me. You interested in seeing it?"

It took Sennett about five seconds to say yes and about thirty minutes for Jackson to go back to his room and, according to him, "rummage around a few things." He came back with the card and handed it to Sennett, who studied it for a minute and then handed it to me.

I looked at the card for a moment. "I've seen this before, somewhere."

"How?" Sennett asked.

I handed the card back to him and thought for a moment and then asked to see it again. For some reason, I remembered Joey's soccer game. That's when it hit me. "His name is Jeff Taylor. I saved his life."

Chapter 34

FREDDIE JACKSON LET US HAVE THE CARD. He said he didn't care what we did with it. I gave Sennett the address, and we made our way to the northern suburbs of Detroit. It took us forty-five minutes in traffic to wend our way to the high-rise offices of Troy. It was clear to both of us that, with Crandall's death, Jeff Taylor was our only link to him and the insurance he was trying to sell Freddie Jackson.

While Sennett drove, I told him about Taylor's episode of choking and how I performed the Heimlich maneuver on him. He said it must be a great feeling to have that kind of power to help someone.

"It's not about power; it's about training. Being a doctor is not about voodoo magic. Just like being a cop is not about being James Bond."

"Right, if I was James Bond, I would be in prison for the rest of my life for violating basic law. But lucky for Bond, he doesn't get scrutinized by the public for every move he makes."

"You're right on that one. Maybe there's a James Bond of medicine. If so, he could tell the malpractice attorneys to go to hell."

Once we reached the Chrysler Freeway, I called Taylor's office and spoke to his secretary. I gave her my name and asked if I could see him that afternoon. She came back in a couple of minutes and told me her boss would be glad to see me whenever I got to his office.

Fifteen minutes later, we turned onto the boulevard at the Troy exit and made our way east past several twenty-story office buildings. A half-mile from the expressway exit we pulled into the parking lot of a shining glass edifice that looked a little like a giant sailboat. I could see why people liked working in the suburbs. Easy in and out, no expensive parking decks, and, whether it was real or not, a feeling of safety.

We walked through a two-story hexagonal lobby with black granite floors and large, hanging LED light fixtures. Taylor's office was on the opposite side from the entrance. We entered his office through two large glass doors into a foyer with expensive quarter sawn oak floors, a large aquarium, and high ceilings that gave the place an air of spaciousness. The receptionist was a young, handsome Asian woman, probably in her mid-twenties, with short box braids, deep red lipstick, and heavy mascara.

Sennett and I took a seat on a brown, modern leather sofa with a metal armrest. On the glass table in front of it lay copies of *Barron's* and *The Wall Street Journal*. Sennett looked through the pile of magazines and newspapers for something to read.

"I doubt you are going to find *Sports Illustrated* or *The Police Gazette* here," I remarked.

Sennett shot me a quick glance. "I was thinking of something more liberal, like *The New York Times*."

"I don't think you will find that here either."

He was about to say something else, when a tall man with long hair and a perpetual suntan walked up and extended his hand. "Dr. Dailey," he said with a smile. "How nice of you to stop by. To what do I have the pleasure of seeing you?"

I shook his hand and then introduced him to Sennett. When I told him George was a lieutenant in the Detroit Police Homicide Department, his smile quickly disappeared, replaced by a curious, scrutinizing gaze. He stiffened slightly as he asked us to step into his office.

Once inside we walked down a paneled hallway past a large conference room. His nameplate was at the end of the hall. From there we entered a man cave office. His desk sat in front of a large glass window that looked out on a landscaped area, sheltered by several maple trees and evergreens. A stocked bar was on either side of a large flat screen TV situated in front of five or six large padded leather chairs. As he motioned for us to sit down, I wondered how many cows they had to kill to furnish this office.

"Can I offer you gentlemen a drink?"

Sennett shook his head. Taylor smiled and offered him a rain check when he was off duty. That seemed to break the ice.

"What can I do for you, doctor?"

"Call me Ben. I remember you said to contact you if I needed anything."

"I think you earned that."

I thanked him and explained how I occasionally worked with the Detroit Police. He looked at me a little funny, not fully comprehending what that meant. That's when Sennett stepped in.

He explained that the Detroit Police Department was investigating the death of a young woman and a police officer. It appeared their deaths might be connected to certain life insurance policies. In the process of following up on information, someone gave us his card as a possible lead.

"How would I be involved?"

"I'm not sure that you are." Sennett replied. He stopped for a moment and then asked, "Do you know a man named Mark Crandall?"

His voice had no hesitancy. "Sure, I know Mark. He has a Beechcraft twin engine a hangar next to my plane. He works for Sturgis and Martin. We consult with them."

Sennett asked him what kind of consultation. He said his company initiated annuity investments, retirement plans, and life insurance stock derivatives. I knew what the first two were, but I had never heard of a life insurance derivative. Neither had Sennett, so he asked him what it was.

Taylor sat behind his desk with his hands in front of him and his fingers forming a steeple. "An life insurance derivative allows a person to buy a policy and then sell it to a fund. The policyholder gets a portion of the value and the fund receives the rest of the proceeds at the time of death. It's called a viatical."

Sennett appeared skeptical, but Taylor assured him it was all perfectly legal. It even traded on stock exchanges. He said Crandall came to him a couple of years ago with a client who wanted to set up a life insurance derivative fund. He didn't know who owned it, but the fund was sold on the Toronto exchange. While he talked, he opened his computer and tapped in a few instructions.

"I've got it. It's called Toussaint Investments. After I made the contact I had nothing more to do with it. Our company facilitates investments, but, in view of the volatility of some products like this, we avoid selling them. If you're going to get out on a limb, it's caveat emptor."

"Any idea how someone got your card?"

"Occasionally we get someone who calls us. I don't know how they get our name, but we tell them we don't deal with individuals. Our company only acts as a facilitator between the stock exchange funds and the investment companies. If they call us directly they get referred to Touissant or other investment companies that deal with that product."

Sennett asked if someone from an investment fund would approach the individual. Taylor shook his head as he searched the screen. Reading the report, he blinked a couple of times. "It looks like things weren't that good. Toussaint recently went out of business."

"Do we know the names of the principals?" Sennett asked.

"Yeah, James MacAllister and Thomas Rhoades. They're in Toronto."

Sennett then asked him if he remembered the investment consultants from the Detroit area that dealt with viaticals. He said that Crandall was the most active and acted as his own broker.

When he finished, I asked Taylor to explain once more how the mechanics of the fund worked. Taylor said that the "investor" would buy the policy for a sum paid to a policyholder and continue to pay the premiums, collecting the value at the time of death. When Sennett told him it was hard to believe, Taylor went back to his computer and printed up a reference article in *The New York Times* from August 2012 by James Vlahos and handed it to me. Taylor said it was grisly but true. I pocketed the article in my jacket.

"No one sells a life insurance policy to an individual with a terminal disease. Isn't that right?" I asked.

"For sure," Taylor replied. "That's why the investor looks for individuals with pre-existing life insurance policies and life-threatening problems. When he finds them, he tries to buy them as a derivative. This product was big when the HIV epidemic started. Sometimes, if you had the right mix, it was a good investment. I know this sounds callous, but the problem for the investor was the development of medication to eliminate the disease. So when cures for HIV were developed, viaticals fell out of favor."

Betting on a dying man. I told Taylor it sounded pretty gruesome. He nodded, but said that for some people, getting that money before they died was important. Besides it was totally legal, so the only crime they might be committing could be construed as avarice. I told him I agreed, but it was still macabre.

Taylor agreed that in general the life insurance business was somewhat depressing, but it wasn't usually complex. First of all, only registered agents sold life insurance. The client filled out basic information, height, weight, and personal habits, like smoking and alcohol consumption. Then they got into health issues. Obviously, the company wanted to know the risk of selling someone a policy.

He went on to describe the various medical investigations. In most cases this was an in-person medical exam that was arranged with a health care professional. During the exam they would take a history, check vital signs, like blood pressure, and get a blood sample and urine specimen. If needed, the underwriter might ask for additional tests, like EKGs, stress tests, and pulmonary function tests. Sometimes they would order more records from a doctor.

"What if I lied about my health?" I asked.

"Bad idea. It's actually a felony," Taylor continued. "If they find out, the claim is denied, the money you're supposed to get never sees the light of day, and you might go to prison."

He had just finished describing the investment when Sennett's phone rang. It was Knudsen. The Lieutenant listened for a moment and then clicked off. He turned back to Taylor.

"What kind of a guy was Crandall?" I asked.

"He was nice enough, a little bit of a hustler, but always straight up. Why do you ask?"

"He was murdered a few days ago." I replied.

Taylor's face immediately went pale and moisture began to bead on his forehead. Sennett asked him if he was okay.

Taylor nodded. "It kind of shakes you up when you know the person. You know what I mean?"

"Yeah, I know what you mean. It's part of my job, but I never get used to it."

Sennett asked a few more questions, mainly about where he got his clients. Taylor said it was usually through word of mouth. Then Sennett asked him if he knew about The Full Coverage fund.

"Never heard of it."

"How about Herbert Knowlton?"

Taylor nodded. He remembered meeting him once at a golf outing a couple of years ago, only because in the foursome ahead of him were a couple of politicos. One of them was the mayor's chief of staff, Tommy Holiday.

Sennett's phone buzzed, and he looked at a text. When he finished, he appeared distracted. "I just had a message from my office. Something came up, and I have to leave."

When we got up, I shook Taylor's hand. "Thanks. I appreciate your help."

"It's the least I can do for a guy that saved my life."

Taylor walked us to the entrance and said to call if we needed more help. We walked out of the building and stood in the late morning autumn sun. The heat felt good in contrast to the crisp, cool air from last night's frost.

"What do you think of Taylor's response to finding out that Crandall had been murdered?" Sennett asked.

"It seemed to be a little too visceral for a casual business acquaintance. How about Tommy Holiday? What do you make of that?"

"Hard to figure." He bent over and pulled out his keys from his pocket. As he did, he saw something on the ground and picked it up. It was new penny.

"My lucky day." He held the shiny coin in front of him and then pocketed it.

AS SOON AS WE GOT IN THE CAR Sennett was on the phone to Knudsen and asked him to look up Toussaint Investments and McAllister and Rhoades. His next call was to Brian MacGregor in Windsor. He wanted as much detail from the Canadian government as he could get on Toussaint Investments in Toronto. By the time we returned to his office, Knudsen had a stack of papers on his desk.

"Your guy must have known somebody," Knudsen said. "Thirty minutes ago, all those papers came through."

Sennett sat down and started going through them. When he finished, he handed them over to me. "Just corporate filing papers with the Canadian government. Nothing that I saw that would give us a lead. Why don't you look through them and see if I missed something?"

I picked up the stack of papers and leafed through them, unsure what I was looking for. Scanning them rapidly, I got three quarters of the way through, then I suddenly stopped. On the bottom of page sixty-four was a handwritten signature. I stared at it for minute, trying to make sense of what I had just seen. Sennett must have noticed.

"What is it?"

"There's a name in the corporate structure you should look at."

"What's the name?"

"Herbert Knowlton."

Sennett stared at Knowlton's name and then picked up the spreadsheets. After a couple of minutes he put them back on Knudsen's desk. No sooner did he put them down, he asked to look at the crime scene material from Knowlton's house.

We spent over an hour going over records from Knowlton's house, fingerprints, checkbooks, computer data, even his address book. Finally, Knudsen showed us photos of Knowlton with a variety of people, even a photo of Knowlton in front of a building next to a railway siding. I immediately remembered the photo from his house. When I showed it to Sennett, he didn't know what to make of it.

We were about to close the file when Knudsen came over with a piece of paper. It was a property tax bill for Knowlton Auto Parts, paid six months ago. Sennett said he thought the family business had folded.

I asked him to go back to the file and enlarge the photo of Knowlton near the railroad tracks. This time I studied it closer and checked the number on the building. It read 13675 and matched the street number on the tax bill, 13675 Tireman Avenue.

"Why would Knowlton still have an auto parts store?" I asked.

"Good question. We need to take a look."

Sennett wasn't in a mood to hang around. He told Knudsen to get a search warrant for Knowlton Auto Parts. While we waited, Sennett said he needed something to eat. I followed him downstairs to a small eating area with vending machines. He bought two sandwiches and two cans of Coke and handed me a Styrofoam plate. We took a couple of minutes to inhale a chicken sandwich and wash it down with soda.

"You know, George, it's bad for your digestion to eat so fast."

He glanced up at me. "Doc, I do a lot of bad things. That should be the worst of my problems."

I acknowledged his comment, but pointed out that a peaceful stomach was the precursor to a peaceful mind.

"Who said that?" he asked.

"Gastromicus, an old Greek philosopher."

"You got to be kidding."

When I told him not everything the doctor tells you is the truth, he began laughing. It was the first time I'd seen him crack a smile all day.

We threw away the cans, wrappers and Styrofoam plates and made our way back to his office. By the time we got there, Knudsen had the warrant. Sennett pocketed it and then checked his revolver. That shook me up enough to check my own.

We were about to walk out of the office when Knudsen spoke to the lieutenant for a couple of minutes. When the sergeant left, Sennett turned to me. "Knudsen told me he talked with McAllister and Rhoades. Both are lawyers and they were both partners in Toussaint Investments. When Knudsen asked him some questions, they told him to fuck off."

"Are you surprised?" I asked.

"Not really, but there was one other thing that Knudsen told me. Apparently, Knudsen's mother came from Montreal and he speaks a little French. He asked me if I knew what Toussaint meant. When I told him I had no idea, he said that in French, Toussaint means All Saints Day. It's the day they honor those who have passed away. Then he added that in Mexico it's called the Day of the Dead. He started laughing about how that was some name for an investment company." Neither Sennett nor I were in a laughing mood.

BY THE TIME WE HAD LEFT SENNETT'S OFFICE, dusk began to darken the western sky. Soon a chill insinuated itself in the air and a light mist began falling. Sennett got behind the wheel and turned on the wipers. They beat out an erratic rhythm on the glass, squeaking as they went back and forth.

"Time for new blades, don't you think?" I asked, trying to break the silence.

"Probably, but I like the beat. Almost like the drums of an army going into battle."

As he turned off the expressway and onto Schaefer Road, I told him I wasn't a touchy-feely guy, but I had a terrible feeling of evil around me. "Somebody is looking at us, knows what we were looking for, and knows how to kill anyone in their way to prevent us from finding out. This evil is personal."

It took him a short while to respond. "It's probably the spreadsheet; true or false, someone thinks you know something."

We exited past Plymouth Road and drove south to Tireman. It was an old, dirty part of town. In its best years it was an industrial area interspersed with low-income housing. Now it was one of those lost neighborhoods in the city.

We drove past dirty, squat cinder brick buildings housing a mélange of low income businesses, scrap yards, and deserted retail stores. A red neon sign flickered on the party store on the corner of Schaefer and Tireman. Two of the streetlights on the corner were out and the third gave just enough illumination to see the beer and wine sign on the front window.

In the distance I could hear the shrill whine of a fire truck. The sound seemed to be coming at us, and when we turned the corner, I could see why. A dull haze of smoke filled the air. The street was closed and spotlights illuminated the carcass of a burnt-out building. I looked up at the circular sign on the front. 13675 was the address. Above the number was a broken clock. It read three twenty. I wondered if that was the time of day when the city died.

We parked as near as we could to the blaze and watched as the fire engines rolled up to the front of the building. The efficiency of the fire fighters mesmerized me. Within five minutes they had hoses hooked up to the fire hydrant and were pouring water on the building. The structure had something to do with lumber, because the smell of burning wood filled the air.

Looking at the smoke and debris, the whole scene appeared like a hopeless mess. Any treasure inside the inferno was in ashes, with no hope of saving the structure and or its contents. Methodically, the firemen controlled the inferno. The blaze was over but the building was in ruins.

After we spent about fifteen minutes watching, a fireman came over and demanded us to leave the site. Sennett showed him his badge and asked to see his captain. The fireman pointed to a large man leaning up against a hook and ladder truck.

We got out of the car and walked toward him, as the fumes and smell of charcoal increased. About ten feet from the truck, the captain looked up through the haze. He snorted in irritation.

"If you two guys, are from the media, I ain't got time to talk." He turned and looked down at some papers on a clipboard in front of him.

"C'mon, Red, you haven't got time for your boy?" Sennett asked.

The captain looked up again and a smile creased his face. "Dammit, George, don't you ever announce yourself?"

They jabbed jokingly at each other for a couple of shared moments about a fire in the Indian Village neighborhood. Apparently, Sennett had been holding a hose when it threw him on the ground. They both laughed about it. When Sennett introduced me, the conversation got serious as he discussed the murder investigation and why we were there. Just as he finished, a fireman came up to Red, hauling a rectangular metal object on a small dolly.

"We found this in the rubble, Captain. Thought you might want to take it with you." It was a safe.

Sennett stared at it as if he had found the Crown Jewels. "Red, this could be important. Have you got some way to open it?"

He told Sennett that they had all kinds of gear to open things and sent his fireman to retrieve a special drill.

"Don't be surprised if everything in that safe is reduced to ashes. Very few things can survive that kind of heat."

The fireman returned with a huge drill and told us to step back. He hooked it up to an electric line strung from a pole and began bouncing it off the lock. After ten minutes he drilled through. When he pulled open the door, we peeked inside with a flashlight and saw several folders. As Red mentioned, most of them seemed withered from the heat. We bent down to examine them and found that one in the middle was, miraculously, still intact.

Sennett reached in and pulled it out. The pages had turned brown, but the writing was legible.

"Mind if I take this with me?"

"As long as you sign for it. City law for all fires requires it, police or not. This might have been arson, so we keep everything we find like this."

Sennett nodded and signed the paper on Red's clipboard. Then he pulled out his cellphone and tried to turn it on. "Shit, the battery is dead. Ben, let me have your phone for a second."

I reached in my pocket and gave it to him. He took it and the folder and went on the other side of the fire truck. "Wait here. I'll be right back." I wondered what he was doing, but you never knew about Sennett.

While I waited for him, the acrid fumes of the smoldering building continued to irritate my eyes. As I rubbed them, I asked Red if he ever got used to these fires. He said, "Not really. It's a job constantly filled with potential danger, often without a hint where it's coming from."

It sounded a lot like being a doctor.

He was about to say something else, but Sennett came from the other side of the truck and handed my cell back. "Let's get this downtown where we can look it over," he said, as he tucked the folder under his arm. When Red told him to be careful, he nodded; and we began to head back to the car only a block away.

CHAPTER 35

As we were walking, I noted that it was now considerably darker—a combination of the smoke from the fire and a dearth of streetlights in a city with too many problems to fix. We had just turned the corner when I felt a shove from behind that knocked me to the ground. The next thing I heard was a loud grunt. I looked over at Sennett. He was bent over on the sidewalk.

At first I thought he was stabbed or shot. Then I heard a loud wheeze. He looked as if he was reaching for his service revolver. Panic surged over me, just as it had when Snake was killed. This time I reached in my coat for my gun. I grasped it and wriggled it out. My hand was shaking.

"Forget it," Sennett shouted. I wondered why he wasn't in action, chasing after whoever attacked him.

He scrambled to his feet and dusted his pants and jacket. Then he staggered for a moment and pulled himself upright. I noticed that the folder was no longer in his hand. "Where's the paper?" I asked. "Are you okay?" If I didn't know better, I would have thought he had a few brews. He tried to reply, but suddenly he collapsed on the sidewalk.

I bent over him and checked his pulse. There was none. I turned my head in both directions, looking for help. There was no one. It was a helpless, terrifying feeling, alone on this desolate street with Sennett dying. My mind raced. Why had his heart had stopped? Forget the reason, I quickly decided. It didn't matter. I wasn't a cardiologist, but I knew CPR. There was only one choice.

I ripped open his jacket and placed my hands over the left third intercostal space. Once there, I started pushing on his chest. The rules of CPR had changed. Don't worry about the airway; just compress the chest. As I did, I yelled for help, not expecting anyone in this deserted neighborhood to see or hear anything.

In the dark, I couldn't tell if what I was doing was helping. I managed to pull out my cellphone between chest compressions to turn on the flashlight. I shone it down on his face; that's when I saw a trickle of blood on the side of his cheek. When I pressed on his wrist, I still couldn't feel his pulse.

"Godammit, George, start beating," I yelled at the top of my lungs. Then I started to push on his chest again.

The muscles in my neck and shoulders tightened and sweat ran down my face, stinging my eyes. The words "Day of the Dead" crept into my mind, and I brushed them away. Alone on a dark, misty street with no help in sight, I fought off panic and kept on compressing his chest. But I knew that this couldn't continue: I had to get help. My cellphone was my only hope. I had to take a chance.

I stopped for a moment, turned on the speakerphone of my cell, and dialed 911. Once connected, I restarted pumping on his chest. Within in seconds the operator came on the line. "Quick! Officer down! Send Help!" Gasping for air from my efforts, I told her in broken phrases the problem I was facing and where I was.

I left the phone on as the operator made the call. She told me to stay connected and encouraged me to keep doing chest compressions. It took another minute or two, but at last I heard the siren. It must have been from the EMS unit at the fire. As they approached, I felt his pulse again. It was now present but faint.

As soon as they arrived, the EMS guys took over, hooking up an EKG lead and giving him oxygen by mask. They started an IV and looked at the EKG strip. When I saw a shallow rhythm starting across the screen, I put my hand over my face, totally exhausted, and slumped forward with relief.

"You got him back," the one tech said. "What happened?"

I raised my head and said I wasn't sure. "He just keeled over." At that moment the other tech looked down at Sennett's chest, bare in the glaring light of his flashlight.

"Unless this bruise is from your chest compression, it looks like he was hit hard by something. My guess is that it suddenly stopped his heart. Good thing you were around. His strip is normal now. We have to get him to the hospital."

One of the EMTs called into City Hospital's emergency department and gave them the information. As soon as he did, his partner ran back to the EMS truck to get a stretcher.

When he got back from the van, he pulled the stretcher next to Sennett. With his gloved hand he put a curved object on the stretcher and shone his flashlight in it. "Take a look at this." It was a tire iron. "This is what must have hit his chest," the fireman said.

"What about the blood on his face?" I asked.

"He probably hit it on the sidewalk. If he was hit hard on the noggin with something like this, we wouldn't be resuscitating him."

By this time Sennett had struggled back to consciousness. His head moved from side to side, but he was silent. It didn't take the EMTs long to get him on the stretcher and into the truck. I retrieved the keys from his pocket, got into the squad car, and followed the EMS van to City Hospital. Although my hands were still shaking from exhaustion, somehow I still managed to drive. Just not very fast.

By the time I reached the emergency department, Sennett was already in the trauma room surrounded by six doctors. I walked in and peeked over their shoulders. He was moving all four extremities, but was still silent.

One of the nurses came over and asked me who I was. I wasn't about to start the whole process of sticking my nose into the medical practice of the hospital again, so I told her that Sennett was my friend, and I was a doctor. It didn't make a difference. She was about to shoo me out when one of the EMS techs saw me.

"Liz," he said, "the guy's legit. He saved the cop's life."

Liz moved aside and I looked at Sennett lying on his back on the stretcher. He was breathing on his own and the cardiac monitor showed a regular heartbeat. I had nothing to do now, except to call Knudsen and tell what happened. When I finished, I told him to notify me of any changes in Sennett's condition.

My legs were wobbly as I trudged out of the emergency department to Sennett's car, but the physical strain was nothing compared to my emotions, realizing how close Sennett had come to dying. I bowed my head in thanks that my friend would live.

I drove Sennett's squad car back to headquarters and explained to the policemen on duty what had happened. He didn't believe me until I showed him my badge. Everyone knew Sennett. He was indestructible. The fact that he was lying on a stretcher at City Hospital really shook the cops up.

"Is he going to be all right?" one of them asked.

"I think so," I said hopefully. With that I went out to the parking garage, climbed into my car, and headed home. On the way back I suddenly remembered the folder that Sennett had carried. Someone knew it was important—important enough to try and kill Sennett.

It was late when I pulled up to the house. When I got inside, Jordan was waiting for me.

"You look awful," she said, ever the truth teller.

"I guess I'd have to admit to that." I went on to explain the night's activity, and when I got to the part about the folder, she looked anxious.

"What was in it?"

"I don't know and probably never will. Sennett had the folder in his hand as he walked back to the car. That's when he got hit on the chest."

Her eyes narrowed and her face was creased with fear, almost afraid to hear the truth. "No, don't tell me. Is George all right?" she cried out.

I went on to tell her about the CPR and the hospital, and explained to her that he was recovering. As soon as I said it, the tightness in her face relaxed and the prosecutor took over. "So any meaningful evidence in that safe is gone. Where do you go from here?"

When an officer of the court asks me what to do, I know this there's a problem. I just shook my head and shrugged. What else could I do?

"Joey is asleep, but I still have dinner ready. Let's sit down and eat."

I washed up and then walked into the kitchen, putting my cell phone on the counter and slumping into the chair at the table. I was sick of being a detective. I wanted my life back.

Jordan made us both a turkey sandwich, put it on the table, and then poured me a glass of cabernet and then one for herself. I took a bite out of the sandwich and a couple of swallows of the wine. As soon as I began to get my thoughts together, I told her everything that happened. No sooner than I began, I heard my cell phone buzz. I wondered if it was from the hospital.

When I picked it up, I saw a text message waiting from my cellphone provider, telling me how much data I had used for the month. It was annoying, but I had to shut it off. When I opened the phone, the camera came on.

That was strange, because I didn't take any photos recently. Out of curiosity I looked down at the little square at the bottom that showed the last picture. It appeared to be a piece of paper. I clicked on it and up came a photo of a yellow sheet of paper with some numbers and letters on it. It was similar to the paper Sennett had in his folder. Then I remembered that he was the last one to use the phone.

"What are you doing?" Jordan asked.

I explained the screen on the cell. "Any chance you could look at this?"

"Sure, just send it as an e-mail, and I'll download it."

The process was painfully slow for me, but after a few minutes of fussing, I managed to send the photo. Jordan, sitting at her computer, took it off her mail. The next thing I knew a sheet of paper came off the printer.

I picked the document up and studied it carefully. It didn't make any sense, only ten lines of numbers in a column. Each column had eight numbers. Next to them were capital letters.

77974411	TD
7788560	JS
77540306	AVE
77184908	CR
77409377	JC
77654380	CF
77476544	HS
77465251	TH

"George took a photo of the original piece of paper. I should have known he wouldn't take any chances. He knew something important was in that folder."

"They must be in a group, because they each start with seventy-seven," she said. "Other than that, it doesn't make any sense. Could those letters be initials?"

"I don't know. They could be anything," I said quietly, feeling the exhaustion of my night's efforts.

Jordan sat with me as we silently finished the food and wine, both of us consumed with our thoughts. Mine were focused on what happened that evening and how near my friend had come to death. Then I realized how close I had come to the same end. Why hadn't the assailant come after me? How did he know Sennett had the folder?

Jordan broke the silence. "You know, Ben, maybe we should go up to Canada for a few days. Get away from all of this."

She was right, but this was not the time for a getaway. Something told me this mysterious adventure was going to get even crazier.

CHAPTER 36

I WALKED INTO SENNETT'S ROOM EARLY THE NEXT MORNING. He was sitting up in his bed, and his face looked like an angry storm-cloud. "What the hell did you do to my chest? It feels like I've been gang tackled without pads."

"You know, George, they say you don't do a good CPR unless you bruise a couple of ribs."

"I'm glad you did a good job," he said ruefully, "but I thought I just had the wind knocked out of me."

"Not hardly," I said.

Then he smiled. "Just be glad I didn't have to do it to you. Paybacks are hell. By the way, thank you."

I smiled and then told him I had spoken to his doctors. They said his heart was fine, but he'd taken a sudden hit to the chest that jolted his heart's internal pacemaker node. They told him they were going to keep him in observation for the day. If everything worked out, he'd be out of the hospital in the morning. I could sense he was chomping at the bit. Pretty soon he was asking me about the photos on my phone.

"You are the master of detail. Why didn't you tell me?"

"It's just a process. If you don't know anything, you can't tell anything," he said. "Did you print them up?"

"Yeah, but when I studied them, I realized they're the same kind of numbers that were in the spreadsheet that Carina Knowlton had given me. The only difference was there were letters with each of the numbers."

I told Sennett that Herbert Knowlton was doing business with Touissant Investments and Toussaint Investments was dealing with life insurance derivatives. Somehow those numbers had something in common.

"We need to get MacGregor on this. I'm going to call Knudsen to contact him right now." He looked around his room for a moment. "I've got to get out of this joint. It's for sick people."

"You just had CPR for God's sake. Let me do this."

"You said I have nothing wrong with my heart. Why should I stay?"

Ten minutes later his cardiologist walked in. He was a portly man in his late thirties with ruddy unshaven cheeks, an open collar shirt with his tie askew, and a stethoscope wrapped around his neck; he'd clearly been on all night call. It was certainly not a poster boy look for his profession.

He introduced himself, then laid his stethoscope on Sennett's chest, narrowing his eyes as he listened. When he was done, he picked up the vital signs sheet and studied it. Again, another frown.

"Looks like your heart is fine. You're pretty lucky. We call what you had commotio cordis, Lieutenant. It comes from a sudden blow to the chest. The condition is pretty rare; you're my second case."

Sennett looked worried. "I'm glad I'm contributing to your education. By the way, what happened to your other case?"

"You don't want to know. Thankfully you're in good shape. There is no permanent damage. As I understand how this happened, it's lucky you have a doctor as a friend."

"You bet; I just didn't know how good a friend."

As soon as he finished speaking, Sennett got up to leave. The doc knew he was a homicide detective in a stressful business and told him so, but Sennett didn't bite. He said his job was mostly routine stuff.

The doctor recommended another day of observation, but Sennett was having none of that. He asked the cardiologist who made the rules. The cardiologist told him that overnight observation was the standard of care. If he wanted to leave, Sennett would have sign a form.

"So if I want to leave, I'd probably be okay, right?" Sennett asked.

"Probably," he said matter-of-factly, "but I don't want to be responsible for anything that happens."

"What if I take you off the hook and sign the paper?"

"That's your choice. But if I do let you go, I would want you to take it easy."

"Take it easy? You bet I will," Sennett responded.

Sennett could sell air conditioners to Eskimos. But that was the way he was, and I wasn't man enough to challenge him. He was over twenty-one.

Immediately on the words "let you go" the lieutenant slung his feet over the side of the bed. The nurse came in, took out his IV, and got his clothes out of the closet.

I tried to help him, but he shrugged me off, so I went outside and waited. After ten minutes I went back into the room to see what the problem was. He was standing next to his bed shirtless with his pants and socks on, looking for something. Gazing at his six pack and massive biceps, I could see why he was one of the most feared cops on the force. However, when he asked where his shoes were, he seemed helpless and aggravated. "At home?" he ventured.

"On the bed in front of you. Are you sure you're okay?"

"Yeah, just so damn irritated being here. I gotta get out."

"Relax. Just think, it could be Allan Davis looking for your shoes."

He laughed as I handed them to him and slid them on. "I guess you're right."

Once he was dressed, we walked to the elevator, but instead of pushing the down button, he decided to go up.

"Where are we going?" I asked.

"To check on Carina Knowlton."

Carina had been in the ICU above us. I called on her several times, mostly talking with nurses. Although she had contracted a lung infection, she was getting better.

Fortunately Carina was young. Most people who get her type of lung infection are elderly and debilitated. After we last saw her she worsened, and her doctors were talking about a tracheotomy. But after a few days of intubation she seemed to rally. Eventually they took her tube out and were ready to send her back to the general medicine floor. It was only Sennett's intervention that kept her in the ICU. It was the most secure place in the hospital, especially with a twenty-four hour cop next to her.

Sennett talked to the policeman and then went into her room. It was a glass cubicle filled with every kind of monitoring device available. As we walked in, I heard the beeping of her heart monitor, the IV sensor, and her pulse oximeter beating out a rhythm that sounded like an Afro-Cuban band. I looked to my left and saw Carina sitting on a chair next to her bed, her hair pulled back in a ponytail and her face free of the thick makeup that went with her job. She looked younger, fresher, more like a college student than a hooker.

Sennett pulled up a chair and sat next to her. He asked her how she was feeling. Her wan smile spoke volumes—glad to be alive but still scared.

"Carina, I want to ask you a few questions, mostly about those numbers you gave to the doc. Did Cal tell you anything about them?"

She said she told me before, she didn't know. Sennett explained that he was looking for a connection to someone else and wanted to know if Calboy ever met anyone when they went to the bar together. She appeared wary of saying anything, finally replying it was usually a bunch of rich guys.

Sennett frowned. "Look, Carina, I can understand you might be afraid, but it's not going to get any better if you don't tell us everything you know. I can't keep a guard on you twenty four-seven for the rest of your life."

She remained silent for a few moments and then blinked her eyes. "It was the mayor's guy. I can't remember his name, but for some reason I associated him with a television program I watched about Wyatt Earp."

Sennett looked puzzled, so, remembering our meeting at the Pipeline, I piped up. "That would be Holiday as in Doc Holiday."

At the sound of the name she nodded. Sennett asked Carina if he had ever threatened her in any way. She said she met him once with Cal at a bar. He talked to Cal about some papers and acted like an arrogant jerk, cursing Cal and getting in his face. "After he left, Cal never talked about the papers, but he did say that Holiday was a bad guy and I should stay away from him. I never asked him anything else."

Sennett didn't have much else to say. He told Carina that she was under protection until this thing came to a conclusion, but she must remain in the hospital. It was her only chance of being in a controlled situation.

Carina nodded grudgingly, and we left. When we got outside the hospital, Sennett stopped and looked around. Across the street, the skeleton of the sprawling medical complex was nearing completion. In the autumn sunlight, it cast a shadow over City Hospital and the downtown.

Sennett seemed engrossed in his thoughts, so instead of talking, I gave him a copy of the paper he photographed on my cellphone. He studied the columns of numbers and letters for a couple of minutes and then put it in his pocket.

"You know, Doc," he said, "there's got to be something on that list that leads to Sandra Wells. It is the one commonality. This paper is the clue. Herbert Knowlton owned an investment company. Toussaint sells life insurance derivatives. Mark Crandall sells life insurance, knows Knowlton, and deals with Touissant. He also knows Patsy Evans. We need to know what Knowlton invested in and who his customers were."

He was right, but getting an answer was going to be hard. All the contacts were either dead or missing.

"Let me ask you a question, George. Why all of a sudden are all these people being killed? It doesn't make sense."

Sennett thought for a moment and then replied, "If I didn't know better it seems like someone is going out of a business and doesn't want leave any of its employees alive."

CHAPTER 37

W E WERE IN SENNETT'S OFFICE when Knudsen came in and explained
that, while Herbert Knowlton's Full Coverage Fund closed six months
ago, the tax records appeared to be correct and the corporate filings were proper. Sennett didn't say anything, so after a few moments of standing silently in
front of his boss, Knudsen left.

"What do you think this all means, Doc?" Sennett asked.

"Herbert Knowlton was selling investments in viaticals. What we don't
know is who got the money. The only thing we have is his name scribbled on
the bottom of a page for a company in Toronto that sells life insurance derivatives and the paper from the safe."

"What do you make of that paper we found in the safe?"

"I'm putting myself in Knowlton's shoes. Let's assume that Knowlton isn't
on the up and up. If I'm him and doing something illegal, I would want to protect myself. In case of trouble, I would need a piece of paper with something on
it that would implicate someone else and keep me from getting hung out to dry.
I could use that paper as protection."

Knudsen walked in the room with some more papers. This time Sennett
told him to leave them on his desk and close the door. I'd known Sennett for
a long time. He always got irritated when he was frustrated, especially when
a company like Toussaint that had the answers was out of business. At that
point I suggested that businesses may die, but there's always a paper trail, maybe in the Toussaint records. That's when he picked up the phone and called
MacGregor again.

Sennett got him on speakerphone and explained that he wanted him to
crosscheck the numbers on the sheet from Knowlton's safe and see if it matched

anything on Toussaint's records. The Inspector said it wouldn't be easy because of the extensive list of numbers in the Toussaint files, but he'd get a crew right on it. When Sennett hung up the phone, he had Knudsen send him a copy of the numbers from the safe.

Waiting in a chair for the answer wasn't in the cards. As I've said, Sennett hated waiting for anything. I knew his cure for impatience was food; so when he suggested we get something to eat, I wasn't surprised. What did surprise me was where he wanted to go—a yogurt shop.

"Let me ask you, George, are you okay?"

Yeah, why? The doc says my heart is fine."

"Then why are you suddenly going healthy on me?"

"You should understand the benefits of low fat yogurt. The healthiest people in the world are the Armenians. They live to be over a hundred. You know what scientists feel is the reason?" He didn't wait for my answer. "Yogurt, that's what."

"How about genetics, doesn't that have something to do with a long life?"

He didn't answer. Like an evangelist, he led me into the shop down the corner from the police headquarters. From my perspective it was a bad location. If you wanted to do good business around a police station, you opened up a donut shop. Boy, was I wrong. When we turned the corner, the place was full of cops.

As we walked in the door, Sennett said it was a whole new world out there. It didn't take me long to find out the reason why George had changed his eating habits. Behind the counter was an attractive African American woman, probably in her late twenties.

"Hi Georgie," she said, smiling.

Sennett responded with his own grin that wasn't the look of a casual friendship. "Hey, Alicia. Meet my friend, the doc, here. Ben, this is Alicia. She owns this shop. Best yogurt in town."

Alicia stuck out her hand and flashed me an electric smile. For a guy that liked high cholesterol and sugary food, this was a sea change. I could see why.

I asked her what to order. She said the pistachio was selling well. I filled my cup, and George did the same. After we found a table by the window Alicia came over to talk with us.

"George told me about you. The Police Surgeon is what he said. He called you one of a kind. Coming from him, that's a pretty high compliment."

"I wish it were true. The lieutenant and I have been through a lot together."

We chatted for a few minutes. While I never saw George with a woman before, this looked special. She knew a lot about him. My tip was when she started talking about George's eating habits. Just when the conversation was getting interesting—preferences in malt beverages—his cell went off. He listened for a minute, and the smile dropped off his face.

"Gotta leave, Doc. MacGregor called." Alicia looked down and sighed when we got up. "Don't worry, Alicia. You know we'll be back."

As we walked to his office, I asked him what the "Georgie" was all about. He kind of smiled and then shook his head. George was a close-to-the-vest guy when it came to his personal life. I knew letting me meet her was a big step for him. But right now he didn't have time for distractions.

When we got back to the office, Knudsen got MacGregor on the line and they talked for a while. The inspector had received the numbers. Every now and then Sennett would nod and write something on a piece of paper. When he was finished, he hung up the phone with a perplexed look.

"The list at Touissant Investments had hundreds of names on it. That's the bad news. The good news is that each of the numbers on the list from the safe matched up with account numbers of deceased individuals. Each account had several policies that were turned into stock derivatives."

"Do we know the names on the policies?"

Sennett nodded solemnly. "Yes, Knudsen checked. They were all on the Surveillance Center records."

"So we know the names of the deceased patients. We also know that each of them had a life insurance policy that they turned into a viatical. The only thing we don't know is the how and the why. Each of them appeared to have died from their illnesses. We saw that on the death certificate."

"An enormous number of Surveillance Center cases were in the Touissant Investments file," Sennett said. "The cases amounted to about $20 million dollars, but the total value of the whole portfolio was in the hundred of millions. It seems strange a portfolio of that size had so many cases from southeast Michigan."

Sennett and I went over the Cancer Surveillance Center list again. I sat down at the desk, placed a yellow legal pad in front of me, and started writing the names in columns again. Next to each name I wrote the diagnosis and the status of the patient's disease at the time of death. Each of the patients had a slow-growing malignancy.

After an hour of work, I put down my legal pad down and looked at the list. Then I glanced at George, sitting across the desk, dealing with some e-mails. "George, all of these people had a life insurance policy. Maybe we should look at them."

He agreed and called Knudsen to get the policies from the insurance company that issued them. It took another hour of bureaucratic haggling to get to the right person. The process of getting the information was difficult because of privacy laws, or at least that's what Knudsen told Sennett.

"Doc, the bureaucracy makes me crazy," the lieutenant said, crossing his arms in front of his chest. "On one hand it is understandable, but on the other, so many crimes could have been prevented if people could talk to one another. Just look at 911."

"You're preaching to the choir, George. I deal with HIPPA laws all the time. You can't talk to anyone today without the threat of violating their privacy. I appreciate what the law represents, but if you have an emergency or you need information from another doctor or relative that may be important, the legal ramifications can be really serious. "You don't get proper clearance."

He nodded. "It's the bullshit I hate. No one has any common sense any more."

We talked for a while longer, both of us commiserating over our legal restraints. I was about to tell him about an incident I had with a patient who almost died, when his phone rang and he answered. As he listened, he signaled to me that he was getting what he wanted.

It took another hour, but the DA came through. Sennett was able to get twenty of the life insurance policies on his computer. I opened them up and started looking through the various sections. At the time of purchase, they included a couple of individuals with high blood pressure and arthritis, but no serious pre-existing conditions.

The next thing I did was to spread out the copies of the signature pages. Next to them I put the list from Herbert Knowlton's safe. I decided to separate the letters from the numbers and write them in a column.

I could see no discernible pattern in the order of the letters, so I wrote each of the pairs of letters on a separate piece of paper. Only one had three letters. When I was done, I noticed something I had missed on first glance.

TD

JS

AVE

CR

JC

CF

HS

TH

My eyes stopped at "AVE." It looked familiar.

I knew I had seen this abbreviation before. Then it came to me. It was Arthur Van Engle's signature, that indifferent, almost illegible scrawl that had trivialized my attempt to save the life of Sandra Wells.

I called Sennett in from the other room and explained what I had found. He looked at the list for a long time, studying all the letters.

"You might be on to something," he said, looking at my list. "If "AVE" is

Arthur Van Engle, then HS could be Horace Stanford."

"What about the other names?"

"Well, "TD" could be Turner Davidson."

"That means that each of these individuals could have invested in the Full Coverage Fund through Toussaint Investments. The problem is proving it."

I didn't wait for his instructions. Instead I picked up the phone and called Jordan. "We're coming over."

CHAPTER 38

I LOOKED AT SOME OF THE LAW BOOKS behind Jordan as she reviewed the sheets of paper on her desk. Then my eyes shifted to her. She flinched her head back slightly and started tapping her fingers on the table. She always did that when she was trying to solve a difficult problem.

"Are you telling me that that this list from Herbert Knowlton's safe may have been associated with the deaths of more than twenty people?" When Sennett nodded, she said, "How is that possible?"

"This was his idea," Sennett replied, jerking his thumb in my direction. "He can explain it better."

I pulled out the article from *The New York Times* about viaticals. She studied it carefully. When she finished, I pointed out the letters from the list found in Herbert Knowlton's safe. Each of them matched up to the initials of members on the board of control for the construction of the new City Hospital.

I also told her that the numbers on Knowlton's list coincided with numbers found in the Touissant Investments. Each of these numbers represented dead patients from the Surveillance Center list. Every one of these patients had turned their existing life insurance policies into viaticals for a stock derivative fund. When the patient died, the policy was paid to the fund.

Sennett then showed her the list from Herbert Knowlton's safe, explaining the letters after the numbers. I could see her eyes open a little wider as she saw the significance. When he was done, Jordan sat down behind her desk and looked out the window at the river below, as if it could help her deal with the situation. Then she turned back to Sennett. "Whatever we discuss doesn't go beyond this room. I'm restricted from telling you confidential information because any leak could affect future investigations of corruption in Mayor

Robinson's administration. If this conversation goes beyond this room, I will deny it ever happened."

"Understood," Sennett replied.

"You are probably right. Six names on this list match with each of the people on the city's board of control for the new hospital construction—Turner Davidson, John Sanford, Arthur VanEngle, Horace Stanford, Jamieson Cartwright, Charles Fitzhugh, and Tommy Holiday. They approved the city hospital project, and it was their committee that oversaw the money earmarked for construction contracts. We vetted each of their investments and bank accounts and found no conflict of interest. We knew about Herbert Knowlton and the Full Coverage Fund. It was perfectly legal. Each of these individuals declared their investment of ten thousand dollars. We even checked out the placement of funds in Toussaint Investments. We found absolutely nothing illegal about it."

Sennett thought for a moment. "Just because their names were on Herbert Knowlton's list does not make them guilty of anything," he said. "Without direct evidence of involvement in anyone's death, conviction is impossible."

"No one knows about the relationship between Knowlton's fund and the dead policyholders," Jordan continued. "However, if a policy funded a return because of an intentional death, that's a felony." While she spoke, my eyes somehow focused on that farming law book I had noticed once before. It was strange that it caught my eye.

"What if you took it one step further and the money was used as a bribe?" I asked.

"What do you mean?" Sennett asked.

I suddenly held my hand up, waving like a student answering a question. The assimilation of what Jordan said and the sudden realization why I had noticed the book gave me the thrilling excitement of solving a complex medical question. "If you took it one step further, a person might want to bribe someone but wanted the money transfer to be legal. If a fund owned a life insurance policy on a person with a terminal disease, killing that individual was like reaping a wheat field you had planted months ago." Jordan and Sennett looked at me with disbelief.

I told them that under my theory, the policyholder sold a life insurance policy into Toussaint Investments, a stock derivative pool made up of viaticals. "The policyholder gets instant cash. At the same time, The Full Coverage Fund legally invests the money in Toussaint. Anytime a bribe needs to be made, the original policyholder is killed using a drug or technique that can't be traced and the money is disbursed as a stock dividend. When the patient reaches the funeral home, the death certificate is signed off as the end result of a chronic disease. Everyone thinks the investor made a wise investment. And by the way, if that person was on the board of control of a large governmental project, he might feel inclined to okay a contract or two."

Sennett chimed in, claiming that Knowlton's list could be a safe passage ticket. "If things got hot for Herbie, he had the list and he could threaten or blackmail anyone that was involved, including the so-called prestigious people on the list. Think that that might make them nervous?"

Jordan agreed. "If you're right, it's taking a Ponzi scheme to a new level."

"Exactly," I said. "Who would question the death of a person with a chronic, fatal disease? I suggest that no one would, including the doctor who signed the death certificate."

I wanted to prove my point so I asked for the death certificate on the guy that was buried at St. Regis. In response, Jordan rummaged through the papers on her desk until she found Reginald Stone's records. After a short while she found his death certificate. The doctor's signature read: John Everson, M.D. in Adrian, Michigan.

"Let's call his doctor and find out if he remembers the patient," I said."

"Before we do that, I need to call him, explain what this is all about, and send him a legal authorization from my office," Jordan replied.

That process took about half an hour. Jordan explained to Everson that she had some questions about one of the doctor's patients and gave him Stone's name. She knew HIPPA regulations existed, and, because of that, she faxed a letter to him from the Justice Department. Along with it was the signed death certificate bearing Everson's signature. He agreed to read the letter and call back.

Fifteen minutes letter, he called. Jordan put him on speakerphone and introduced Sennett and me. Then she apologized for all the red tape.

"No problem," he said. "I've been in practice for over forty years, and when it comes to regulations, I think I've seen them all. It's one of the reasons I'm retiring. Now what's this about Reggie Stone?"

Sennett then explained that they were interested in the death certificate he signed. Everson replied that he was surprised that Reggie died. He said that before he signed the certificate, he reviewed Stone's medical records. This patient might have had chronic lymphocytic leukemia, but he surely didn't show any outward signs of the disease.

Jordan asked if he had actually seen the patient. He replied that the funeral home called him to sign the death certificate. It was an unattended death, so no direct proof of what he died of existed. But, Everson added, he did have chronic lymphocytic leukemia. And while it was possible that Stone had a heart attack, what difference did it make? He had a terminal disease and no family contact.

"You're right, unless this wasn't a natural death," Sennett said. "That's no implication that you did anything wrong. I can understand what happened."

"I sure feel bad if I missed a criminal aspect to this. I never thought of that," Everson replied.

"No reason to feel bad. However, I do have a question, doctor," Sennett said. "What kind of a person was Mr. Stone?"

Everson said Reggie was a solitary guy. "No family; resided on a small place on the outskirts of Blissfield. He lived off of his Social Security and VA benefits."

There was a moment of silence and then Everson continued. "Come to think of it, I do remember one thing. It was weird. The funeral director called me after I signed the certificate. He said that when he was laying him out, he noticed something strange."

"What was that?" Sennett asked.

"Part of his little finger on his left hand was missing. I had no idea what that meant and just passed it off. It sounded strange, but like I said, Reggie had a terminal disease "

Sennett thanked him and said he would keep him informed if anything materialized. After he hung up, the room remained as quiet as a morgue.

"Okay," Jordan asked, breaking the silence, "Stone was murdered, and this wasn't a random killing. Now how do you find out who is organizing this?"

"If it was me," I said, "I'd play the telephone game."

Sennett gave me a blank look, so I explained it to him. "A dozen people sit in a circle and someone whispers to the person next to him that Mary is going on a car ride with John. By the time the message goes around the circle, the message is: Did you know Mary is pregnant? How about telling each of the people on Knowlton's list that we know something. It might get someone nervous."

Sennett nodded. "I know just the way to do it."

He called Jordan and me back an hour later and said he contacted Horace Stanford at his office. He told him that Sandra Wells's death was now considered a murder. Because of her job, the investigation included all the people involved with approving the contracts for the new City Hospital. As part of that investigation, they all had one commonality—an investment in a fund called The Full Coverage.

I asked him what his response was. Sennett said he replied that investing wisely is not a crime. "I told him no one was accusing him of anything, but we had to turn over all the stones."

When I asked Sennett what was next, he said, "You were the one who suggested the game. As you know all too well, all we can do now is wait."

Just as I was about to hang up he said, "By the way, I almost forgot. Mildred Walters called me. Man, she is a woman on a mission. I could hardly get a word in, she was so upset at the callousness of the police."

I asked him what she said. "Patsy Evans has been at her house for the past couple of days. Mildred didn't know anything was wrong until she saw a spot on the evening news that reported Patsy missing."

"How is she?" I asked.

"Now that she is with Mildred, everything is okay. It seems Ms. Evans finally found a real friend. I settled things down with Mildred when I explained this was a murder investigation. We sent a social worker over there, and from what I could tell, they think Patsy is going to be okay. When I spoke to her personally, she told me that Crandall had asked her to see what she did at work. She brought her computer to his home and the rest is history."

When I asked Sennett whether she was going to be in trouble, he said no jury in America would convict that poor girl after what she went through.

I STOPPED AT MY OFFICE TO PICK UP MY MAIL feeling frustrated. It reminded me of my time warming the bench in college, waiting for my number to be called. This detective work was definitely affecting my life. I hadn't seen Joey in a couple of days, and my medical practice was suffering. I decided to stop by the office.

I wasn't going to see any patients, but, when I walked in, Karen told me she found a package at the front door when she was locking up yesterday. She went to her desk and handed it to me. There was no name or return address on the outside.

I was apprehensive as I walked back to my desk. I set it down in front of me and opened the top. Inside was a grass-stained Michigan football. I stared at it almost paralyzed; it was an oppressive, smothering sensation. My hands were clammy and I started to sweat as I realized the terror so close to my family. Somebody had sent Joey's ball from our backyard.

I gazed out the window from my desk and saw my Wagoneer sitting under a flood lamp in the parking lot, alone except for Karen's car. Blood pounded in my ears as I pulled out a whole pack of gum, ripped off the wrappers, and stuffed all five pieces in my mouth. When I was under control, I dialed Sennett and told him what happened. From the wrath in his voice he sounded more upset than me.

"Somebody is playing with us. Maybe it's Tommy Holiday. I can't find the sonofabitch! Even his office doesn't know where he is. I think he knows we're on to him."

"What are you going to do?"

"We're not going to wait for a grand jury. I put out a warrant for his arrest on suspicion of bribery. Once we get him, he can deal with the grand jury."

I got home in time to have dinner with Joey and Jordan. The first thing I did was search for the football to make sure I wasn't mistaken. I looked everywhere. It was gone. Someone was taunting me. I swore; if Tommy Holiday touched Joey, I would kill him. I knew that, regardless of my reluctance to use a gun, this situation was different. This was my family.

I let Joey stay up late and watch Sports Center. About eight o'clock he had passed out on the couch, and I put him to bed.

Jordan was waiting for me at the bottom of the stairs. "Did you ever think how bizarre this case is? It's almost like Sandra Wells is leaving hints to us from the grave."

"You might be right. From what I know about her, she was pretty methodical and never left anything to chance. She must have known she was in danger."

"Why didn't she tell her bosses what was going on?"

"That's the missing piece. You'd think she would have. It makes me feel she didn't have it wrapped up. Somebody must have known just how close she was to the truth and tried to kill her before she solved that last piece of the puzzle."

"And Holiday is the someone."

"Sure sounds like it," I said.

"Have they found him?"

"No, but trust me, they're looking. I'm worried about a guy like him. He is capable of doing anything."

Then I told her about the football. "That's it, Ben," she said angrily. "We need to move out of the house and go to my parents in Miami."

"You're right, but I've got to stay. Until the crime is solved, we could never come back to the house."

It was hard to argue with her logic. I was a doctor and not a policeman and my family came first. After an hour of discussion and a call to her parents, I gave in and bought airlines tickets for the next day.

When I finished arranging the flights, I said, "I have to meet with Sennett early tomorrow to clear up a few things and then we'll leave."

Jordan, satisfied that we had a plan, went upstairs and started packing a couple of suitcases. In the meantime I went outside and told the night watchman what happened. Then I let Bucky into the backyard for the night. I would talk to Sennett tomorrow and see if he would watch him until we returned.

I SLEPT POORLY THAT NIGHT. My dreams were unsettling. I was walking on a city street at night when a man with a large knife came after me. Suddenly we were in cars racing down a street in Birmingham, when my car spun off the road and slammed into the wall of a building. I looked in the rearview mirror and saw blood streaming down my face. Then I looked to the right. Through the open passenger window I saw a man with yellow crooked teeth. He gave me a grim smile, took a knife from his coat and reached out to cut my finger off. Suddenly I woke up, my heart pounding. Sweat poured off my face.

I slipped out of bed and looked at myself in the mirror. This case is making a wreck out of me, I thought. It had to stop. I washed my face, and then went down the hall to check on Joey. He was fast asleep with his mother's cellphone on the nightstand next to the bed.

I went back to the bedroom and slipped under the covers. Jordan stirred slightly, but she quickly went back to sleep. I was glad. I didn't want her to see me like that.

CHAPTER 39

WHEN I WOKE UP, I LOOKED AT THE CLOCK. I had overslept. Shaving quickly, I got dressed and went downstairs. Joey and Jordan were already up and having breakfast. Jordan was reading the paper, and the TV blabbed on in the background.

Joey was deeply involved in his mother's I-Phone, pushing buttons and asking questions. Jordan showed him how to use a game.

"Are you sure you want to do that with a 7-year- old kid?" I asked.

"I'm not worried, he's already texting." As she spoke, I glanced at a news story on the TV. I listened carefully to the reporter.

"Breaking story in Detroit. A massive search is going on right now for Tommy Holiday, Mayor Robinson's chief of staff. Unsubstantiated reports link Holiday to possible involvement in a money-laundering scheme associated with the new City Hospital. The Mayor has declined comment pending further investigation. Political pundits are already questioning what effect this will have on the upcoming election." I was sick of Holiday, his arrogant disregard for the law and his possible involvement with a scandal at City Hospital. When the reporter went on to describe Holiday and his career, I turned off the TV. If they caught him, I hoped they strung him up by his balls.

"What does all this mean, Ben?"

"It means that our biggest lead in the death of Sandra Wells is now gone."

I didn't have time to discuss it further. I told Jordan that I had planned to meet Sennett at his office and help collate the medical information on the spreadsheet before we left.

I skipped breakfast and rushed out to the garage. Five minutes later I was on a side street, pulling onto Woodward Avenue. A cold, misty rain clogged the sky, looking like it had the chance of turning to snow. I fumbled with my keys and dropped them under the Jeep. I was upset with my inability to control my nerves and pissed off at the prospect of leaving town, a poor combination for driving in rush hour traffic in bad weather.

After I reminded myself that even though I was in a four-wheel drive car, it was no substitute for careful driving. My thoughts turned back to the Wells murder. I had the distinct feeling that this case was slipping away in a tangled web of murders and obscure information sent from a dead woman. Once on the highway, I melded into the morning traffic.

I was near the interstate when I realized I had left Bucky outside overnight. I called Jordan to ask her if she would bring him in. After six rings, the phone went to voicemail. Strange, she should have heard it. I tried her cell once more. The same thing happened. Then I tried the landline.

At that moment my cell phone rang. I heard a quick, "Ben, there's an intruder. Come home now!" Then nothing.

I was scared, more scared than I had ever been in my life. I had to go back. At the first turnaround, I made a Michigan U-turn across the median and headed north. Traffic was busy, but not impossible. I swerved in and out between cars, honking my horn and trying not to get caught at a red light. I barely made it through the last light and turned into Birmingham, when I saw my cell flash. It was Jordan's phone. I stopped at the curb and looked at the text. My heart almost stopped. The words no parent wants to see: "Daddy, help."

No time for hesitation, something bad, very bad was happening. One thing I did realize, whatever was going on, Joey and Jordan were in separate parts of the house. Jordan called on a landline. The most likely spot was the kitchen. But Joey called from Jordan's cellphone. I knew where he would hide. We played hide and seek dozens of times. He was in the attic.

I called Sennett, but it went to voicemail. "Something is going on at my house," I yelled into the phone. "Call the night watch to find out!" Determined to protect Jordan and Joey, I hung up. I wasn't going to wait for a response. Instead, I resolutely brought down the gearshift and sped down the quiet side street toward what I believed might be the end of my family.

I parked in front of Mrs. Barker's house, two doors east of ours, next to a huge oak tree still hanging on to the last of its brown leaves. The light was on in the kitchen. Joey loved going over to see Mrs. Barker. She always gave him what he described as the "best cookies ever."

The first thing I looked for was the night watchman. He was gone. Then I looked at my watch. The police always left at seven. Whoever was in the house knew that.

Before I opened the car door I put my revolver in my coat pocket and slipped out of the front seat through the passenger side. Hiding behind the tree,

I circled around to the backyard of the Thomases. They were a quiet, elderly couple, who kept to themselves and probably weren't up at this hour.

A dense line of almost impenetrable arborvitaes separated our houses. Having spent time in them searching for Joey's baseballs, I knew how impermeable they were. The only way through them was to stay as close to the ground as possible.

Dropping to my knees, I crawled under the trees on my stomach and entered the backyard. My first thought was why Bucky wasn't barking. Looking to my right in the dull morning light, my eyes focused on a large motionless object on the grass. My heart almost stopped. It was Bucky.

It was a struggle to keep my emotions under control, but somehow I made my way to the back door and found the hide-a-key "stone" near the steps that led to the basement. I managed to get there, staying away from the kitchen window and looked for the box. As I opened it and stared into the empty container, my jaw fell. Whoever was threatening my family knew what he was doing. A paralyzing fear gripped me like a crushing vice as I realized that a killer might be in my house.

I had one other choice. I found the pole for the aluminum ladder next to the house and slowly raised it to the railing on the balcony. I was hoping it wasn't tangled. I was in luck. I reached up, placed the hook on the folded ladder and pulled down. With a dull scraping sound it slid off.

The bottom rung reached about a foot from the ground. I pulled on the sides of the ladder to check its stability. It held firm. Grasping the side chains, I inched my way to the second floor. The French doors opening from our bedroom were locked, but I had hidden a key in the corner of the balcony.

I found it, unlocked the door, and crept slowly into the bedroom. Luckily, I was wearing rubber-soled shoes. I made my way silently over the area rug and headed for the attic door. It was Joey's secret hiding place.

I could hear something in the kitchen, a woman's voice yelling for help. Desperation pushed me to go to Jordan, but my first goal was getting Joey out. I opened the door. The floor made a slight creak as I entered. The large room was crammed with old furniture, boxes filled with memorabilia, old sports equipment from college, and several antique Persian rugs from Jordan's mother.

"Joey," I said softly. "It's Dad. Don't say anything. I know you are in here. We're going to get out."

I heard a rustling sound and then saw Joey emerge from behind the door. He was holding Jordan's cellphone. I grabbed him and held him tightly. As I did, he wrapped his arms around my neck.

"Okay, pal," I said, trying to sound confident. "We need to get out through the bedroom." Slowly, I explained what we were going to do. When I finished,

I asked him if he understood. He nodded his head. I looked at him closely. He appeared concerned, but not afraid.

We were about to leave when I heard the sound of steps coming up the stairs. There wasn't much time. Frantically, I looked for somewhere to hide. Then I saw the rugs.

"Joey," I whispered. "Listen carefully. We are going to hide in those rugs. Dad will protect you. Just hold onto me."

He didn't say anything but followed me to the Persian carpets. I quickly unrolled an eight by ten rug from the top and laid down on it, pulling Joey with me.

"Now we're going to play a game," I said. "You and I are going to roll the rugs over us."

I pulled the edge of the rug over my shoulder and held Joey as we rolled over a couple of times. I had one hand around Joey and the other in my pocket, where it clutched my gun. There was room to breathe, but I couldn't see much. Just then the door to the attic opened. I heard the slap of a shoe on the wooden steps and could see light coming from the open end of the rug. It must be the intruder.

After a few moments, thrown boxes and breaking glass reverberated on the wooden floor of the attic. The noise stopped for a moment and then I felt something hard poking against the rug, maybe like a stick or a baseball bat. To my surprise, Joey remained quiet.

I heard some words uttered angrily in French that sounded like "nick a mare" and "say days canaries." I had no idea what they meant, but I was sure it was not wishing us happy holidays. Finally, the words stopped, the light went off, and the door closed.

It was time to take a chance. We unrolled from the rug into the dark attic, illuminated only by a small amount of light coming in from the attic window. I helped Joey up, and we walked to the door. He still clutched Jordan's cellphone in his hand.

"Joey, we're going into my bedroom. When we get there, I am going to get you out of the house by the ladder."

"Why can't we go out the front door?" he asked.

"There is someone there I don't want you to see. Now I want you to walk softly and not talk. And one other thing, put Mommy's cellphone in your pocket."

Joey slipped the phone into his cargo pants, and we walked cautiously out of the bedroom and onto the deck. I looked down on the ladder, and suddenly felt my pulse bounding in my chest. Inside the kitchen I could see a shadow of someone, and it wasn't Jordan. I swung my leg over the balcony and steadied myself on the ladder. Then I reached for Joey's arm and lifted him on to my back. "Put your arms around my neck, son."

Sweat dampened my forehead and my leg muscles tightened. Slowly I made my way down the ladder. It swayed slightly but held under the weight. As soon as my feet hit the ground, I let Joey down and told him softly to let me have the cellphone. I quickly opened up a text and struggled as I typed in Sennett's number and sent a short message. I gave him back the phone and said, "Daddy's depending on you. Run to Mrs. Barker's house as fast as you can." I had to get Jordan.

I watched as Joey made it under the trees and into the Thomas's backyard. I was consumed with both relief and fear. He had to make it to Mr. Barker's house.

I climbed up the ladder, swung over the balcony railing, and edged toward the bedroom. Stepping inside, I tiptoed to the stairs leading into the kitchen. I was half way down when I heard the moaning of a woman's voice.

With my gun was in my right hand, I flattened my back against the wall. Looking in the full-length mirror in the hall, I could see into the kitchen where Jordan was tied up in a chair. Behind her was a short man with a big chest, huge arms that bulged out of his cotton sweater, and surprisingly small hands holding a knife at Jordan's throat. Her computer was on the kitchen counter.

From the police description this must have been Pinky LeBeque, except he looked worse than the drawing. He had alligator eyes, his small pupils peering out from underneath dark, heavy eyebrows. His swarthy skin was marred by a long scar on the left side of his face. It was the face of a demon from a nightmare.

I was tempted to rush him, but I couldn't risk the chance. Instead I watched, almost helplessly, waiting for an opening. By this time he was circling Jordan, moving his knife from one hand to the other.

Jordan remained silent as he continued to move around her, holding the knife at her throat.

I saw Jordan's horrified face. "You'll get nothing from me. I would rather die."

He smiled as he stroked the side of her neck, almost as if he was enjoying this torture. He must have heard something outside, because he stopped and turned to look out the window. That's when Jordan turned her head and saw me in the mirror. Her eyes darted from side to side, as if she was trying to tell me something.

LeBeque turned around, grabbed her left hand, and placed it on the counter. As he moved, he muttered to himself in French. They were the only words he spoke. With her hand in his strangulating grip, he brought the knife above her left pinky finger and waited. Why didn't he kill her? It was then that I realized he knew I was there and was baiting me to show myself. I knew it was me he wanted.

With the blade on her little finger Jordan screamed in horror. Time seemed to stand still waiting for me to do something. This wasn't a game on a field;

this was a life and death battle with a trained killer. I was torn between making a rash act that might cause her death and watching him torture her. I had no choice. I crept down the stairs out of sight of the mirror. When I got to the door, I stood up, holding my gun tightly in both hands. I was strangely calm and focused.

"Put it down or you're dead," I shouted.

He turned and looked at me with a snarling, contemptuous grin. Then he grabbed Jordan's hair and jerked her head back with the knife at her throat.

"Ben, help me!" she yelled.

Once again a noise from outside forced LeBeque to look out the window. At that instant, Jordan braced her feet against the kitchen counter and pushed back with all her strength.

He toppled backward along with Jordan in the chair. The knife clattered to the floor. As he got to his feet to pick it up, I nervously pointed my gun and fired. He dodged and fell as I recklessly fired three shots at his chest from close range, but missed. To my surprise he got up, this time with the knife in his hand. He grinned silently as he moved toward me.

I was surprised at his quickness. He was on me with his stiletto before I could fire back. The blade slashed at my arm, cutting the jacket but missing my flesh. However, in my effort to avoid him, I clumsily fell backward. My gun crashed to the floor. As he jumped toward me, I rolled toward Jordan. This time, he had me cornered against the counter. From the floor I saw the glint of the knife come down at my neck. Just as he was about to strike, Jordan threw herself at him on the chair, knocking him to the floor with thud. I leaped away.

Pinky's smile was gone now. Jordan had tumbled over, still lashed to the chair. I'm sure he knew he could take care of her later; that's why he turned toward me. This time he wasn't going to wait. He came at me again with the knife raised. I knew he wouldn't stop until he plunged the blade deep into my neck.

As he stalked me, he saw my gaze move to my gun on the floor. He jumped to pick it up, but I got there just before he did and grabbed it with my right hand. This was my only chance. He dove at me with the knife extended, fury in his eyes. I jumped to my feet. No shooting instructor's instructions, no time to steady myself. It was reflex and instantaneous. I had one second. I pulled the gun up, aimed for his head. A loud reverberation filled the room as I pulled the trigger. I saw a flash, and he fell to the floor, the knife just missing my neck. His body jerked for a moment, but I didn't stay to watch him die.

Instead, I quickly moved to Jordan, pulling the chair upright, and took a knife from the drawer to cut her bond. I held her tightly as she shook uncontrollably.

"You're okay," I said, consolingly. "He's dead."

"I was so scared," she cried." She stopped for a moment, her body shaking and her breath coming in short gasps. Then almost as if she had awoken from a dream, she asked, "Where is Joey?"

I continued to hold her close to me. "I found him and sent him off."

She gently moved out of my embrace and held my arm. "Let's go. I'm okay, but I need to see him," she said firmly.

We rushed out of the kitchen without looking back, opened the front door and ran outside. By this time, I could see six squad cars silently creeping down the street and Sennett charging like a bull elk down the sidewalk. When he saw us, his head sagged with relief.

I waved at him, but didn't wait to explain what happened. Instead we rushed into the Barker's house. I apologized to Mrs. Barker as we entered. She just smiled and pointed to Joey in the kitchen. I thought he would be hysterical. Instead his cheeks were bulging cookies and milk.

We both ran to him. Jordan got there first. She picked him up and hugged him. That's when she broke down, tears streaming over her cheeks. I held both of them in my arms as Jordan sobbed with joy. Joey would have no part of it. When he saw me, he jumped down and reached into his pocket for Jordan's cellphone.

"Dad, did you see the text I sent you?" he asked proudly.

"Yes, Joey. I'll never forget it as long as I live."

It was several minutes until Sennett came to the front door. By this time, the cops were milling all over the block. When I saw Sennett, I took him outside and stopped on the sidewalk. "I killed him," I said as softly as possible. I hated to think about it, but I had a certain pride in being able to pull the trigger and defend my family.

"Doc, I know dead people, and I didn't see any."

I was shocked. "Wait a minute. I know the bullet hit his head. He was bleeding, then his body jerked a few times and stopped."

Sennett shook his head in disbelief as I explained what happened.

"Was this the same person we saw at Sean Richardson's house?"

"It might have been."

"If it was, you just fought with one of the deadliest Mafia guys in Canada."

"He might be the deadliest Mafia guy in Canada, but he also has nine lives. No way he could have lived through it. I shot him in the head, for Chrissakes."

"Did he tell Jordan anything, like what he wanted?"

"He wanted me and the computer. I'm sure of it. My family was the bait to get me there."

"He probably would have killed both of you had he been able to," Sennett said with a deep sigh. One other thing. I think you better take care of your dog. He's barking a lot. Seems a little wobbly, like he doesn't know where he is." I had forgotten about Bucky. He was alive! I looked over at Jordan. The tears had returned.

"Ben, I know this is a tough time for you, but I've got to find LeBeque. Did he give you any indication where he was going?"

Jordan heard the question and answered quickly. "He kept mumbling something weird to himself, while he was tying me to the chair. He said Hangar H."

"George, we need to get this killer or we'll never be safe. That's got to be an airport hangar and the only one around here is at Oakland."

CHAPTER 40

OAKLAND AIRPORT IS A HAVEN for most of the private jets in the metropolitan Detroit area. The downturn in the economy may have hurt the auto industry, but with its recent recovery and a lot of rich people who still lived among the four and a half million souls who made up the Metropolitan Detroit area, a need still existed for a private airport. And that was part of the problem—finding the killer's plane.

Sennett didn't wait and neither did I. Within a minute we were in his car rolling onto Maple Road with the siren on and lights flashing. The windshield wipers were already fighting off a cold, steadily misting rain that was blurring our windshield. By the time we reached Telegraph Road, the speedometer read sixty miles an hour. Luckily, the morning traffic had eased.

He slowed at Telegraph Road, a packed six-lane highway, and watched as cars pulled to the side. It looked as if we had enough room to turn north until we saw a woman in an SUV driving and texting. Sennett blared his horn, but she was oblivious to everything else around her. It was too late. We were already in the intersection.

"Hang on, Ben," Sennett shouted. I clutched onto the door handle as he accelerated between two cars just in front of the oncoming vehicle. The woman realized the danger at the last second and slammed on her brakes. I braced my feet on the floorboard and clamped my hand the door handle. Our car fishtailed on the wet pavement but made it through. As soon as we made it to the other lane, I shoved the last of my gum in my mouth and waited for my pulse rate to go down. Sennett looked at me and nodded.

We accelerated with our light flashing, passing dozens of cars at eighty miles an hour. The faces of the drivers in the cars were a blur. It was like watching a police pursuit in an Imax theater, except this was real life. The car passed through Pontiac and exited on M-59, heading to the Oakland Regional Airport. On the way Sennett tried to called Knudsen, but his cell didn't work. I tried mine but it didn't work either.

At Airport Road, Sennett slowed just enough to find the entrance, an angled, glass-enclosed building on a circular drive. There was a security guard on duty. Sennett pulled in, showed his badge, and asked for directions to Hangar H.

The guard told him how to negotiate his way through the airport to the twenty or thirty hangars at the northwest corner. When he finished, Sennett asked him if they had trouble with cellphone coverage. "The tower is out because of the weather," the guard said. "Not even planes are taking off."

Sennett pulled out his card and gave it to him with instructions to call his office and ask for Sergeant Knudsen. "Tell him we need a backup at Oakland Airport immediately. It's urgent."

The guard's eye widened when he heard Sennett's command. I guessed he must have been in the military from the way he said "Yes, sir." As soon as he finished, Sennett took off.

We drove around the service drive to the north end of the landing strip. Hangar H wasn't hard to find as we drove down the alphabetically organized hangars. The closer we got to Hangar H, the more congested it became. We dodged five or six Gulf Streams and made our way to the far western edge of the airport.

I saw a ten-passenger jet on the edge of the tarmac of Hangar H with a large sign on the tail emblazoned with Empire Investments. The covers were still on the jet engines and the chocks were in place on the wheels. If LeBeque was going somewhere, it wasn't on this plane.

A workman was walking around the plane, so Sennett pulled up his car and we got out. The cold drizzle, now accompanied by a light wind, stung our faces. The man, in a rain slicker and overalls, looked at us quizzically, then asked us what we were doing.

"Have the owners been out here?" Sennett asked, brusquely.

"Who wants go know?" he retorted.

Sennett pulled out his badge and gave him that wilting look that created an instant attitude change.

"Nobody's been out here. As far as I know, this plane isn't scheduled to leave for a while."

Sennett looked pissed. Something was going on and he had no idea where to turn. He didn't bother thanking the man, as he got back in the car and closed the window. Just as he was about to pull away, the man tapped on the car window. Sennett rolled down the window again.

"Say, Lieutenant, you might want to check over at Hanger H-2. Sometimes this company uses a Beechcraft over there to go to northern Michigan."

Sennett leaned out the window and handed him his card. "This is my office number at Detroit Police Headquarters. There is a possibility that we might have a problem. Call this number and tell the man who answers to send a back-up." Sennett wasn't taking any chances.

We made our way through a series of narrow strips just wide enough for a prop plane until we came to H-2. The gray metal siding building was as far away from the main terminal as you could get. It was still wet outside, as the dark, drizzling shroud was deciding on whether to turn into snow.

We stopped a hundred feet from the entrance. Sennett took a flashlight from the car, then got out his revolver and checked the chamber.

"You carrying?" he asked. I patted my jacket pocket, and he nodded grimly. "You might need it." I didn't try to glorify my encounter with the killer in my house and how he had gotten away. I have to admit I was angry with myself that I could not kill LeBeque at point blank range.

The sliding door to H-2 was unlocked. Sennett nudged the door open and we both walked cautiously through the entrance. The only light was from his Maglite and whatever the outside atmosphere could muster. On a dank, drizzly day like this, that wasn't much.

We shoved the sliding door wider and stepped deeper into the hangar. The air was listless with the pungent odor of oil, aviation fuel, and mildew. It was cold enough to see my breath. In front of us was a clean, white Beechcraft Bonanza. The only sound I heard was the muffled, drumbeat of rain on the metal roof. Sennett pulled out his gun and swung his light around the building, exposing the oil drums and spare aircraft parts that lined the walls. In the distant corner the light reflected off small puddles of water that dotted the oil-stained floor.

"Nice plane, huh, Lieutenant?" a voice behind us suddenly asked.

I spun around, startled to see Mark Crandall with a gun pointed at Sennett. As he turned on an overhead light my mouth went dry and the gum I was chewing turned tasteless. "Now drop the Sig on the floor." Sennett dropped his gun and Crandall bent down and picked it up.

I looked at him as he moved toward us. Dressed in a leather jacket, jeans and black work boots, he had morphed into the uniform of the criminal he was. Gone was the reassuring face of an insurance salesman. In its place was the cold, calculating look of a killer. I noticed a thin cloth bandage on his left hand. With his right hand he methodically patted me down and found my gun.

"Nice peashooter," he said examining my pistol. "The next time you try and kill someone, make sure he's dead. Not scratched but dead." He put my gun in his pocket. "Isn't that right, Pinky?"

From the shadows behind him, the guy I had "killed" at the house walked up. He wore a gray cap to cover a gauze dressing swathed around his head. When he saw me, he snickered with a look of loathing that started a cold sweat running down my shirt. Crandall picked up Sennett's gun and gave it to Pinky.

"I thought you were dead," I said.

"Think again, eh," he grunted, in his French Canadian accent.

Crandall pushed Sennett and me toward the ladder on the side of the plane. "Move!" Crandall yelled. "We don't have time to monkey around with you two. Now get up the stairs."

We walked up the steps and into the fuselage with Crandall and Pinky behind us. I noted two rows of two passenger seats on short metal legs inside the cramped space and facing each other. In front of the seats was the cockpit. Across the aisle against the side of the plane were two cement blocks. Tied through each block were two lengths of rope lying on the floor of the plane.

Crandall pushed each of us into the seats, next to each other and facing the cockpit. While Pinky guarded the door, he pulled out a roll of duct tape from his jacket and methodically wrapped each of us around the chest separately. We both struggled, but with our upper arms immobilized in front of us, we were helpless.

When he finished, he took each of the two ropes and handed them to Pinky. LeBeque then silently tied the ends onto the cement blocks. He then took the other ends and secured them on each of us, one around Sennett's left ankle and one on my right ankle, each with four or five feet of slack. He checked the knots a second time and then walked to the airplane door and waited.

I looked over at Sennett. Ferocity filled his eyes, and his jaw muscles bulged as he clenched his teeth. Crandall didn't know he was messing with a wild tiger that didn't like to be caged.

He wasn't alone. I would find a way out; I had to.

"We've got them locked down, Pinky" Crandall gloated. "Now take care of our other business, and we'll start the plane. We've got to get over Lake Huron before it gets too dark." He stopped for a moment and turned to face us. "I have to hand it to you. You guys are smart. But not smart enough."

I felt a pounding in my ear as fear began to grip me. "You'll never take off in this weather," I said.

"Think again. This is mild compared to Alaska."

As Pinky left the plane, I studied Crandall. He was in charge now. I assumed, like most intellectual criminals, he was probably a narcissist. He had to tell us of his greatness before he killed us. We had to keep him talking until we found an opportunity.

"What about your finger?" I asked.

"It was the price I had to pay. Pinky cut it off. I knew that if the police found my finger, and not the body, they would figure I had been murdered by Pinky and that was that."

"You know you'll get caught." Sennett said, his neck corded with bulging veins.

"Oh really, you think so. Sandra Wells almost got us. Now look where she is."

"What about Tommy Holiday?" As Sennett spoke, I looked for a way out. There was nothing.

"Tommy? He didn't know shit. He was just following you and your doctor friend around to find out what you knew. Pinky shadowed him. That's how we found out about the spreadsheet. We knew his every move, and we plan to take care of him right here at the airport before we dispose of you two."

Sennett violently rolled his shoulders, to no avail. "All this for money, huh?"

"A once in a lifetime opportunity with my Mafia friends in Canada. I planned every step. They get the contracts at City Hospital, and I get a cut. It was perfect; it was a scheme no one could break. When that spreadsheet got out, my bosses told me to shut down The Full Coverage Fund and anyone with knowledge of it." As he spoke, he bent down and tightened the knots on our legs.

"How did you kill those people from the surveillance center?" I asked.

"Succinyl choline. You should know. It's untraceable. Anesthesiologists use it all the time to paralyze patients before they go under. I'd call Pinky in to take care of business. No big deal. After all, they all had terminal diseases," he said mockingly. "And the best thing is, nobody cared. They had no relatives."

"What about Calboy and Sandra Wells? Was killing them all part of protecting your sick scheme?" I asked.

"You forgot Herbert Knowlton and that pimp, Aurelious Jones. And yes, it was all for money. More money than you can ever imagine."

I sensed a tingling in my neck as the hair lifted off of my skin. "You're a sick fuck."

His face reddened. "Oh yeah? We'll see how sick you feel begging for your life before I drop you and your lieutenant friend in the drink for a swim."

I could feel my jaw beating on the gum in my mouth as fear began to take over my senses. Oddly, the more I chewed, the more it stirred something primal in my brain. For right now, I had to keep him talking, make him angry.

"I bet you were always a loser," I said. "All you ever wanted was to get money, be rich. You'd show everyone."

I hit the right button. His lip quivered and his eyes narrowed. He pulled out my gun from his jacket.

"You know, Crandall," I continued. "People like you are just petty assholes. Killing people for money, ruining their lives. You're going to die and rot in hell."

"How do you know?

"You're wearing a cross. You believe. Now you know where you are going.

There's no confession that can help you. God hates you. Hell is your home. How's that for a confession?"

The reference to hell made his face grimace in anger. Instead of using his gun, he raised his bandaged left hand and pressed his thumb against my right eye. The pain was excruciating. As I winced, he laughed. "You asked for it. I'm going to torture you until you beg for mercy. Fancy big shot doctor now, aren't you?"

Chewing the worn out wad of gum to stand the pain, the primal path to survival crystallized my thoughts. I had no other weapon other than my jaw and the muscles that made it move, the strongest muscles in my body. With all my strength I arched my head forward, opened my mouth, and clamped my teeth on his partially amputated finger. Crandall let out a scream and dropped the gun on the floor. He recovered quickly and raised his other hand to the side of my head. I ducked and missed the direct hit to my temple.

By this time Sennett had managed to get to his knees. He lunged at Crandall, knocking him loose from my jaw and onto the floor of the plane. Once he was down, Sennett wedged his elbow on Crandall's head.

Crandall struggled against the weight of Sennett's body, throwing him backward, and managed to sit up and reach back with his left hand for my revolver. When I saw the gun, I fell on top of his arm, knocking it out of his hand. The two of us were now on either side of Crandall with our heads in the aisle and our legs on top of his. He struggled to get to his feet. My arms were aching from the tape around my chest as I lunged for his bandaged hand again, and this time my teeth didn't let go.

This momentary diversion took his attention away from Sennett. It was too late for Crandall. With the smooth ease of a yoga stretch George swung his left leg in the air over Crandall's head, wrapping the rope around his neck and pulling him forward. It took a couple seconds to realize he was creating a hangman's noose. Instantly, I released my grip on his hand and painfully swung the rope from my right leg in the opposite direction around his neck, exactly as Sennett had done. When it was completely around, I tried to do it again. This time I could feel my leg muscles cramp with excruciating pain. I made one last effort, rolling to my side as I lifted my leg, and once more managed to loop it around his head.

As soon as the lines were in place, we both slid in opposite directions in the aisle, tightening the ropes on his throat. A look of panic filled Crandall's face as he realized his head was now trapped in the snare. The more the rope tightened, the more his congested face turned an increasingly grotesque blue color. A moment later his tongue swelled outside his mouth, and his eyes bulged wildly. I looked at him with complete disgust.

I hated this man for what he did to his victims and my family. Crandall was an evil, despicable human being and deserved to die. But I knew something else. I'm a tough son of a bitch, but I'm not an animal. There is a time for death, but what we were doing was the worst kind of murder. As the scumbag lapsed into unconsciousness, I released my leg.

"George, let him go," I panted. "He'll be better to us alive. A bunch of his people are wishing he was dead. We need his testimony. Keep your rope around his head in case he revives and rolls over to me. We still have to deal with LeBeque."

Sennett must have agreed, because he released his leg too and slid over to me. As he did, a gurgling noise wheezed out of Crandall's mouth. I looked at him; he was breathing but still motionless.

Rolling onto my side, I slid toward the cement block where I was tethered. I staggered to my knees and bent over the ragged edge of my anchor. Stretching my arms as far apart as I could, I moved back and forth. I could feel the tape give slightly as I moved. My stomach and back ached from the effort. My eyes stung as sweat poured over my face. Suddenly I heard a faint ripping sound and the lower piece of tape tore open.

My arms were now loose enough that I could use them. I moved over to Sennett and grabbed his tape with my fingers. It took a minute or two, but I was able to tear it in half.

Sennett kneeled, shaking his arms. When his circulation returned, he turned to me and released the rest of my bondage. Once mobile, we both un-tied our ropes. For a moment we stood up and looked at the inert killer on the floor. Then we bound him in the cords that were meant for us.

"I'm glad to see you visit your dentist on a regular basis," Sennett said, when we finished.

"Me too. The doc tells me I have no cavities. By the way, if we get out of here, I'm taking yoga lessons," I replied, looking out the open door of the plane. That's when I saw LeBeque standing in front of another man. I couldn't see who the person was, but he appeared to be bound. What I did see was LeBeque releasing one of his arms and reaching for something in his belt. It was his knife. Next to it I saw Sennett's gun. LeBeque turned the man to the left and brought the knife to his neck. It was Tommy Holiday. Even with his eyes searching desperately for an escape, he didn't seem scared. That's how tough that character was.

Frantically, I looked for my gun. It was on the floor next to the seat. I bent down and scooped it up. Sennett looked over at me and yelled, "What are you doing?"

I had no time to answer. I bolted to the door and shouted at LeBeque. "Drop it!"

As I yelled, LeBeque spun the man around and smiled. It was the faceless, malevolent smile of death. The look lasted only a split second, but that was long enough. When Holiday saw me, he reacted with a fighter's instinct, slamming the sole of his boot onto LeBeque's instep, forcing him backward.

This time my chest felt light, and I breathed easily. Bending my legs slightly and raising the gun with both hands, I whispered to myself: "Front sight, front sight, smoothly squeeze the trigger." Suddenly, my shot echoed in the empty hangar.

A moment later I heard a siren in the distance.

EPILOGUE

IT WAS TWO WEEKS AFTER SENNETT and I had escaped our death at the hands of Mark Crandall and Pinky LeBeque. The newspapers and local and national networks stations were all over it. As far as Sennett and I were concerned, we had enough of this horrific crime and wanted to put it in the past.

Mark Crandall turned out to be a canary. He quickly confessed to plotting the murders, but made a plea bargain—divulge his Mafia connections and he might get away with a lesser sentence. Thankfully, although it was a Federal crime, Jordan wasn't involved.

For my part, after a week in Florida visiting Jordan's family, I went back to work. It was the best way I knew to avoid living in the past. Don't get me wrong, justice was served. After all, Crandall was in custody, Lebeque was dead, and the entire scheme exposed. Each of the "investors" in the Full Coverage Fund were indicted, including Charles FitzHugh. I admit great satisfaction when the TV newscast showed him doing the "perp" walk into court with the other defendants.

Whether any of them would be found guilty or not would take years. Tommy Holiday for his involvement in the matter came out as a hero. He had been working for the mayor, doing his own investigation. Typical for him, he said if Sennett and I weren't so interfering, he would have cracked the case. That said, he managed to thank me, which was pretty good, coming from a hard ass like him. And, by the way, he said his hearing had recovered.

But all of that didn't really matter, I was grateful for having my family intact and appreciative that I was a doctor again. It took a couple of patients to get back in the groove. I could tell they wanted to talk to me about the case, but I said I wasn't legally allowed to discuss it. Heck, I didn't even talk about it with my staff. Maybe some day, but not now.

Around ten o'clock that morning I got a phone call from the office of an attorney, Carlyle P. Thomas. His secretary told Karen that Mr. Thomas had a letter for me from Sandra Wells and wanted to speak to me about it.

I was furious. Intruding into my life with phony calls really pissed me off, especially when it involved the death of an innocent person, like Sandra. I went to my office, picked up the phone and immediately started chewing out the person at the other end.

Before I could finish, a man's voice came on the line. "Dr. Dailey, this is Mr. Thomas, and I can assure you this is not a crank phone call. I have a letter that Sandra Wells wrote to you, with specific instructions for me to present it in person."

The tone of my voice deepened. "I tell you what, Mr. Thomas, call Lieutenant George Sennett at Detroit Homicide and tell him what you just told me. Now goodbye."

I hung up, wondering how people could be that cruel. My wonderment lasted about thirty minutes, and then George Sennett called me. "Ben, this guy Thomas is legit. He faxed me documents and his credentials. After I looked them over, I checked with some attorneys I know. They said he is a well-respected lawyer. I think you better go."

IT WAS A CLOUDLESS EARLY WINTER DAY when Jordan and I drove to Thomas' office on Jefferson Avenue. His digs were in a thirty-story skyscraper overlooking the Detroit River and the skyline of the Motor City. Both of us were reluctant to go. What could be in this letter that was worth re-opening the events of the past few weeks? After all that had happened I thought the whole episode was history, and the less we saw of it the better.

We parked in a covered lot off Lafayette Avenue and walked a block to the building. Signs of the city's rebirth were everywhere, apartment buildings, restaurants, and retail stores. In the distance, like a glittering jewel, the glass on new City Hospital sparkled in the sunshine; a clear sign to all that Detroit was rising from the ashes. That glow even passed onto Mayor Robinson. A grand jury cleared him of any misdeeds with Sandra Wells.

As we entered the lobby of the Penobscot Building, I looked at Jordan. I could tell by her quiet demeanor and hesitant step that she still did not want to look at what had almost happened to her family. I was sorry I had talked her into going. She waited for me to push the elevator button and stood quietly next to me with her head down.

The elevator took us to the twenty-seventh floor office of Thomas, Dingman, and Peters, P.C. The secretary was expecting us, and we were ushered into a wood paneled conference room with a highly polished mahogany table. A well-dressed gentleman, whom I guessed was Mr. Thomas, sat in a large leather chair with a No. 10 envelope and several folders spread out in front of him.

He was an officious looking man in his mid-fifties with thinning brown hair touched by gray on the sides. His pleasant smile and warm handshake took away anything ominous in his appearance.

As we sat down, I gazed out the window, wondering what kind of information Sandra Wells had in her will and how it would affect us. Thomas reached for his reading glasses on the table and then picked up the envelope.

"Sandra Wells was a client of mine for a couple of years," he said. "During that time, I found her to be an extraordinary young woman. I don't think I have ever met a more organized or thoughtful person in my life."

He took out a handkerchief from his pocket, breathed on the lenses of his glasses, and then cleaned them. When he was done, he methodically put them back on.

"Dr. Dailey, I read your story in *The Free Press*. Quite amazing. How did you get involved?"

"I have too many friends that I didn't know I had," I replied.

Thomas looked bewildered. "Are you talking about the police officer that was murdered? Cal something?"

"Cal Finney."

"Well, reading the article, it's clear you have quite a reputation."

"True, but I'm trying to shake the notoriety. It just won't go away."

"If you don't mind, I have one question I wanted to ask, mainly because in some small way I feel part of the whole affair. What happened to that poor woman who was abused by her father?"

"Carina?"

He nodded.

"I got a letter from her. She's on the mend. Her boyfriend is a medical student and apparently they are together. She's going back to school and trying to get her life in order. I think she will. Carina's a strong person."

As I looked at him, my gaze flicked upward. These questions were irritating, and I wasn't interested in rehashing this sordid story. Aside from breaking up a huge bribery scheme and a murder ring, I saw no good for me, or my family, in keeping the story alive. I think Thomas understood my irritation. "Sorry, it was such an unusual story, I couldn't resist finding out more about it."

"Don't worry. You're not the first person who asked me. In your position I'd ask too. But I'm more curious as to why you invited my wife and me to come here today."

"Sure. Let's get down to business. Several months ago, Sandra asked me to write a will. In the document is a personal letter to you, which, at her instructions, I have read. After you look at it, I think you will understand a lot more about her." He handed me the letter and an opener.

I picked up the envelope and opened it. Jordan leaned on my shoulder as I read the contents.

Dear Dr. Dailey,

If you get this letter, it is because I instructed Mr. Thomas to deliver it to you as part of my will.

My parents both died and I have no relatives except for my dear cousin, Charmayne. I always wanted a family, but I never knew for sure that I would get married or, perhaps, something would happen to me before I found the right person. I decided that the only way I could assure myself that my child would be born was to have a frozen embryo. If I married and had children, I would put the embryo up for adoption. Accordingly, I had a sperm donor for my eggs. His name is Jonathon Edwards. He is currently a lawyer practicing in Chicago. Jon was a good friend of mine from law school, but we were not romantically involved. When he made the donation, he signed all the legal documents that gave me control of the embryo. He did not want to be the legal father.

Both Jonathon and I had genetic testing. These results are included with the letter. I checked with my obstetrician, and he indicated no significant markers.

I also prepared to finance the growth of this child by selling the proceeds of a life insurance policy to a stock derivative fund. I want to make it clear that the money I received was obtained legitimately. The documentation for this income is also attached to this letter.

You might be wondering where this is leading. As you know, I was in your office several times. I admit that in a way I came to interview you. I read about you and your exploits. They were so unusual I wanted to see if the articles about you were true. I believe they were. I really enjoyed our conversations. I found that, in fact, you are an intelligent, kind, and decent person. I do not know your wife, but I had some friends in the McNamara Building who work with her. They all said wonderful things about her

All of this is a roundabout way for me to ask you and your wife a question. I need someone to be the trustee of my embryo. If something should happen to me, I would want to know that he, or she, would be given to the right family for adoption. It would be my honor if you and your wife would accept my offer to be the trustee of my unborn child. I only ask of you that the surrogate and recipient of this gift would somehow add my name to the child so that in some way I will continue my family's legacy.

I know that this is a lot to ask, but after talking with you on my visits to your office, I know you and your wife are my first choice. If you do accept this offer, I would love it if you would someday show this letter to the child. Thank you very much!

Respectfully,
Sandra Wells

I was stunned. So was Jordan.

"How well do you know this person?" She had a slight edge to her voice, as if I had something else going on.

"All I can tell you is that she saw me on several occasions for minor problems. You know how I like talking with patients. I remember striking up conversations with her. It was mostly questions about being a doctor, my profession, and my family. I never realized at the time that she had this in mind."

A thought quickly crossed my mind. "What if my wife carried this embryo to birth? Is that acceptable?" I spontaneously asked Thomas. The quick realization of my hasty question surprised me. I'm not impulsive, but the words came out almost as if I was thinking aloud.

The room fell silent. As Jordan quietly squeezed my arm, I looked at her face. She blinked her eyes rapidly and followed up with a fixed stare. "Are you sure?" she asked, with an excitement I hadn't seen in months. "For me it would be so much more personal than an adoption. Oh, Ben, can we?" Her eyes closed in prayer, and suddenly the room was silent.

"I see no reason why that would not be possible." Thomas, as wide-eyed as a child, appeared taken aback at the question. "I would presume that if she felt comfortable enough to have you and your wife as trustees, you certainly would be fit as parents. This is certainly an implied offer to you, so I can make the arrangements."

My mouth had pushed me into a corner I shouldn't have walked into, but my brain urged me to stay. I looked down at the table and fumbled through the papers in front of me, half-reading them and half wondering what to do next. We had spent months talking about having another child and exploring the options. I raised my head up from the documents and turned to look at Jordan. Hope shone in her face, and this time it was a joyful tear that sparkled in the morning sun.

My words were slow and deliberate. "We accept."

GENE RONTAL is a head and neck surgeon. Born in Detroit, he attended the University of Michigan, where he received his medical degree. After completing a residency at the University of Minnesota, he went into private practice in the Detroit area and began teaching at the University of Michigan Medical School. He is currently a professor in the Department of Otolaryngology/Head and Neck Surgery. His writing career started twenty years ago when he published his first novel, *Sterile Justice*. Since then he has three other books in print (*A Lethal Dose*, *The Cruelest Cut*, and *The Police Surgeon*) and has participated in promoting them with book signings and radio and newspaper interviews. In addition to his mystery writing, Gene Rontal has published over fifty scientific articles, authored chapters in medical textbooks, and has been quoted in a number of lay publications, including *Time*, *Science*, *National Geographic*, and the *Wall Street Journal*. Doctor Rontal and his wife, Ellen, enjoy skiing, traveling, and spending time with their family.

CPSIA information can be obtained
at www.ICGtesting.com
Printed in the USA
LVHW091112120121
676264LV00007B/90

9 781603 817356